Push It To The Limit

Lock Down Publications
Presents
Push It To The Limit
A Novel by *Bre' Hayes*

Lock Down Publications
P.O. Box 1482
Pine Lake, Ga 30072-1482

Visit our website at www.lockdownpublications.com

First Edition April 2016
Printed in the United States of America

Lock Down Publications
Like our page on Facebook: Lock Down Publications @www.facebook.com/lockdownpublications.ldp
Cover design and layout by: Dynasty's Cover Me
Book interior design by: Shawn Walker
Edited by: Mia Rucker

Dedications

First, I would like to give honor and praise to the Almighty, whom I passionately refer to as my Lord and Saviour Jesus Christ for blessing me with the talent, and the opportunity to be everything that I am today, good and bad.

Next, I would like to dedicate this book to my four children D'Armonie, Amahre', Ronald, and Rahmi' Johnson.

To my parents, Tinya and Edwin Williams, Sr.

To my mother-n-law and father-n-law, Kenneth and Patricia Eugene.

To my sisters and best friends, Brandi, Yannie, Teedy, Bria, Lavenya, Treniece, Charlene, Shelita, Ronnisha, Kimberly, Celeste, Nika Vaughn, Taravia, and LaShawn. To my Hayes, DeVare, and Williams family.

To my boyfriend, Kendrick Anderson, who motivated me, and pushed me to finally finish the book.

To my brothers, Kada, Telly, E.J., and Hurt. Praying that blessings fall down on my brother Kada, and he is set free.

To my group/fans on Facebook, I love ya'll from the bottom of my heart. Without the help, promotion, and belief in me from my group I wouldn't be where I am right now.

To my belated grandmother, my sweet lady, Betty, and my grandfather Rayfield.

To my whole Lock Down Publications Family, especially Cash and Coffee, for giving me what I feel is the opportunity of a lifetime.

To my D.T.R./B.F.L./BAKERBOY family for just being who y'all are. To Rachelle Gardner for introducing me to Cash.

To Shannon Batiste for her creativity when I needed her to come through for me.

To Edward Dunn for all that he has been to my group on Facebook.

To Gus (a.k.a. Bliss) for being one of the best promoters that I could ask for.

To my bff/cousin Mukk for EVERYTHING (the videos, the shares, etc.)

I would like to say keep your head up, and praying for all of our family on Lock Down:

Bryant Hayes, Jr. (Kada)
Lorenzo Eugene (O-Dog)
Jermaine Weber (Joe-Joe)
Damien Hall (Frog)
Courtney DeVare (C-Nile)
Calvin Taylor (Tooka)
Cleveland Mitchell (Clink)
Juan Alexander (Spue)

Prologue

She was pacing back and forth in his apartment. He had given her the key while they were at the funeral so that they could meet up when it was time. Her fists were balled so tightly her nails dug into her palms, but her anger blocked out the pain.

How in the fuck could this bitch ass nigga try to play me like this? What type of flunky ass bitch does he take me for? He better have my money so that I can get the fuck on. He has me all the way fucked up.

Her eyes watered as she thought about what he had just done. She started to tremble at the thought of him touching another woman after he told her that he would never hurt her again.

Lying, no good bastard.

Taking a deep breath then exhaling slowly, she tried to calm herself as she made her way over to his living room window, parted the blinds, and looked out just in time to see him pull up.

Hurry up, motherfucker.

Breathing out of her nose, she briskly walked back across the room and snatched her bag off of the couch. Inside of it, she found exactly what she was searching for. Yesterday, her home-girl, who was a pharmacist, had provided her with the needle that was now in her hand. It was filled with something that would neutralize the size and strength advantage he had over her when she struck.

Today, his ass would pay for every single dishonest act he had made against her.

When she heard him put his key in the door, she slid the needle into her pocket, and stood ready to pop off on him. She couldn't believe that she had to hear her nigga fucking another bitch. After all of the chances that she gave that motherfucker, he still tried to play her to the left.

He walked in the door as if he didn’t know that she had already heard everything. But when he looked up at her, her expression confirmed what he already suspected. He was busted.

She was extremely red in the face, and breathing frantically.

“Nigga, you got me fucked up,” she yelled as he closed and locked the door behind him and turned to face her again.

In three strides she was up in his chest, swinging a hand at him violently.

He tried to move but reacted too slowly. The phone in her left hand caught him upside the head, opening a small gash over his brow. “Ah,” he winced.

“You bitch ass motherfucker.” Her arms flailed widely as she pummeled him with punch after vicious punch.

He threw his arms up to cover his face. “Baby, chill the fuck out.”

“No, nigga, you should have chilled. Bitch, where the fuck is my money?” she spat.

“Let me explain.”

“Explain? Explain? Nigga, either you better have my drugs or my motherfuckin’ money. If you don’t, I don’t want to hear shit else that you have to say. Tell it to the bitch I heard you fucking on the phone.”

“What the fuck are you talking about?” he dummied up.

“I’m gonna show you what the fuck I’m talking about.” She backed up a few steps and pulled a gun from her waist. With a scowl on her face, she cocked the *glizzy*, and pointed it at him. She was looking him dead in his eyes, no blinking, with a clip full of bullets. “First, you break my heart, and then you play with my money?” she asked gripping her lips with her front teeth.

“Baby, listen to me,” he pleaded softly while deciding to admit to what she’d obviously heard. “I didn’t mean for it to go there. It—it—it just happened. That bitch meant nothing to me. I love *you*.”

His claim sounded sincere, maybe because she desperately wanted to believe him. Her heart shattered all over again and tears poured down her face.

Sensing her weakness, he cautiously stepped toward her, and then leaned in to hug her. “Baby, we can get through this. Let me make it up to you.” He pressed his lips against her cheek and kissed away a few tears.

“I don’t know if I can trust you.” She sniffled back fresh tears that threatened to escape from her watery eyes.

“You can trust me, baby. I promise you. Please put down that gun before something bad happens.”

She hesitated a moment then let the gun slip from her hand and fall to the floor. His body relaxed against hers and he placed a trail of kisses down her face.

Usually his lips set her body on fire, but she had just heard another bitch moaning from his touch. Add to that, all the other shit she had forgiven him for.

She felt him hardening against her, and that shit pissed her off. The motherfucka had just taken his dick out of another bitch, now he had the nerve to be rocked up for her.

That sealed his fucking fate.

She eased her hand in her pocket and retrieved the syringe. “You wanna try again?” she asked in a forgiving tone. “You promise?” Her arms went around his neck.

“Yeah, baby. And this time I won’t let you down.”

“Ha. Nigga, do I look like a fool?”

Her sudden change of tone confused him. “Say what?” he asked.

“Bruh, you got the wrong bitch.”

With her thumb she flicked the cap off of the needle head. In one swift motion she jabbed the needle into his neck and released the fluid. He let out a pained cry and pushed her away.

"Bitch, what the fuck did you do?" His hand shot up to his neck, where the needle was still lodged. A second later his body hit the floor and he began to lose feeling in his limbs. She had injected him with an instant paralysis drug.

She looked down at him unmercifully. "Nigga, I told you not to play with my money, but you thought a bitch was playing with you. Bruh, I do this, and I'm tired of telling you niggas not to play with me."

Spittle ran from the corners of his mouth. He tried to say something but his jaws locked up. She shook her head at him in pity, but only because he had tried her one too many times.

Moving with purpose, she began to ransack the house. She went from his living room to the attic, destroying everything. Finally, she stepped onto a loose piece of wood on his bedroom floor. She stopped, lifted it up, and found stacks of money.

Flipping through the bands of cash, she saw that it was mostly large bills. With a trained eye, she estimated it to be at least fifty thousand dollars, which was double what he owed her. In addition to the money, she found a whole brick of cocaine.

A smile crept on her face as she stuffed everything into a pillowcase and exited the room. She stormed into the living room and gathered up her bag and the gun she had dropped on the floor. It was only a few feet away from where that nigga laid, so she couldn't help but look down at him again.

A pang of regret shot from her head to her heart, and a tear stung her eye. *Why did it have to come to this?* she couldn't help but wonder.

She had to force her legs to move or she might've stood there for hours pondering the answer to that question.

Finally, she headed to the door, leaving him motionless on the carpet. He was temporarily paralyzed, but not dead. In an hour, or so, he would slowly began to regain use of his limbs. Maybe now he would realize how badly he had fucked up.

As she opened the door, she thought about how letting this nigga slide would have other niggas thinking that they could test her. *You can't have that. These streets ain't no joke. You gotta make niggas respect the way you operate, and nothing earns their respect faster than cold-blooded murder.*

She shut the door, took a silencer out of her bag and screwed it onto the glizzy. *Fuck it. I'ma do his ass,* she decided as she retraced her steps.

His eyes widened when he saw her return with the nine in her grip and a murderous look on her face.

"Why did you have to do me like that?" she asked. "I forgave you for everything. I never planned to hurt you. You've been lying to me since the day that I met your fake ass. I really fell for you."

Saliva was pouring from his mouth, and onto the floor. He never answered her because he could not form the words.

She cocked her tool and aimed it at his head. "You're a real bitch ass nigga. When you reach the other side, say hello to the other niggas I sent there."

She squeezed the trigger, letting off one shot. Pieces of skull and brain splattered onto the floor, and blood splashed up on her face and her clothing. A pool of blood began to drain from his head, and she breathed out a deep sigh.

"Fuck it, the nigga had to go," she said as she turned and headed for the door.

She had never loved a man as much as she loved him, but his deceit had turned her heart cold against him. She looked over her shoulder and caught one final glance at his dead body.

"All grimy motherfuckers get dealt with, eventually," she uttered to herself as she slipped out of the door.

Chapter 1

Keeky stepped outside of her one-bedroom apartment in Houston, TX with a pair of high-waist pussy shorts, a hot pink crop top that read *The Baddest*, and a pair of all-black Jordans.

It had been a hot summer and the day was not very humid. Most people stayed inside because the heat index had been dangerously high for the past few days during mid-day hours. At one hundred two degrees, it wasn't safe to be out and about.

"Say red," she heard a male voice say as she was getting ready to hop in her 2015 candy apple red Nissan Coupe.

She moved her eyes to the right so that she could see who was trying to get her attention through her peripheral. She could see a pearl white Cadillac Escalade with 24's to match the body of the SUV.

"Whoa," Keeky said, trying to keep her cool as she answered him. She hated for a man to refer to her as *red* when he was trying to get her attention. She felt it was annoying and disrespectful.

She bit down on her lips and tilted her head to the side a little as she began to turn around and make eye contact.

He was staring her up and down as if he wasn't expecting her to be so beautiful. She was 6'1", and a slim, fine, red bone. All of the hood niggas wanted her because she was smart and sexy, but still 'bout that gangsta shit. Keeky had naturally long, curly, brown hair with blonde streaks. Her eyes were gray and her lips were a cherry red, but plump. Her titties sat just right and she had an ass to die for.

"What's your name, ma?" he asked.

"Keemari, but everybody calls me Keeky."

"Well I'm not everybody, so I'm gon' call you Keemari pretty lady. Where you headed to?"

"You real nosey to say I ain't catch yo name, and I'm definitely not about to tell you where I'm headed. I don't trust nobody, especially you niggas. I live out here, but I'm from the N.O. so I'm extra careful around you country ass Texas niggas," she said in her New Orleans accent.

"I feel you, shawty. Well, let me get your number so that we can get to know each other better."

Keeky hesitated at first, but dude was stepping out of the Escalade, and homeboy was fine. He was dark-skinned with a sexy bald head, and a nice lined up beard. He had on a pair of joggers, a white tee, and oreo colored Jordans.

Look at the dick print on this God, Keeky thought as she was biting her lips. He reminded her of Tyrese, but with a set of gold teeth on his top and bottom vampire teeth. Dude was hot so Keeky couldn't help but to give him her digits.

"What's yo name?" Keeky asked.

"Zay, baby, just call me Zay."

"Well, Zay, I have to go, but you can give me your number, and I'll text you mine."

As Zay began to call out his digits, Keeky noticed a black Tahoe creeping by. She watched the SUV as it passed. Zay realized that she wasn't paying attention so he stopped calling out his number, and looked around to see what it was that she was watching. She kept her eyes on the Tahoe until it turned the corner. When she glanced back at Zay, she noticed that he was looking around with her.

"I'm sorry for being rude, but I like to watch my surroundings," she said.

"I understand, ma," Zay answered with his eyes now locking with hers.

"You can finish running your digits. You have my undivided attention now," Keeky said as she tried to focus on him.

She noticed the Tahoe coming around the corner again, but this time she didn't take her attention off of Zay. She stayed quiet as the vehicle pulled up behind him, and a nigga wearing a black hoodie jumped out.

"Give it up, nigga," the voice said from the hoodie.

Zay was facing Keeky, and dude was staring her down as he put the gun to Zay's back. His hoodie was drawn up tightly, but she could see the sweat trickling down his face. As dude got ready to reach in Zay's pockets, Keeky pulled a .9mm off of her door.

"No, bitch, you give it up. Yo, Zay, you want me to *yea* this nigga, or you good?" Keeky would have dead him at the go of Zay's word.

Zay was standing there with his hands lifted mid-way. He was breathing heavily, and he seemed to be stiffened. Keeky could tell that he hadn't been robbed at gun point before because he froze as everything was happening. He was slightly shaking, and she noticed that his hands trembled, as well.

Keeky walked over, pulled the nigga's hoodie off, and put the gun to his head. He had a nasty scar on the side of his face that reminded her of a horseshoe. His skin was high yellow, and his hair had deep waves. "Say, today I'm gon' let you live, but I wouldn't mind rocking your ass in broad daylight since you didn't mind fuckin' up my day. Next time you stunt in front of my shit, I'm gon' leave you laying in front of my shit. Nah gimme your piece, and get the fuck on."

Dude handed Keeky his gun. She knew that he was inexperienced because of the way that the whole thing went down. He would have never taken his eyes off of her at any time if he had done this shit before.

Zay turned around, and to Keeky's surprise, he threw a wild punch that hit dude in the nose. After that punch, he didn't stop throwing blows. "Nigga, what you thought I was just gon' let you slide like that? Huh, bitch?" Zay had spit flying out of his mouth as he was yelling at dude. "You tried to catch the wrong nigga down bad today, motherfucka."

"Get the fuck off of me, nigga," dude could barely get out a word as he was being beaten. He never had a chance to fight back. Zay started stomping him as he tried to ball up and protect himself. "Uuuggghhh." He let out a groan as Zay repeatedly kicked the parts of his body that he had access to.

By this time, damn near the whole block was coming outside to see what was going on. Keeky pushed Zay off of dude to snap him out of it. He ran back at him, and began stomping him again.

"Chill the fuck out," she said as she pushed Zay again. "You gon' get us caught the fuck up."

He did not want to quit. "I bet you this nigga gon' remember me everytime he look in the mirror," Zay blurted out. He was moving all over the place as if he thought that he was Superman. He never noticed the crowd that was beginning to watch. Keeky pushed him again, and he stared at her with fire red eyes.

"Calm the fuck down, and follow me," Keeky told him. She grabbed his arm, and pulled him towards her. He stepped over dude, turned his head around to slowly mug him once more, and then ran to his Escalade.

They hopped into their rides, and Zay followed Keeky down the street. She drove until they were a safe distance away from the scene. She pulled into the driveway of an abandoned home down the street, and Zay pulled up behind her. She stepped out of her car, and started walking towards Zay's vehicle.

"Baby girl, you snapped," Zay yelled as he hopped out of his truck and stood in the driver door. At first he was only being flirty with Keeky because he was trying to hit, but now he knew that he had to have her. Keeky was the bitch that every street nigga dreamed of.

"Yeah, I told you I don't trust no nigga so I keep my .9 nearby," she chuckled. It was obvious that she didn't take any shit. She knew that it would be best for them to get out of the neighborhood altogether so she got straight down to business.

"You can run me your number really quick, and then I have to go."

Zay called out his number, and Keeky started walking off.

"Don't forget to hit a nigga up, ma. Use them digits that I just gave you." As he hopped in his truck to roll out, she waved for him to put his window down.

"You owe me," she said with a smirk on her face. He was already thinking the same thing.

"That's a bet. I got you, Keemari," and he rolled off.

***

Four days had passed, and Zay was preparing to go to the barbershop. He went at least once a week in the mornings. He put on some basketball shorts, a muscle shirt, and some Jordan slippers as he walked over to the kitchen table to grab his keys.

Black hat, black shades, black diamonds oh behave... no he can't with the fuckin' seats back, got the paint job tho and the fuckin' seats cracked, I'm a d-boy... his Lil Wayne ring tone was going off in his pocket as he was trying to leave.

"Hello," he said.

"What's good with you?" a female voice said from the other end of the phone.

"I'm chillin', who dis?"

"Keeky."

"Ooooh, what's up, Keemari? I thought you forgot about a nigga."

"Nawwww, it ain't like that. It's just that school and work had me tied up."

"What are you going to school for?"

"I'm a math major."

"Where do you work at?"

"You ask too many questions, and I'm not a phone person. I just wanted to holla at you. You have my number so hit me up when it's good for you."

"A'ight ma, that's cool. But before I let you go, can I get you to say yes to going out on a date with me? No, better yet, I owe you. So, how about you come to my spot, and I'm gon' hook something up for you?"

"Your spot? Where you stay at?" she asked as him inviting her over sent up a red flag for her.

"I stay on the southside, baby girl. You'll be safe with me. Don't worry." He laughed because he could sense the tenseness in her voice.

"I don't do house visits."

"Well, I don't just invite anybody over to my house like that, but I'm taking a chance on you, so why not take a chance on me?"

"I hear you. You know what, you did say you cook, huh? Damn right, I'll come over."

"Tomorrow, 8:00. Is that good for you?"

"Address?"

"I live in North Teal Esatates Circle."

"See you tomorrow."

After they hung up, Keeky called her best friend, Dymond. She wanted to let her know that she had a date on tomorrow.

"Waddup, girl?" Dymond asked Keeky as she answered the phone.

"Chillin'. You know that I haven't really been dating, but a few days ago I met a nigga that got my attention. He almost got smashed in front of my spot, girl. I had to pull out my .9 on the nigga who was trying to smash him."

“Wait. Bitch, what happened?” Dymond was at full attention now.

“I’m gon’ run all the details later when we link up at the trap spot, bruh. Right now I need you to help me to get ready for this date. I have to be fly when I go over to that nigga house.”

“Well, sis, I’m on my way to your spot so that you can run that tea while I help you find something to wear, and fix your hair because I’m not waiting until tomorrow for the tea, girl. You got me fucked up. I’m on my way.”

Chapter 2

It was a beautiful day outside. The birds were chirping, the sun was shining brightly, there was a little breeze passing through, and the atmosphere seemed to be peaceful. Zay locked up his spot, walked to his truck, and thought about what he could do now that he had gotten Keeky to agree to come over. No way was he letting her get away that easily, so he had to bring it.

"Wassup, shawty?" Zay asked as he answered the phone. It was Fendi. She was one of the women that he dealt with every now and again when he would feel like being bothered, or when he just needed a female friend to entertain him.

"Nothing much baby. I wanted to go and get my hair and nails done. Do you think that you could look out for me?" she asked him.

He hesitated before he answered. He was tired of dealing with the same types of women all of the time. The ones that would rather have their hands out than to get it on their own, the ones that could not think past their looks, the ones that were materialistic and had no goals set in life, etc. He was fed up with their kind, and it was beginning to show.

"You know what? Hell no, I can't give it to you. I have my own shit to do today, and it doesn't include spending my hard earned money on your ass. If you need it that bad, you better call the next nigga 'cause Zay ain't upping a damn thing." He hung up the phone and shook his head. He didn't expect to hear from her again because money was her motive. If he wasn't giving up the money, then she definitely wasn't trying to hang around, and he knew it.

He made it to the barbershop to get his beard lined up, and trimmed. He asked the old head there what was something special that he could do for a young lady that he had his eye on.

"She might be the one," he said to the old head as he lined him up.

"Well, first things first, you have to be yourself, but you also need to bring that romance back. You young niggas today don't know how to treat a woman. That's why y'all end up losing the good ones, and they come running back to old heads like me that know how to spoil them," he chuckled while tilting Zay's head backwards so that he could line up the bottom portion of his beard. He cleaned up his razor and continued, "You see, the problem is that none of y'all youngsters know what it is that y'all are looking for. If all you're ever interested in is a nice ass and a pretty face, then that is all that you will ever look for. If you want something more, you have to look for something more in a woman."

"That's what I'm doing with this one. She's more than just a pretty face, and a nice ass to me. I mean, I can't lie, shawty is fine and all, but I can see that she has a lot of potential," Zay explained.

"Well, if she's all that and you don't know what to do with her, bring her to me. I'll show you what to do with a woman like that," he laughed.

"I hear you old man," Zay said as he sat up in the chair. The old man handed him a mirror so that he could check out his work. He admired himself for a minute, and handed it back. He passed his hand up and down around his beard area, and then underneath his chin. He handed him his money, dapped off the other men in the barbershop, then made his way out of the door.

He thought about the conversation that he had just had, and the old head was right. If he wanted Keemari on his team, he had to do something that he had never done, to get the type of woman that he'd never had.

Zay headed home to wash up. *What can I cook to show off for this woman,* he thought to himself as he was driving home.

He had a few hours left to play with, so he decided to make a stop at the grocery store. He took out his cell, and made a list of the ingredients that he would need in his memos. He got out of his ride, walked towards the store, and grabbed a buggy from the outside near the doors. As he made his way inside, he noticed an elderly lady with two young children who seemed to be searching her purse for something that she obviously could not find. The two little kids seemed to be hurt that the old lady had to leave whatever it is that they were buying at the store.

"Excuse me, miss," Zay said as he tapped her on her shoulers. He did not know exactly what it was that she needed, but he assumed that it was money because she was preparing to leave the items that she was trying to purchase.

"How you doing there, suga'?" she looked at him and said. She had a slight tremble in her hands, and a small hump in her upperback.

"Can I help you to purchase your things? It would be my pleasure." She had food items and toiletries. He could not figure out why the kids looked so sad if there was nothing on the belt in particular for them.

"Thank you, young man, but I will have to decline." She was very stern with him.

"Well, consider it a blessing. I've been blessed abunantly, and now I would like to bless you."

"Well, since you put it that way, okay." She allowed Zay to pay for her things, and she gathered the children so that they could leave. Zay began to walk off, but the old lady sent one of the kids to tap him so that he could turn around and return.

"Yes, ma'am?" Zay asked. "Did I forget to pay for something?"

"No, you didn't. Take a walk outside with me." She motioned for him to follow her. He did not know what she could want with him outside, but he agreed to follow. "These here are my grandkids," she said pointing to the children that accompanied her. "They belong to my daughter. My daughter is not stable right now. I have not raised a child in a long time. I've been praying daily that my child can get her life together, and come take care of her kids. It's been a struggle with them, and I've barely been able to make ends meet. I forgot my check book at home. I was going to write a check for the items that you bought for me, and hope that it didn't bounce. Instead, God sent you. My grandkids were disappointed because they had not eaten in a while. I just can't afford it. I just wanted to say that God has a blessing with your name on it. Thank you. Blessings like these don't come too often."

"It is I who was blessed, ma'am. Blessed that God has put me in the position to be able to help you, and you are most welcome." He hugged her, and shook hands with the kids before walking off proudly. He was a firm believer of doing good to people because he felt as if it would bring good back to you.

He had about three more hours left to prepare for Keeky's arrival. She deserved for him to go all out for her, not just because she had saved his life, but also because she had the potential to be the woman that he needed. It was not that he had been searching for a lady to make a life with, but if a good woman was sent to him he surely would not pass up the opportunity to have her.

He found everything that he was looking for in the grocery store, and he prayed that Keeky would like it. He purchased his things, and made his way back home to get prepared. He still had to bathe, prepare the food, find the right clothing to wear for the evening, and he had to make sure that his place was spotless. After about two hours had passed, he had a thought that he was sure would win Keeky over. He took his cell phone out of his pocket, and called her.

"Hello," Keeky answered.

"Yo, wassup? I have an idea," Zay said.

"Run it then. I'm listening."

"I was thinking. Since you said that you don't feel comfortable with house visits, how about we go out to eat. I bought everything to prepare a nice meal for you, but by no means do I want you to feel uncomfortable with me."

"That's wassup. I would like that."

"Would you like me to pick you up?"

"Nawww, I'm good. I'll let my homegirl bring me. Where is it that we are we going, by the way?"

"To Brennan's of Houston. Meet me there at eight."

"That's a bet. I'll be there."

They hung up, and Zay rushed to prepare for the evening. He prayed that there would be openings at Brennan's because he would need to make reservations in order for them to have dinner there, he still needed to freshen up, and he definintely needed to stop at the bank to get enough money to wine and dine Keemari for the night. He seemed to be getting lucky in every area that he needed to address as he was on his way to meet her.

His cell phone went off at 7:59. "'Sup Keemari?"

"I'm at the door," she told him.

"I'm walking up now."

Zay made his way to the door, and was mesmerized as Keemari stood there in an all-white Bebe dress with red heels and the purse and accessories to match. Dymond had whipped her hair into a mohawk style, and her makeup was on point.

"Got damn," said Zay, damn near drooling. Keeky's body was banging.

"You don't look too bad yourself," she said, smiling. Zay had on a black and white polo button down, with white Levi pants. He had on a pair of white Cole Haan's, and his cologne had Keeky's nose wide open.

This nigga smells good as a motherfucker.

Zay held the door as they walked inside. The hostess met them at the reception area and asked if they had reservations. He gave her his last name, and she showed them to their table. He pulled out a chair for her, and then walked around the table to seat himself.

"Would you all like anything to drink?" the hostess asked.

"Yes, ma'am," Keeky responded, "I would like a glass of lemonade please."

"What about you, sir? Would you like anything to drink?" she asked Zay.

"Yes, ma'am. I would like a glass of water to start off with."

The hostess wrote down their drink orders, and then handed them their menus. "I'll be back shortly with your drinks. Please look over our menu, and I'll be glad to take your orders when I return."

As she walked off from their table, Zay took Keeky's hand, and held it in his. He looked into her eyes, and rubbed his thumb across the rest of her fingers. "I don't know what it is about you, but I'm really feeling you, ma." She could tell that he was serious because of the way that he looked at her. It was something about how a man looked at the woman that he really cared about.

"How do you know that you really want me if you've only been around me once?" she asked with a stern look on her face.

"Because it doesn't take long for a man to know what he wants. We know when we first meet a woman what our intentions are for her."

"I'm sure you do. So when you first met me, what were your intentions?"

"Honestly, Keemari, when I first met you, my intentions were to try and have sex with you, but it was something about the way that you handled yourself that made me realize that you are not like the rest."

"And what's so different about me?"

Zay started to answer her question, but was interrupted by the hostess. "Are you all ready to order?" she asked.

"Yes, ma'am," Keeky answered. "I'll have the alfredo stuffed lobster please."

"And what about you sir?" the hostess asked Zay.

"I'll have the same."

"Would you all care for a glass of wine while you wait?"

"No, ma'am. We are fine."

"O.K. I'll return shortly with your meals." The hostess walked away, and Zay wasted no time continuing his conversation.

"I don't even have to eat. I can just sit here and stare at your beauty all night long."

Keeky thought to herself, *I hope this nigga don't think that he's getting some. He can eat me, but he cannot fuck me*. "Is that right?" she asked. "I cannot imagine you passing up such a good meal to stare at me the whole night." She chuckled, but she was flattered inside. The hostess returned with their meals, and Keeky's eyes lit up. She was amazed at how good everything looked.

"Enjoy your meals. If there is anything else that I can do for you, please do not hesitate to ask."

"Thank you," Keeky and Zay said in unison.

They began to eat slowly. "A nigga never did no fancy shit like this for me before," she said.

"As beautiful as you are, I'd do this type of shit daily." Keeky smiled and continued to eat. She blushed at the thought of him willing to wine and dine her daily.

"I believe that you would do things like this for me, but you cannot make me believe that you would do this everyday. It's impossible. It would be nice, but we both know that ain't happening."

"I don't know what type of niggas you're used to, baby girl, but I'm aiming to please."

"That's wassup. I like that. You're quick with your responses, but I will be the woman to make you back those words up."

"That's fine. I'm willing to back up every word, in every way. Let me explain something to you, this is not something that I do for every woman that I meet," he said as he looked at Keeky while she continued to eat. "I do not believe in leading people on. I have come to realize that I cannot treat every lady the same, and I cannot love every lady the same. I believe that the right woman is worth going all out for. That is why I decided to go above and beyond for you."

"Is that right?" Keeky said with a kool-aid smile on her face. She was starting to turn red, and she definitely was beginning to soften up. She felt warm and tingly inside. That was a feeling that she had not gotten since her days with Jakobe'. Jakobe' was her first real love, her first lover, and her first heartbreak.

As they finished up, she put her mint in her mouth, and took out her cell to call for her ride. "What are you doing?" Zay asked. He knew that she was trying to get away, but he could not let her do that just yet.

"I'm calling for my ride. I don't want to be sitting here when you leave."

"I could take you home."

"No, thank you. I'm fine. I'd rather call my girl to come and get me."

"What if we go catch a movie?"

"You know what? I would like that, but how about we go over to your place and catch that movie instead?"

"My place? You really want to go over to my place?"

"Yeah, let's go to your spot. I wanna see how you're living anyway."

He agreed, and they got up from the table. He left a nice tip for the hostess, then walked over to open the door for Keeky. As they headed to his vehicle, he let it be known that a man is always supposed to treat a lady like a lady. He opened doors, he said please and thank you, and he gave her his undivided attention. It took them approximately thirty minutes to make it to Zay's place. As they arrived, he opened her door, grabbed her hand to help her out of the vehicle, and walked her to his door. He unlocked it, and flicked on his lights. They stood in the entrance of what seemed to be a family room.

"This is my living area," Zay explained.

He had a 70" TV, white leather sofas, white carpet, white coffee tables, and small artwork to accent the area perfectly. They walked to his master bedroom. He had a 60" flat screen mounted on the wall over the fireplace, and a California King sized sleigh bed.

"Have a seat," Zay said pointing to his bed, "I won't bite."

Keeky rolled her eyes at Zay, and then looked at his bed. She did not move. She stood there staring at him as if he had said something that cut her spirit deeply.

"I'm tired of telling you that I don't trust you niggas. I really did come over here to watch a movie with you, only."

"Chill, baby girl, and let me finish making it up to you."

"Whatever," Keeky said as she stared at his bed again. She was not willing to sit down and have him catch her off guard in any way. She was beginning to tense up because she felt as if he was being a little too persistent.

Zay pushed her back, pushed her dress up, and started to kiss her from her thighs to her ankles. His lips were so soft, but she still did not want to give in so easily. She pushed him back, and tried to get up. There was no way that she was going to let him take advantage of her so quickly. She was used to being the dominant one in the bedroom, and Zay was moving so fast that she didn't even have a chance to say no, or play hard to get at first.

"You got me fucked up," she said. "I didn't come over here to let you have your way with me. Either we wait, or you can let me leave. We can do this in my time, or we can let this shit go altogether."

"Shawty, I'm not trying to take advantage of you. You have to learn to relax, and let a man be a man. I'm in charge in this bedroom, whether you like it or not, baby girl."

"Well, I'm out then. Do your thing. Thanks for the meal. I'll holla."

"You really think that I'm going to let you leave like that after I've worked so hard to get you here?" Zay was not about to give up and Keeky could tell. His aggressiveness was actually a turn on to her because she had never had a man that was so willing to go after what he wanted.

He picked her up, threw her back on the bed, and pushed her legs towards her stomach. While pinning her in that position, he used his tongue to go up her thighs, and straight to her clit. He grabbed her legs tighter so that she couldn't move, and he began to tongue the pussy like it was a peach. He wiggled it from side to side so that he could stimulate her clitoris. He loosened his grip just a little bit so that she could begin to swish her hips enough to give him the rhythm that she wanted.

He turned his head sideways, and put his lips in between her pussy lips as he sucked on her clit some more. She could not keep still as his tongue flickered her pearl tongue. Her legs began to tremble, and her heart rate picked up. She started to moan as he began to slurp her wetness. He waited until she came and he made sure to slurp all of that, too. He leaned up to kiss her and she could feel his rock hard dick pressing against her still sensitive clitoris. She wanted that dick badly, and she was beginning to let it show as her juices flowed down her legs. She pulled him closer and his dick felt like a heartbeat.

"You want that dick, huh?" Zay asked.

"Yeah, I want it right now, baby."

"Well, not tonight, I'm good. I just wanted to make it up to you from the other day," he said and stood up.

Keeky lay there, heart pounding, not believing that this nigga was about to leave her hanging like that.

"Get up, ma. I hope you didn't think that all I wanted to do was hit, baby girl. I ain't that type of nigga."

Zay gently helped her up and pointed her to the bathroom so that she could go wash up. Keeky couldn't believe this nigga flipped the script on her like that, but she respected the hell out of him for it, and it made her crave him even more.

"Baby girl, you never told me where you work at," Zay said as Keeky began to run the water in the bathroon.

"I told you that you ask too many questions. Nigga, where do you work at?" she shot back at him.

"The streets is my occupation, but I'm not a flashy type nigga. I try to stay low-key, which is why I moved to this area, and I started a construction business to keep the laws off of me," explained Zay as he was talking loud enough for Keeky to hear him over the running water.

"Yo, that's wassup," Keeky said with a smile on her face, "so why don't you have a female on your team? I know you have options."

"Yeah, I do, but I got too much going on to hook up with the wrong bitch and have her get me caught up. I really started from the bottom so I move carefully. I've done jail too many times and my T-Lady done cried over me so much I can't even do it to her anymore. My moms really loves me, baby girl. I'm her only son."

"Real. Well since you kept it 51/50 with me, I might as well do the same," Keeky said while walking out of the bathroom.

"My life hasn't been easy and I'm not trynna run my history to you, but I had to learn to hustle to take care of myself. My people died in a car wreck when I was seventeen so I've been gettin' it out the mud ever since. My brother was a trapper before he got murdered, and that's who gave me the game. His murder really made me cold-hearted on some shit. He got rocked by his homeboy. Them niggas was friends since birth. I can remember how close those niggas were to each other. I can still see that nigga crying hard at the funeral, and having to be escorted out several times. When I found out that he was actually the nigga who rocked my brother, I couldn't keep myself together. My brother was my best friend. He didn't bring me around them niggas so they really didn't know much about me. It was only fair that I made that nigga family cry, too. School is going to be my way outta this shit one day."

"Damn, lil' mama, you been poppin' that pistol, huh?" Zay asked in shock, but loving that shit at the same time.

"Maybe, maybe not."

"I think I love you," Zay laughed.

Keeky tooted up her top lip, and then she shared in on the laughter with Zay right before her phone rang, taking her attention off of him.

"Hold up." She reached onto the dresser to retrieve her cell. It was Dymond. "What's up? You know…"

Dymond abruptly cut her off. "We need to meet ASAP." She hung up the phone. Keeky already knew what that meant. Every time she tried to chill and wind down a little, something always reminded her of why she had to stay on beast mode.

"I'm gon' have to holla at you later. I got something that I need to handle. Can you take me home?"

Zay grabbed her, and kissed her gently. Then they walked outside to his car.

He opened the door for her, and then walked over to his side to start it up. He popped in a CD, and the music started blasting. *What they told me don't do do from small, I grew up doin' different. Told me stay away from drugs, I grew up doin' business. Mama know I'm doin' wrong, I'm on a grind I can't hide it, she seen me broke Monday had a big knot by Friday*, Kada rang out through his speakers.

"What is that you listening to?" she asked him as they were bobbing their heads.

"That's my nigga, Kada. I'm trying to get his shit heard out here in Texas. He cold, huh?"

"Fuckin' right. Where he from?"

"He's from the boot. Them Louisiana niggas is poppin' right now. Here's a CD. Check my nigga out."

Keeky was so into her coversation with Zay that she didn't notice her phone lighting up. It had been on vibrate, and Dymond seemed to be blowing her up. "You on your way?" Dymond asked when Keeky finally answered the phone as she was pulling out of Zay's driveway.

"Yeah, bitch. Why you in a hurry? What the fuck done happened now?" Keeky snapped.

"Some nigga just pulled a strap on me while I was at your spot. I went over to chill until you called me to come and get you. I decided to go take a ride, and I was getting in your car, dude just walked up on me. I should have let you take your own car, bitch," Dymond said jokingly. "Nigga said to let you know that he got you for that shit that you and dude pulled on him the other day."

"What did the nigga look like? You saw his face?" Dymond could hear the rage in Keeky's voice.

"Oooohhhh snap. Bitch, I bet that's the dude you pulled your nine on, now that I think about it? Nigga really looked fucked up, and he looked like he was on some other shit, too. That nigga had that same scar that you described to me so that had to be him. I'm glad that boy ain't rock me, yo, but we gotta end this nigga before he becomes a problem. I'm ready to sleep the nigga tonight if you with the shit."

Keeky was in a rage. "I'm on my way. Grab me a black hoodie, some black tights, my J's, and my Ruger. Meet me at the other spot. Zay is gonna drop me off."

Chapter 3

Dymond was just like Keeky to a certain extent because that's who she learned the game from. She was a twenty-four-year old streetfighter from the Bronx. Fighting was how she made her money before she and Keeky started hustling full-time. Dymond and her brother, Blayden, moved to Texas when they were thirteen and fourteen, after their parents separated. Their father had custody of them because their mom started losing all of their money when she became a heroin addict. Dymond met Keeky when she was sixteen, and they'd been best friends ever since. Being that Dymond was a tom-boy, she really did not have many boyfriends. The ones that she did have, they dated for awhile. She spent most of her time being overprotective of Blayden since she was the oldest. She was always a fighter, but she became a killer when she and her cousin Zah met Keeky. They all started out with hard lives, but losing Zah about three years ago was what really shook Dymond up.

"You got what I asked for, sis? I'm about to pull up." Keeky called to ask Dymond.

"Yeah, I got it, my girl. The only thing that I had trouble finding was that damn Ruger, but because I know your ass so good, I ended up finding it. Check it out though, picture I had my people trace that plate number. This nigga stays on South Taylor Street."

"I know you lying. So this nigga close?"

"Yeah, bruh, let's do this shit 'cause we got money to make. Blayden just called and he got a sixty thousand dollar dope sale."

"That's why I fucks with Blayden. If he wasn't your brother, I would have made him my nigga a long time ago."

Dymond rolled her eyes because she hated hearing females talk about how fine her brother was. That shit was disgusting.

"Bitch, I don't wanna hear that shit. I'll see you in a few, I have to click over."

"A'ight then. We'll run it when I make it."

"That's a bet. Bye, girl."

Dymond clicked over. "Waddup beautiful?" Dymond's boyfriend asked when she answered the phone.

"Nothing, daddy. About to go make a run with Keeky. Waddup?"

"I want you to stop by my spot when you're done, bae. I got something special for you."

"That's a bet. I'll be there."

"Love you, girl."

"Love you too, bae."

Dymond was hard on the outside, but she had a soft spot for Bliss, whom she frequently referred to as daddy. They had been together for four years now, and she was hooked on him. She arrived to the spot, and realized that Keeky had already made it there.

"Yo, Keeky, you ready to ride out? I just got a text from Khalil," she yelled out.

Khalil was Zah's boyfriend before they lost her, and he was also Blayden's best friend.

"Gimme five more minutes, I gotta finish puttin' this shit in the duffle bag," Keeky said. "A'ight. I got that other shit that you asked for, too." Dymond told her.

"Slide it in here," Keeky said. "I won't be long getting ready." It took her about ten minutes, but Keeky finished up what she needed to do for their sale, and she was ready to roll.

As Keeky walked up, she just stared at Dymond. Dymond's legs were cocked up on the coffee table, and she sat slumped back into the couch. "You think you sexy, huh, bitch?" Keeky chuckled as she joked with her. Dymond was thick, fine, caramel skinned tone, wore braces, and stood about 5'6". Looking at her kind of reminded you of Delicious from Flava of Love. She was banging, but she was a tom-boy. She grew up playing sports, but she mostly boxed because her dad was into it. Taking shit off of anybody was not of her demeanor. "Come on, I'm ready," Keeky said as she was getting short winded from carrying that heavy duffle bag.

"A'ight, let's roll out. My man just called me so I'm trying to finish this shit quick."

"Bitch, you act like you have to go running everytime that nigga call."

"I do. How do you think that I kept my nigga all of this time? This street shit is how I eat, Bliss is how I cum."

"You nasty, braud," Keeky said with a disgusted look on her face.

They laughed and walked out of the door.

Keeky rolled down her windows so that they could enjoy the breeze on the twenty-minute ride to Khalil's place. When they pulled up to his apartment to drop off the duffle bag, Dymond stayed in the car while Keeky went inside. Whenever they went to make a transaction of any kind, they always left one person behind to lookout, and make sure that things stayed settled on the outside.

"Yo, Khalil, it's me," Keeky yelled as she banged on the door so that he could hear her.

It took him no time to answer the door, and let Keeky in. She was fascinated with his place. She stepped inside and noticed that Khalil had his place set up like a bachelor bad. He had never gotten serious with another woman since Zah was reported missing a few years ago. He had a bar set in the kitchen area with almost every brand of liquor imaginable. There was a fifty-inch aquarium in the living room wall with exotic fish, a projector coming out of the ceiling, and a nice bar-sized pool table in the middle of the floor. He had a chocolate leather sectional in the corner, and windows were everywhere. It was the perfect duckoff. Hard to imagine that this was an apartment.

"I'm trying to live like you when I grow up," Keeky jokingly told Khalil.

"Shiidddd, I'm trying to be ballin' like you and Dymond. Y'all the ones with that work."

"No doubt, no doubt. This is a whole lot of work that we're trusting you with, though. Do you think that you're going to be able to move that shit?" Keeky got right down to business.

She didn't believe in beating around the bush, or lettin' a nigga chop it up about everything except for what she went over there to talk about.

"So, you have two bricks, that's one hundred twenty thousand dollars. Since we fronted you, we gon' need ten thousand dollars on top of that. I'm making sure that you gon' be able to push that because we been knowing each other too long for you to make me have to choose between you, my drugs, and my money. I already don't believe in frontin' a nigga, so don't take my kindness for weakness. You already know what choice I'm gon' make if I have to choose."

"Yeah, I feel you. I already know y'all rules."

"All I suggest, playboy, is if you fall asleep, and you don't wake up one hundred thirty thousand dollars richer, don't go back to sleep. I would hate to have to be the bitch to wake you up, just so I can put you back to sleep my nigga. It's always business over bullshit."

"Standing here listening to you is really making me miss Zah right now. I know she would have been right by y'all side."

"Fasho. I loved that girl like a sister, bruh. If we ever luck up and find the motherfuckers responsible for Zah coming up missin', I'm gon' drop them bitches where they stand."

"Real talk."

"Well, I'm gon' holla, nigga. We have something that we need to get to ASAP."

"That's a bet," Khalil said.

She went outside and hopped back into Dymond's black GMC Yukon Denali with the cop tint, and all black 26's, and they headed out.

They pulled up on the corner of South Taylor Street within about thirty minutes. The block was quiet except for about five niggas standing around in the front yard of a run down old house. It looked like a trap house.

"Yo, you ready?" Keeky wanted to know from Dymond.

"Yeah, you want me to pass by, and then spin this bitch around? We could bust at 'em on our way passin' back like we used to do."

"Fuck no. Bitch I gotta walk down on this nigga. When I leave I gotta know for sure this nigga ain't breathin', but you could pass by so that we could make sure we have the right nigga first."

Dymond slowly drove down the street, and passed the house that the men were occupying outside. The guy that they were looking for was standing at the head of the driveway with his hands inside of his pockets, and he was smoking a cigarette. Nobody could see inside of Dymond's SUV because of the dark tint that she had, but the occupants of her vehicle could see what was happening outside. One of the guys tooted his head up as if he was speaking to them as they passed. She drove around the block to the next street, they parked, and got out of the Denali.

They walked through a couple of back yards until they were able to see the nigga that they were looking for. He was still standing at the head of the driveway. They pulled up their hoodies, and walked up on them from behind.

"Bitch, lay down," Keeky yelled as she walked up on him.

Before any of the other guys could run, Dymond ran up with a choppa, and made everybody else get down. "Where y'all niggas thought y'all was goin'? Move, or I'm gon' start dumpin' on you niggas."

Keeky was in a rage by this time. "Didn't I fuckin' make myself clear when I told yo' ass not to come by my spot again? That's the problem with y'all niggas now. Y'all motherfuckers too hard headed. I told you I was gon' lay yo' ass out if you play with me again. Nah, bitch, beg since you act like you don't have no understanding."

"Fuck you," he yelled out, "Bitch if you was a killer you would have done me in the first time."

"Nigga, be quiet, these hoes is serious," one of his potnahs yelled.

"Hoes," Dymond said. "Nigga, I got yo' hoe", and she kicked him in the face.

"You right, nigga, fuck me. But since you think I'm playing, I'm gon' off one of your niggas first." Keeky let out three shots to the nigga laying across from him, one to the head and two in his back.

"Bitch, that was my lil' brother," he started screaming.

"Nigga, fuck yo' brother. Open your mouth, or I'm killin' somebody else."

"Bitch, I'm not..." he tried to say before he was interrupted by Keeky.

The street was quiet, and the neighbors seemed to be asleep. Not a car was riding by, and it seemed as if they could do what they needed to do and leave. Keeky stuck the Ruger in his mouth, and bent down to look in his eyes. "Suck it," she said moving it slowly in and out of his mouth. "How that bitch taste? You look like you done sucked dick before ol' wide mouth ass nigga. Oh well, I just wanted you to know what the Ruger tasted like before I send you to meet the Reaper, bitch." She shot him in the mouth, then she stood over him and let off six more rounds before she stopped shooting.

Dymond watched as Keeky finished, then she told her that they needed to go. Dymond didn't believe in leaving witnesses so she let the choppa sing on the rest of the niggas.

They ran through the cut and around the block to where the Denali was parked.

"Bitch, start this truck up and roll out before somebody spots us. After all them rounds we let off, I know the neighbors are bound to start coming outside," Keeky told Dymond.

"Yeah, plus we have to meet Blayden in about thirty more minutes. You know that nigga is impatient."

"Shit, I forgot about that. Roll out. You gon' have to move this bitch lightly though, Blayden gon' understand. We got a brick in here, and illegal guns."

"I feel you, put the windows down though. I need to smoke somethin' after that shit we just pulled."

"Now why would you let the windows down if we ridin' dirty?"

"Bitch, ain't no cops out right now, and plus I don't like my truck to smell like that shit, whether I smoke it or not."

Keeky just did as she was told. Dymond looked in her rearview as Keeky put the window down. She gasped, "Oh shit!"

"What the fuck is wrong with you?" Keeky looked at Dymond and asked.

"Bitch, the nigga you just offed, his Tahoe is behind us." Dymond looked spooked.

"I made sure that nigga was dead. How the fuck did his Tahoe get behind us? Bitch, ain't no way that boy was still breathing."

"Be cool. I'm not gon' let them know that we see them following us. Whoever the fuck that is gon' follow us straight to Blayden."

"If we weren't ridin' dirty, I'd bust at the bitch right now."

"We good. Let me hit up Blayden real quick."

"What's up, sis? I'm waitin' on y'all at the spot," Blayden answered as if he was aggravated.

"Nigga, we on our way, but we're bein' followed. Meet us on Tab Lane," Dymond hurriedly explained.

"A'ight. I'm gon' find a duckoff to pull into, and wait til I see y'all."

"That's a bet." Dymond and Blayden hung up.

"That nigga on his way Keeky so stay calm, bitch, I'm tellin' you. We ridin' too dirty for you to try and pull off some dumb shit."

"Man, I'm calm."

Ten minutes later, they pulled up into a yard on Tab Lane. Dymond and Keeky strapped up, then hopped out as if they were walking inside. The house that they parked in front of was beautiful. It was a two-story home with a half of circle driveway. It was surrounded by palm trees, and had a huge fountain in the front.

They heard a door close from behind them, and when they turned around, they had their straps pointing straight at a dark-skinned chick who had her strap pointed straight back at them.

"Man, this whole time you was a bitch ridin' behind us?" Dymond asked disgusted.

"You bitches murked my lil brothers," she said as tears rolled down her eyes. "I saw y'all running back to y'all ride, and I followed you bitches. Yoooo, Reign, I got these bitches. Come out."

A soft voice spoke from behind Keeky, "Drop the gun now, bitch. Don't make me tell you twice."

Keeky slowly put her gun down.

"Now kick it over there to my girl, and tell your homegirl to put her shit down, too."

"Dymond, don't you lay that pistol down. This bitch gon' have to kill me," Keeky said clutching her teeth.

Reign cocked her gun. "So, you think that I'm playin'? You think this shit is a game? Tell your homegirl to drop the gun."

Dymond bent down to drop the pistol, but came up out of her sock with a .22. She pointed it at Reign, and kept the other pistol pointed at the dark-skinned chick.

Blayden pulled up, and hopped out of his whip. Dymond, being the overprotective sister that she was, felt that it was way too much trigger play so she told Blayden to hop back in his ride.

"I got this, bro. Me and Keeky have to handle this shit ourselves. This shit is personal."

"I'm tired of talkin' to you bitches," Reign shouted and let off two quick shots. Blayden screamed and took off running towards them.

"Who the fuck are you?" Keeky asked Reign. To their surprise, Reign had put two shots in the chest of the bitch who had hired her to kill Dymond and Keeky.

Blayden was running full throttle because he could not believe this shit. He had to see what was actually going down. He thought to himself, *what the fuck is really going on? How in the hell could this chick really kill the female that she came here with?*

"Yeah, bitch, who the fuck are you?" Dymond demanded to know, clutching tighter to her .22.

Reign still had on her skii mask as she began to speak. "When I went over to meet ol' girl a little while ago about some other shit, we heard gun shots ringing outside. After everything seemed to be settled down, we ran outside, and her people was dead down the street from their house. We turned around, we saw y'all two running through the cut. Ol' girl told me to keep the ten thousand dollars that she had just given to me, and said that I could use it as a payment if I would do y'all in. She's not a killer, none of them are, which is why they were trying to hire me in the first place. I accepted because this is what I do, and it was on the spot money. When I told you to tell Dymond to drop the gun, I didn't recognize y'all names at first. When Dymond went down, and came back up with the .22 out of her sock, then looked towards me, I recognized her face. You couldn't see me through this mask, but I could see you." Dymond looked at Reign confused.

Keeky got aggravated and took the gun from Dymond. "Bitch, who the fuck are you?" Keeky asked as she lifted the gun to Reign's head. She took off her skii mask and said, "It's me, Zha'Reign."

"What the fuck?" Dymond said. "Bitch, this cannot be real. I mean, what the fuck? How the hell? Man we've been missing you for years," Keeky said before they all started crying.

"I have to call Khalil," Blayden said taking out his phone.

"No. No. No. *Please don't*," Zha'Reign yelled out.

"What do you mean, please don't? This man has been hurting since the day you disappeared," Blayden said.

"*Don't*," Zha'Reign screamed. "He's the reason I was missing. Remember back then when I decided that I would start doing the hits for money? Well, I had a fifty thousand dollar hit from a nigga named Kayne. Khalil came with me. When we got to the spot where the hit was supposed to go down, that nigga Khalil gave me one to the stomach, and one to the chest. He took off with the money I had on me, and left me for dead."

"How the fuck are you still alive then?" Blayden wanted to know.

"I don't even know. All I know is that I woke up in a hospital bed in Alabama where the hit was supposed to go down at, and a nurse was fuckin' telling me that I wouldn't be able to have any children. It took me a while to get my memory back, but once I got it all the way together and they released me, I was on a mission to find and kill that bitch ever since."

"So, you're tellin' us that this sheisty ass motherfucka knew what the fuck happened to you after all of this time?" Keeky yelled.

"Yeah, but it's cool. I got a cake baked for this nigga. I've been putting this shit together in my mind for years, but I couldn't find him."

"Yo, let's roll out," Dymond said. "We can catch up later. Y'all are forgetting that we have a body out here."

"We can go," Blayden said, "but I have something to tell y'all first."

"Hurry up nigga," Keeky said.

"Y'all gotta promise me that y'all gon' let me be the one to set this nigga up for Zha, please. When she disappeared and didn't show up for years, I couldn't figure out for the life of me why this nigga didn't ever want to hook up with another female. I thought it was because he was in love with Zha, and he really had hopes of her return. But listening to her talk, and eavesdropping on this nigga ol' suspicious ass conversations, I've finally figured out what it was. He didn't move on because he was, and still is, fuckin' the nigga that asked Zha to do the hit."

They couldn't believe what it was that they were hearing. Khalil was down low. They did not have the time to let that shit register.

Keeky, Dymond, and Zha hopped in the Denali, and Blayden ran back to his car. They rode home in silence. Keeky and Zha decided that they would go over to chill at Dymond's place until she came from Bliss'. Dymond didn't have a problem with it because it would be just like old times. As they were on their way, they talked about the old days, and how things could finally go back to the way they were. Dymond called Bliss to tell him that she was on her way. "I'll be there in five minutes," she said when Bliss answered the phone.

"I'll be waiting, baby girl."

As she hung up the phone, she wondered if Zha was still the same after all that she went through, and all of the time that she was away from them. They arrived at Bliss' place, and Dymond reassured Keeky that she would call when she was ready for her to scoop her up. She hopped out, and walked straight through the door of his spot.

"Hey, babe," Dymond called out.

"Come in the room. I'm back here," Bliss hollered.

Dymond opened the door and Bliss was standing there naked with a rose in his mouth. His dick was standing at attention, and his body was glowing. Dymond walked over to Bliss, gently grabbed the rose out of his mouth, and placed her hand around his piece. Bliss started undressing her, and slowly walked her over to the bed. As he lay her down, he gently rubbed her down her sides as he began to undress her. He kissed her softlty, and as their lips peeled apart, he used his tongue and his bottom lip to slide his mouth across her bottom lip. She lay perfectly still as he caressed her body, and made his way inside of her. It was never easy for them to get started because Dymond was always as tight as a virgin.

"Uuuhhh," Dymond gasped as Bliss penetrated her. He loved that sound. The sound that a woman makes when a man first enters her.

"Damn, this pussy is always tight, bae. That's the shit that got a nigga hooked. Fuck."

He began to go in a circular motion that had Dymond biting her lips, and damn near losing control.

"Naawww, baby girl, you can't bust right now. Turn that ass over."

He watched with excitement as Dymond turned over, and got into the perfect position with her ass tooted up in front of him. Bliss pushed down on her back to make the perfect arch as he grinded in and out of her.

"Fffuuucckkk me, daddy," Dymond yelled out. Bliss worked his penis slowly, as he admired his long stroke. He enjoyed seeing his piece go in and out of Dymond as he admired all of her wetness accenting it. He worked her slowly while gripping her ass with both of his hands as she threw her ass backwards towards his pelvis.

"No, baby, you fuck me," Bliss told her.

Bliss pulled out, layed down, and grabbed Dymond to put her on top of him. She was overflowing. Her pussy was so wet that it made that gushy macaroni and cheese sound that happens when you're mixing it up. Bliss knew she was feelin' right. As she began to ride him she tightened her pussy muscles as she went up, and let go as she came down. It made a nigga feel like he was getting his dick sucked by the pussy. That drove Bliss crazy. He grabbed Dymond by the neck, kissed her, and began to fuck her from the bottom as if he was the one on top.

"Chase that bitch, bae. You goin' get it?" Bliss moaned in Dymond's ear.

"I'm goin' get it right now, daddy."

"Go get it," he told her. She began to ride him wildly with excitement.

"Get it outta me," she moaned loudly.

"Go get it," he repeated himself. She couldn't control herself.

"Go get it," he was making himself more and more excited as she rode him faster because of how turned on she was.

"Well, we can catch that bitch together."

Bliss grabbed her tightly, and she clutched down on him. They both came and Dymond fell flat on top of Bliss. Her body was shaking. He let her lay there for a moment so that he could enjoy his work. There was nothing that he enjoyed more than lying there and feeling her heart beat against his after he finished being everything that she needed him to be in bed.

"Let me take a shower baby," Bliss said as he lifted Dymond up. "I have a meeting in about an hour. If I close this deal, you can stay out of them streets, and move in with me."

"Babe, quit that noise. I'm gon' chill when it's the right time," she answered.

Bliss owned a very successful promotion company called "Ecstatiq." He didn't care for Dymond being in the streets, but he met her that way so he learned to deal with it. Dymond snuggled herself up under his covers, and plucked on the television as she waited for him to finish showering up. She enjoyed being in Bliss' bed. It was one of the few places that she felt safe from all harm, and where she felt what one might call a perfect peace if only for a moment.

She kept the TV muted because she loved to listen to Bliss as he tried to sing while in the shower. It was definitely his comfort zone. *"I got sunshiiinnne, on a cloudy day, ooouuuu, when it's cold outside, I got the month of May."* She chuckled and bobbed her head as he sang out loud. She could hear the shower turn off as he finished up, walked out of the bathroom, and admired her as she walked in. Her body was perfect to him. He sat on the bed, and made a few phone calls as he waited for Dymond to finish freshening up.

When he heard her shut off the water, he had her clothing laid out on the bed for her so that she could get dressed, and he could get to his meeting. She stepped out of the restroom, and he kissed her good-bye. He left, and she stayed. She had to wait on Keeky to pick her up. She walked out of the room, and into the living room where she had left her phone. She needed to call

Keeky so that she could be on her way. She picked her phone up off of the coffee table, and dialed Keeky.

"I'm ready," Dymond uttered to Keeky when she answered the phone.

"On my way, leaving your spot. Zha will stay here and chill 'til we get back." They hung up.

Dymond sat down to watch TV in the living room. She clicked on Criminal Minds.

"We interrupt this program for breaking news," the reporter said from the TV screen. "The police have found the body of what looks to be a forty-five to fifty-year-old female under her house. Neighbors are identifying her as Dianne Spencer. She has been beaten to death. Last seen at her home, was an unknown African American male subject. She seemed to be very well known by neighbors here in the Bronx area. Authorities believe that he could be headed out of state. He's traveling in a black 2010 Ford Fusion with license plate reading XLT 333. The car has been stolen, and the suspect is considered armed and dangerous. If anyone recognizes this victim, please call New York Police Department, as she lived alone, and neighbors say they never saw family at her home. This is a very sad story. Now back to your regularly scheduled program. We will return as details unfold. This is Matt Scotts, with National News 7."

Dymond's cell rang disrupting her daze as she tuned into the news. She picked up. "I'm outside," Keeky called and told Dymond.

"On my way out," Dymond answered.

Dymond locked up Bliss' place, and went to get in the car with Keeky. She was still thinking about that news broadcast concerning her home town.

"Bitch, what's wrong with you?" Keeky asked as Dymond got into the car.

Dymond seemed to be concerned, and there was a sort of hurt in her eyes. She looked at Keeky with tears running down her face. “They just flashed my mom on the news.”

Dymond sat on the passenger side with her head held down. After not seeing her mom for years, she sure did not want things to end for her in this way. No matter what wrongs their mom had done to cause their family to separate, she was still their mom. She only cried because it was her mom, but they never had a real relationship. It was hard to feel bad for, or show emotion for a woman whom she felt did her wrong most of her life as a mother. It was her mom’s fault that their family was split up in the first place, but it was also devastating to know that she passed away without them ever being able to make things right.

“Motherfuckers done her down bad. I have not seen my moms in years, yo. Now I gotta go bury her.”

“That’s fucked up. You know I got you if you need me, no matter what it is.”

“Yeah, I know. No doubt about it.”

Dymond started to search through her phone to find the number to her homeboy from the Bronx. She wanted to know if he may have possibly heard anything. Her homeboy was a street nigga, but he was a nosey nigga. If anybody knew anything, or could find out exactly what happened, it would be his grimy ass.

Keeky stopped at a nearby gas station to use the restroom. She ran inside, and paid for gas on her way out. By the time she used it, and pumped her gas, Dymond had already made her phone call home to find out what she needed to know.

“Say, Keeky, I just hit up my nigga from the Bronx. He said they know who smashed my moms. The nigga’s name is Stone. The streets is talkin’ out there. He said she was trying to change, dawg. Nigga killed her because she ain’t want to get back in the streets for him. Son raped my moms first, and took everything she had, too. That’s what the news broadcast didn’t speak of.”

"Damn, my girl. What you feelin' like?"

"Bitch, I'm feelin' like this nigga owe me his life. My people said he's supposed to be in Cincinnati. Dude owed him some money and made a phone call to him to set up a meeting. I told my nigga I'm gon' run him whatever dude owe him, plus interest if he set that up for me."

"When the meeting for?"

"The day after tomorrow at five."

"Well, we gotta start preparing tonight."

"Stop by my spot first so I can let Blayden know what's up."

It was about 11:45 pm, and they needed to book the next flight out. They needed to make it before daybreak in order to get things moving on their end.

They arrived at Dymond's place and Blayden was lying on the couch in tears.

He had already seen the news.

"Yo, Dymond. Tell me you got something up your sleeves."

"I'm on my way to the nigga right now."

"I'm comin', sis. Fuck all of that overprotective shit, I have to roll with y'all. Even if I have to just watch you do your thing."

"Come on. I ain't even trippin'. All I see is blood right now. I'm gon' make sure this bitch feel me."

Chapter 4

Blayden found flights online for four hundred thirty-eight dollars a piece. He wrote down their confirmation numbers, they packed their things, and headed out. Their flight was scheduled to leave at 6:30am. It would be a two hour and twenty minute flight from Houston to Cincinatti.

"Dymond, call your people, and let them know what time we gon' drop down," Keeky said. She always had to be organized. "Ain't no way I'm going all the way down there, and all your people have on deck is a few pistols that we can use. Tell that nigga I want some good shit, and make sure he got something lethal we could use."

Dymond called up Lyle, her homeboy from the Bronx. She told him exactly what they would need him to bring for their meet up in Cincinnati. He would be driving there so it was going to be easier for him to move with the weapons they needed. Things would have to be in order for them to pull this off the way that they wanted to.

Although Dymond and Blayden's mom wasn't a part of their lives, it was only fair that they take her killer out because family was family no matter what. They did not have time to get much rest because they needed to pack and arrive at the airport at least two hours early.

Zha would stay at Dymond's until they came back so that she could watch the place and send off everything that the state of New York would need to cremate Dymond and Blayden's mom. They left for the airport and made sure to reassure Zha of the instructions that she needed to follow while they were gone. Although they were moving quickly, everything seemed to flow smoothly, and on time.

Zha took them to the airport. "If y'all need me," she said, "be sure to hit me up. I'm only one flight, and one phone call away."

"That's a bet. No doubt." Keeky answered Zha.

"Call me if you need anything, or if you're unsure of how to handle business regarding my mom," Dymond said as she stepped out of the vehicle.

"No doubt about it. I got y'all. I told you that I'm gonna handle it, cuz."

"A'ight. See you soon."

Zha watched them walk into the airport before she decided to pull off. They made it in just enough time to check in and prepare to board their flight. Blayden had gotten them the best seats that he coud find. Their ride was smooth, and seemed to be over in no time.

"We are now arriving in Cincinnati, Ohio," said the pilot over the intercom of the plane.

It was 8:50am, and they needed to find a hotel. They rented a car from the airport, and noticed a motel across the street.

"You go check in while we go handle some business," Dymond told Blayden. "Do not use your credit card. Pay with cash and use that fake I.D. that I gave you a few weeks ago.

"A'ight, sis. Y'all be careful. Do y'all thing."

"You got your money together?" Keeky asked Dymond.

"Yeah, I got everything the nigga owed him, plus interest. Just like I promised."

"Put it in the duffle bag. We ain't handing nothing over until I see the nigga that we came here for. Shit better be legit at five tomorrow when we link up with these niggas, I'm telling you," Keeky told Dymond with that serious look on her face.

"We're good. If not, we know how to take our money and get gone, and I can find the nigga at my own convenience," Dymond answered. She knew that Keeky would go from zero to a hundred if anything went wrong.

They were on their way to peep out the meeting spot early, just in case something could go wrong. They got out of their rental, and scoped the place. It was a small two-bedroom house, similar in style to an old shack. It was quiet in the area because almost the whole block was run-down and abandoned. There was only one dim street light flickering, and the other two street lights near the house were out. The grass wasn't too high, but it was not freshly cut, either.

"I'm glad this nigga isn't expecting us until tomorrow," Keeky said. "I told you that we had to make it out here first so that we could be one step ahead of these niggas. You see that street light right there, we have to make sure to stay in that area because that spot will have the most light even though it's flickering. The other two looks like they've been shot out."

"I've been picturing this nigga murder since this shit happened. My people said they call him Stone.

"I see he a ol' mad ass nigga. He can't keep his hands to himself when his feelings hurt. Typical version of a bitch ass nigga," Keeky stated as she started to get angry just thinking about what dude had done.

"Exactly. Let's be out, though. We need to turn down a little before tomorrow. I'm glad it starts getting dark early now. That way we don't have to do anything in broad daylight. We gon' let them run it, and we gon' show up at 5:45. I'm gon' let dude know he gotta stall for awhile."

"That's straight. Let's go."

They headed back to their hotel. It didn't take them to long to get there. They ran it with Blayden for awhile. Keeky and Dymond were tired, but none of them had eaten since they heard the news about their mom.

Keeky ordered room service for them all. Dymond was a picky eater so she had corn, mashed potatoes, and salisbury steak. Keeky ordered a steak, well-done, and a fully loaded baked potatoe for herself. Blayden had a double cheeseburger dressed with everything, and seasoned fries.

They finished up, Keeky called to check on a few sales, and Dymond rolled a blunt for herself and Blayden. She had just copped some fire purp, and brought some cigars from the gas station down the street from the hotel.

"You blowin' with us?" Dymond asked Keeky.

"Hell no. Bitch, you know that I don't smoke," Keeky answered.

"I know, but you should try this. I'm tellin' you. This shit fiya."

"I'm good. That shit fucks with my concentration."

"Well, that's on you and your body, bitch. Come on, Blayden. Put a wet towel along the floor in front of that door to keep down the smell. This shit is loud, my nigga."

Blayden did what Dymond told him to do. They turned Keeky's phone onto Pandora, and they let the music play while they smoked and chilled.

"This that shit that we ride to. This that shit that we vibe to. This that shit that we get high to. That gangsta' music, nigga. And you can try, but you ain't Lil Boosie, nigga, no," Lil Boosie Bad Azz was rolling on Pandora.

Dymond puffed twice, and then she passed the blunt to Blayden. She was choking. "Damn, nigga, this some good shit," she said in between coughs.

Blayden took a puff. He laid his head back, and let the smoke flow out of his mouth slowly.

"Smoking on this purple I done got a bag for cheap, nigga eyes barely opened, and I'm glued to the back seat. Boosie took another hit and then he passed the blunt to me," Webbie was running his verse through the speakers of the phone. Blayden tried to rap along, but he was too loaded to continue.

They fell asleep once the blunt was gone.

Keeky sprayed the room with some blunt power to get rid of the marijuana smell, and then she laid down to fall asleep as well.

***

At 12:00pm the next day, Keeky's Lil Wayne ring tone went off, *"And you know that Imma ride with my motherfuckin' niggas..."*

"Let me take a shower," Keeky said as she was waking up. Dymond and Blayden decided to get up too.

She took her shower, brushed her teeth, and slid her hair into a ponytail. Dymond followed after her, and did the same. Blayden showered up, then pulled his hair into a ponytail as well. They were dressed in all black, and by the time they had freshened up, ate, and went over their plan again, it was time to go.

Chapter 5

Lyle and Stone met up at their meeting spot so that Stone could pay off his debt. Things seemed awkward for Stone because he knew that he was on the run, and that he should not trust anyone.

"What's been up with you? You good, huh?" Lyle asked Stone.

"Yeah, I'm straight. I just don't feel safe anywhere that I go, knowing that those cops are on the hunt for me, and my face has been all over the news," Stone said with a cold look in his eyes.

"I know, homie. That shit's crazy. I really don't see why you did that shit like that, though, my nigga. That's a female that you offed, potnah. Them people ain't gonna let that shit slide."

"You right. That bitch deserved it, though. She knew that I didn't play that shit with her. I had to make an example out of that bitch. I didn't mean to kill her ass at first, but I couldn't stop beating that hoe. She's lucky I didn't cut her fucking throat. I…"

"Hey my people," Lyle yelled out, interrupting Stone as Keeky and Dymond arrived.

When Stone noticed them walking up dressed in all black, he started to move, but Lyle pulled a nine on him. "Don't you move nigga," he said.

Stone dropped his backpack and froze in place. Keeky and Dymond walked up slowly. As they walked towards him, Stone knew that something was wrong. He began to shake. Lyle never put the gun down.

"Yo, what that is that you brought for me?" Dymond asked Lyle. "Gimme the tool."

"Give her the tool," Stone said, now pissed. "What the fuck does she mean give her the tool? Who the fuck is this bitch?"

Lyle ignored Stone, and pulled out a sniper rifle, but he told Keeky and Dymond to drop.

"You really thought I was gon' let any of you motherfuckas leave here alive? I want it all, from all of y'all."

Keeky and Dymond put their hands up as they dropped to the ground.

"What the fuck are you doing? I thought we had a deal," Dymond said to Lyle.

"I told you that we shouldn't have trusted this motherfucker," Keeky said through the grit of her teeth.

Blayden stood in a duck off waiting on the right time to come out. He had been given specific instructions by Keeky, just in case something like this happened.

"I don't wanna discuss nothing with you hoes," Lyle said. "Let me get everything that you bitches came with, or this rifle starts spittin' head shots." He slowly moved towards Keeky and Dymond, and then he grabbed the duffle bag.

Blayden waited for him to lift up, and then he crept up from behind, swinging a dark gray and black Magnum Kukri Machete, slicing Lyle's head off with one stroke.

"Y'all straight? Get up," he told them.

Keeky and Dymond always scoped things out first, just in case some flakey shit might go down, or in case something went wrong. They gave Blayden the weapon that he was most comfortable using, and placed him behind the house where Dymond figured he was safest.

"Give me that sniper rifle," Dymond told Blayden. He bent down where Lyle's body was, and handed her the rifle. She walked over to Stone, who seemed to be frozen from the shock of what was happening, and stood face-to-face with him. "Nigga, do you know who I am?"

"No, bitch, who the fuck are you?"

"So you still gon' talk dumb, even though I'm the bitch with the gun? Nigga, that was my moms you beat, and fucked over in the Bronx."

"Oh, so what you came here to kill me?" Stone chuckled at Dymond. "Bitch, do it." He had a blank stare on his face as if he wasn't intimidated at all. He looked into her eyes, and she stared back into his. He quickly moved his head to the right, and he pushed her gun to the left. He charged at her, and the gun dropped. She fell backwards onto the ground, Blayden ran over to Stone, and Keeky ran over to the gun.

"I don't know who you motherfuckas took me for, but I ain't going down without taking one of you bitches with me," Stone was yelling. Blayden tried to hit him with a jab, but Stone was too strong. As they fell to the ground, Stone climbed on top of Blayden, and Keeky shot him in the leg.

Pow.

The sniper rifle ripped through his leg, and he rolled over onto the ground yelling, "Kill me, you crazy bitch. I'm ready to die anyway." Stone's eyes were squinting, and he was sliding on his back using his good leg.

Keeky handed the gun to Dymond. She had fire in her eyes.

Pow.

She shot him in his other leg.

Blayden and Keeky stood and watched after they picked up the backpack, the duffle bag, and the nine Lyle was holding before.

"Aaaahhhhhh," Stone yelled again with spit flying out of his mouth. "Bitch, kill me."

Dymond dropped the sniper rifle, and grabbed the machete from Blayden. She bent down and sliced off both of his hands. The more he yelled, the better Dymond felt. She cut off his pants, and pulled a blade out of the back of her tights. She sliced his dick off, and put it in his mouth.

"That should keep your bitch ass quiet." His eyes started to roll behind his head. Dymond kicked him, "No, bitch, you better not die yet. I'm not done." She walked behind him, bent over, and lifted his head up. He looked into her eyes, and she asked him what was her mom's last words. He didn't answer because he could no longer speak.

"I guess you don't have anything to say, huh?" She slit his throat. "Now, bitch, you can die." She stared at him until he stopped breathing, and let his head fall to the ground. "Come on y'all let's go."

They started to walk off. Keeky turned around, walked back, and let off one shot to his head with the nine they took from Lyle. "Oh, bitch, now I feel better. I didn't come all this way just to watch y'all two do y'all thing. Let's roll."

"Bitch, you are a few types of retarded," Dymond laughed at Keeky.

They turned to leave, and Blayden's phone rang. "Wassup, Khalil?" Dymond and Keeky continued to walk ahead of him as he answered the phone.

"Where you at, nigga?" Khalil asked.

"On my way back home in a few. Wassup with you?" Blayden could tell that something was wrong.

Khalil whispered, "Nigga, I got jacked. Keeky and Dymond gon' kill me."

"Nigga, you better figure out something quick then. I'll holla when I touch back down in the hood." Blayden hung up the phone, and put it in his pocket.

"You straight, boy?" Dymond asked him.

"Yeah, everything good. Nothing that has to do with me."

"What time does our flight leave?" Keeky asked.

"It's 7:00 right now. We have to be to the airport by at least 8:30. Our flight leaves out at 10:30," Blayden answered.

"Well, let's get back to the hotel then. We have to gather our things, and get rid of these guns."

They drove back to the hotel, and called Zha to find out if she had handled that business with getting their mom's cremation taken care of. She also needed to know what time they would be expecting her to pick them up.

By the time Dymond hung up with Zha, they had made it to the airport. It was a late flight so things were expected to go as smoothly as the night before. Zha would be there waiting on their arrival.

The flight was very smooth. They slept until the time that they landed. It was good to be back home in their comfort zone with the people that they loved.

"I'm gon' holla at y'all tomorrow," Keeky said, "I ain't have no dick in a minute and I'm trynna fuck something tonight." Although she never really worried about men, or about having a steady relationship, it was something about Zay that secretly drove her crazy inside. She hugged everybody good-bye and walked out of the door. Her cell phone was in her back pocket. She grabbed it, and dialed Zay.

"Hello," Zay said as he answered his phone.

"Please tell me you trynna give me some dick tonight. I really got some pressure built up." Keeky got straight to the point.

"Come through then." Zay loved the way that Keeky talked to him. That fiesty attitude made him crave her even more.

"Be there in an hour. I gotta freshen up."

"Okay. The door will be open." They hung up the phone.

***

Damn, what can I do real quick to make this girl feel special, Zay wondered. He came up with what he thought would be perfect. He took out his cell, and googled ways to make a woman feel special at home. There were thousands of choices, but he needed to find the right one. He took his forefinger, and he scrolled through his choices briefly. He found what he thougt was the right choice, and he quickly pieced everything together. It took him about forty-five minutes to get it the way that he wanted it to be. He stood back, looked at what he had done, and smiled as he admired his work. It was about time for Keeky to arrive, so he went to his bedroom to wait on her.

When Keeky made it to Zay's place, she opened the door, and walked in to see a note on the table with candles lit around it.

It read: NOTE #1- I know you're trying to fuck tonight, and I don't wanna be a tease. So, drop your top right here, and prepare for ecstasy. (Walk over to the fridge, and inside of it you'll find note number two).

She walked over to the fridge with a huge smile on her face.

NOTE #2- Grab the whipped cream, and shake it up for me. I don't want it to splash while I'm licking your body. Take a few strawberries and don't you squeeze them too tight. I need them to be perfect as I eat them off of you tonight. (Walk over to the radio. There you will find your last note).

She walked over to the radio.

NOTE #3: Here's your last note. Click play on the remote. (The music started to play, *"Let me lick you up and down, 'til you say stop. Let me play with your body baby, make you real hot*). Now walk your ass up in here, and let me show you what I know. Come to me.

Keeky walked into the bedroom. Zay had the room covered with rose pedals and candles of all sizes that he had found in a closet in the hallway of his home.

He picked her up in his arms when she walked through the door, and kissed her softly. Just being picked up by Zay had Keeky's juices running over.

He grabbed her nipples tenderly with his lips as he prepared to lie her down. Keeky had a tight grip on Zay. He took her panties off with his teeth, and gently pulled off her skirt.

She was breathing heavily now. "Damn, shawty, you are about to lose control," he said as he enjoyed the fact that her body was craving his. Sex with Keeky was different. Her pussy was wetter than the other women that he was used to dealing with. It juiced up instantly at Zay's touch. He knew that he had to take his time with the pussy because everything about sex with Keeky was special.

He put his face close to hers so that he could hear and feel every breath that she was taking. "You must miss me, huh, girl?" he asked Keeky while looking into her eyes, and making his way down to her opening with two of his fingers.

"Yeeessss," she moaned. He slid his two fingers inside, and she bit down on her lips in the sexiest way. He moved them back and forth a little just to get her wetness onto them, and then he slid them out.

"What are you doing?" she hurriedly asked. "Don't stop."

"Just chill, baby. Let me do my thing." He was enjoying the fact that she did not want him to stop. He used the same two fingers to gently massage her clitoris. He pushed up her legs, and climbed in between them as he continued to finger her. He bit her lips, and then kissed her gently as he slid inside of her.

"God damn," Keeky moaned.

Zay's dick felt as if it was touching the inside of her stomach. He lifted up a little, and took off his t-shirt. His chest and stomach were covered in tattoos. He kept his gold cross around his neck. It swung with every move that Zay made.

Keeky thought to herself, *Lord this nigga is about to fuck me with nothing but his chain swinging.*

She grabbed Zay's waist and pulled him back towards her. As he went in and out, he long-stroked her slowly, and then pulled out to eat the pussy. He spread her lips, tongued, and sucked her clit until it started to swell. Keeky was rocking her hips harder and harder as she got closer to coming. Zay stopped sucking her clit because he didn't want her to cum that way. He grabbed her, bent her over, and went back in.

"This pussy gon' be for me," Zay leaned in and said in Keeky's ear. "Throw that ass back for me."

She loved that he took control in the bedroom. She was so dominant in the streets with these niggas that she needed a nigga to take over when she was in the bedroom. Keeky was biting her lips, rolling her eyes, and throwing that ass back like she was told. Zay grabbed her neck with one hand, and her waist with the other.

"You ready to get you, ma?" he asked Keeky.

"Yyyeessss," she moaned.

He pushed her down, slid out, and ate that pussy from the back until she lost control. While she was coming, he went back in, squeezed her ass with both hands, and deep stroked her until he couldn't hold back anymore. He pushed inside of her, and then held his position just to enjoy the dick sitting inside a little longer. He repeated that same motion, and then he pulled out and came all over her back side.

Upon finishing, he took the whipped cream that Keeky brought in, and sprayed it down the spine of her back. He put three strawberries along the whipped cream line, and bit them off one by one.

"Wait," Keeky interrupted. "Why would you wait until after sex to pull out the sexy shit?"

Zay smiled as he responded, "I waited because I wanted to make you feel just as good after sex as I did while we were having sex. I just don't want this shit to be over. It seems to be an in and out thing with us, so this time I just wanted to enjoy you."

As he began licking off the remaining whipped cream, someone started to beat at his door. He jumped up, put on his pants, and hurried to answer the knock.

"Who the fuck is it?" Zay said as he answered the door.
"Zayvier Thomas, we have a warrant for your arrest."

Chapter 6

After reuniting with her people, Zha was still kind of quiet around them at first because she didn't know who to trust. "Yo, Dymond." Zha called out. She was still at Dymond's place trying to sort some things out. "What do y'all do 'round here when y'all ain't hustlin', cuz?"

"Sometimes I drop in at the clubs that my ol' man works at."

"He ain't workin' tonight? I don't have a hit, and we don't have nothing to do. You wanna roll?"

"Yeah, we can go, but I know you ain't trying to go looking like that, huh?" Dymond stared.

She was 5'5". Her hair was long, thick, and straight and stopped in the middle of her back. She had a tongue piercing, and a clit piercing, also. Her skin was a smooth chocolate color, and her eyes were a beautiful brown. Her stomach had an exotic butterfly tattoo with tiger eyes on the wings to cover the section where her bullet and surgery scar was. She had a large tatt of a hooded reaper covering her left breast to remind her that killin' Khalil was engraved on her heart along with the bullet wound that he gave her. She had small C-cup sized breasts, with an ironing board belly, and an ass like Nicki. This bitch was fine, and her body was all natural.

Although she was short, she was very feisty, and her mouthpiece was off the charts. She didn't sleep much at night because her body had gotten used to staying up due to the fact that she would do her hits between ten and five. She needed to change because she had looked like the day before. Her hair was brushed back, and she was in her sweats.

"A'ight, I got some clothes in my truck. I keep an extra fit on deck at all times. Never know what I might have to get into. It's become a habit for me." She had gone back home to her apartment to get her truck while the girls were out of town. She didn't like having to use other people's things for too long, no matter who they were.

"Well you get ready, and I'm gon' holla at my dude to let him know that we're about to come through," Dymond explained.

Zha hopped into the shower, and put on a sexy powder blue, ripped mini dress. The back of it dropped low enough to expose her spinal tattoo that had the words "to die for." She had on a pair of silver six-inch heels, with all of the accessories to match. When she wasn't doing her street thing, she liked to act like a lady. She was kind of the best of both worlds for a man. She and Keeky had similar styles.

Dymond put on a pair of blue jeans that were ripped at the knees, and a purple belly shirt that covered only her breasts. She wore purple and black Jordans, and a black fitted hat to match.

"Dymond, you really goin' to your ol' man's club dressed like a nigga?" Zha asked, staring at Dymond.

"Fuckin' right. Bitch, I do have my stomach out so be satisfied."

"Yo, you take this tom-boy shit too far."

"Fuck you, bitch, let's go."

Dymond didn't want to drive so they hopped in Zha's SUV. She had to be doing well with those hit jobs because she was driving a copper colored 2013 Range Rover that sat on 26's. She had her sound customized, but no tint on her windows. Dymond rolled a blunt for them to smoke, and Zha found some music for them to listen to.

Her sound was pumping, Z-Ro was blasting through her speakers, *"I don't need no help, my nigga, I can do bad on my own, and I don't need no company, lil mama, stop ringin' my cellular phone. When I be down and out, nobody wanna come and kick it, I'm a nobody until I can shine. Though my money is long I don't need nobody to visit, leave me lonely like you did last time."* That was Zha's theme song.

They arrived at the club. It seemed to be a casual environment because everybody outside was dressed comfortably with the exception of a few women who were overdressed. The ballers were in one line, and the regular hood niggas and chicks were in another. The line was wrapped around the building. They walked past everybody else, and straight to the front. Bliss was right there waiting.

"Hey, baby," Bliss said as he grabbed Dymond's hand and gave her a kiss.

Dymond and Zha got their wrist bands, and followed Bliss into the club. He escorted them to V.I.P. and ordered a bottle of Ciroc Pineapple for them to drink. The section they had was official. They could see the whole club, and watch everything that went on. The crowd was hype, and the music was pumping.

"I'm about to hit this dance floor," Zha yelled through the music.

"Do that," Dymond said. "I'm gon' chill right here and sip on this Ciroc for a minute."

The D.J. was rolling, *"I used to pray for times like this, to rhyme like this. So I had to grind like this to shine like this,"* Meek Mill was blasting. The whole club was bobbin' and rappin'.

"What's your name, ma?" a dark-skinned guy asked Dymond as he walked up to the section where she was.

"Dymond," she said with an aggravated look on her face.

"You in here with somebody?"

"Why the fuck are you asking me all of those questions, nigga. Yeah, I'm in here with my nigga. Get the fuck out of my face."

"You a smot, bitch. Well, fuck you then."

Dymond smirked, squinted her eyes, and tilted her head to the side while staring at him.

"Bitch, you got a problem?" The guy asked, then he spit in Dymond's face. She could tell that he was drunk, but his disrespectful ass had gone too far.

"Nigga, did you just spit on me? I got your bitch, homie," she was yelling as she jumped up from her seat. Security hurried to get in between them.

"What's goin' on?" Bliss ran over to ask.

"That bitch ass nigga just spit in my face."

"My people gettin' him outta here, babe, I gotchu. Enjoy yourself, and let me handle shit my way with that nigga." Bliss always knew just how to calm Dymond down, and she knew that his word was bond so shit would get handled if he said it would. He wiped her face, gave her a kiss, and walked off. She sat down to gather herself, but the thought of that guy spitting in her face seemed to keep playing in her head. She rubbed her face up and down, and gripped her bottom lip with her top row of teeth.

"You good, cuz?" Zha asked Dymond as she was walking up. She noticed Dymond's head down, and something seemed to be wrong. She was too busy getting it in on the dance floor to even notice what had happened.

"Let's go to the bathroom," Dymond said.

They walked into the bathroom and Dymond started scrubbing her face once more.

"What happened?" Zha asked because the suspense was killing her.

"Security just put a bitch ass nigga outta here for spitting in my motherfucking face."

"I just saw them takin' a lil' black ass nigga outside of this bitch. That nigga looked like he was all the way twisted. I wonder if that was him?"

"That had to be his pussy ass. You thinkin' how I'm thinkin'?"

"Let's do it then, bitch. I'm with it, but let's hurry up 'cause I'm trynna finish partying. Nigga ain't about to fuck up my night."

They went out of a back exit door, and walked around the building. They watched as security finally got the nigga out into the street. He started walking towards the alley that Dymond and Zha were standing next to. They waited until he came close enough, and Dymond went with her move.

"Remember me?" she said as she came out of the alley. He looked up, and Dymond punched him straight between the eyes. He stumbled backwards a little, but he was able to keep himself from falling to the ground. "I told you that I got your bitch, didn't I?"

"I'm gon' beat the fuck out of you, bitch." He was yelling, and running back towards her. She put up her set, and positioned herself for the fight. Zha peeped around to make sure that everything was still good. She didn't want anybody to pop up while Dymond was handling her business. When he was about an inch away from her, she starting swinging, but he grabbed her neck, and locked both hands around it. She couldn't breathe, but her hands were still free so she used them to try and loosen his grip around her neck.

"What type of nigga do you take me for? Bitch, I will kill you," Spit was flying in her face as he yelled while continuously choking her.

Zha could barely run in the heels that she had on, but she was moving as fast as she could. Just as she approached them, Dymond took out a taser and hit him in the side with it. His hands dropped from around her neck, and she fell to the ground. The liquor and the current from the taser must have gotten the best of him because he damn near passed out.

"Bitch stay up," Zha said as she squatted down to slap him in the face a little. When he opened his eyes, she stood up, stood over him, and extended her right arm with her glock in her hand.

"Don't do it," they heard a voice yell out from behind. "Put the gun down."

Zha turned around, and pointed her gun towards the alley. "Ay-yo, whoever that is, if you come closer, I'm squeezin' my glock on that ass. When I shoot, I don't miss. I'm gon' fuck clean over you."

"Shit, it's Bliss," Dymond murmered.

"Don't shoot, it's me, Bliss. Dymond, baby tell her to put the gun down."

Reign always remained focused so putting her gun down was not an option. She simply took the gun off of Bliss, and pointed it back towards the guy lying on the ground.

Bliss walked up, and grabbed Dymond.

"Yo, fuck all that mushy shit. I'm already outchea in these motherfuckin' heels, holding a purse. What y'all gon' do, cuz?"

"Chill, ma, give me the gun," Bliss told Zha.

"Oh no, I feel you on that everybody don't have to die shit you talkin', but I don't give up my gun for no nigga. I'm sorry, can't do it."

Dymond interrupted, "Well, come on, let's go. No need to be arguing out here about the shit. Fuck it."

Zha put her strap back in her purse. Bliss looked around to make sure that he was still in the clear. Everyone had finally gotten into the club, and the alleyway that they were in was dark.

Pop. Pop. Pop. Pop.

Bliss was standing over ol' boy. "Nigga, that's mine. Don't ever disrespect what's for me."

"Well check this nigga out," Zha said, smirking at Dymond.

"I told you, cuz, that's daddy," Dymond said as she grabbed Bliss' hand. He was still breathing hard from the rush, but they needed to clear the alley.

They could hear the music bumping as they made their way back to the club. The club was going crazy as the D.J. started to run Webbie's hit *I got my people with me*. Zha ran back to the dance floor, and Dymond walked to V.I.P. with Bliss.

"I love you, baby girl," Bliss said as he kissed Dymond.

"I know, daddy, I love you, too. Hold on, baby, my phone's vibrating," Dymond told Bliss as she looked at her phone screen. It was Keeky. "I gotta go to the bathroom and answer this call."

"Be careful, and make your way back this time," Bliss said sarcastically.

Dymond smiled as she walked off. By the time she made it to the bathroom, Zha was already in there on the phone with Keeky.

"We gotta be out," Zha said when she saw Dymond walk in.

"Why, what's wrong?"

"This bitch Keeky having a hell of a night. Her nigga went to jail, and she said Khalil just called and told her that he got jacked out of all y'all shit."

Chapter 7

"Where's Jade?" Khalil said as he called up Kayne.

Kayne was a big deal in the Houston area. He was a multi-millionaire club owner that despised the ground that Keeky and the others walked on.

"I'm not sure, why?" Kayne answered.

"I just had to tell that bitch Keeky that a nigga jacked her shit from me."

"How the fuck did you let that shit happen, nigga?"

"I went to make a drop to a Jamaican nigga that Jade told me about. When I got there, the nigga pulled a strap on me, and about five more of them niggas came running from behind the building. Them niggas took everything I had, including the blunt I was smoking."

"Damn, you know that bitch Keeky gon' want your head over her money right?"

"Nigga, she made sure she let me know that shit when she dropped it off to me. I'm hoping she spare me on the strength of Zha. God rest the dead."

"Don't mention that name while we're talking."

"I'm sorry. I was just hoping that her name still has some pull because I don't know what else to do, or who else to use."

"Make sure you let her know that you know who jacked you. She will have no other choice except to spare you, at least until you lead her to them niggas."

"Right. Well, I'll hit you back. Let me try and catch up with Jade's ass. She's the reason that all of this shit happened to begin with." He quickly ended his call with Kayne so that he could call Jade.

Khalil kept dialing, and redialing her number. She never picked up. He paced back and forth, knowing that Keeky did not play behind her drugs, or her money. She really only fucked with him because of Zha, and he knew that it was a strong possibility that she wouldn't take him being Zha's ex-boyfriend into consideration. He had hoped that she would come alone because his chances of talking to her would be better, but if she brought Dymond along with her, he knew that together the two of them would dig in his ass, quickly.

Forty minutes later, Khalil heard a knock at the door. It was Keeky and Dymond. Zha stayed ducked off in the car so that Khalil wouldn't see her.

"Open up the motherfuckin' door, Khalil," Keeky yelled as she was banging outside.

"I'm coming," he responded.

Khalil opened the door, and Dymond hit him in the nose. He fell backwards. Keeky pulled out a Smith & Wesson and cocked it.

"Bitch, I told you not to make me choose between you, my drugs, or my money."

"Wait. I know who has it. I just couldn't get it back alone. Please don't kill me, Keeky. Y'all like the only family I have since Zha's been gone."

"Bitch, don't mention Zha's name in this shit," Dymond said as she put her foot on his neck.

Keeky bent down. "If you know who got my shit, nigga, you better tell me."

"I can show you," he barely could speak as Dymond's foot was choking him.

"What's going on?" a female voice said from behind them. Keeky and Dymond turned, and a small dread-headed chick was standing behind them in a nursing uniform.

"Jade, I've been trying to get at you all day," Khalil said, now gasping for air as Dymond lifted her foot.

"Me wuk tahday," she said in her Jamaican accent.

“Yo, who the fuck is this bitch?” Keeky asked, turning her gun on Jade.

“Ya nuh see it?” Jade answered.

“All I see is a bitch that’s interrupting me trying to recover my shit.”

“Reespek. But yu nuh easy. So lemme explain. Dis neegah yah, he like me blood. Take care of me when I was on da streets.”

“So what the fuck does that have to do with me?” Keeky blurted out.

“Feel no way. I just don’t want yah tah kill me brudda.”

“Well, this nigga better lead me to my drugs, or the bitch better have my money.”

“Come on, let’s go. I’ll show you where the niggas at who jacked me. Them niggas you sent me to, they jacked me, Jade.”

“Dems a dead man bwoy. Bumboclot.”

“Come on, I ain’t got time to waste,” Keeky said.

“You better pray we find them niggas,” Dymond told Khalil.

They walked outside to their cars and Zah peeped a little while she was laid back.

“Who’s the chick he’s with?” Zah asked as Keeky and Dymond got in the car.

“I don’t know the bitch,” Keeky answered.

“Me either,” Dymond said.

“Yo, that bitch looks real familiar to me,” Zah said with a serious look on her face.

“Well whoever the fuck she is, she better know how to help that nigga get our shit,” Keeky snapped.

“Why did y’all even front that nigga?” Zha asked.

“Because of you. We only still fucked with him because he fucked with you. We didn’t know anything about all of that other shit that happened with you,” Keeky said as she turned to look at Zha.

Keeky and Dymond had decided a long time ago that they were not going to front anybody. They felt that it would keep down confusion, and that it would eliminate them having to go to jail behind beating or killing a motherfucker over their money. Besides, if someone had a habit, they should be able to support that habit, and if someone wanted to hustle, then they needed to have the money to buy what they needed. If not, then they didn't need to do it was their motto. They would rather lose a little business for the day, than to have to run after a nigga or female for their money.

About an hour later, they arrived in front of a building that looked like a garage in downton Houston. The door wasn't open, but the lights were on, and the blinds were closed.

As they came to a stop, Zah yelled out, "Yyyooooo, I know I recognized that chick. That's the nurse who explained to me that I'll never be able to have kids."

"What?" Keeky asked. "How the fuck did this bitch end up in your hospital room in Alabama?"

"Yo, I don't know what the fuck is going on, but I'm about to rock this bitch Khalil right now," Dymond said.

"No. Y'all promised to let me do it. Please, just wait for me to do it," Zha pleaded. "I've been sitting back waiting for the perfect time to ge at him. It's all that I dream about. It's like I can see me doing it to him, but then I remember that I loved him so much. It will be probably be the hardest thing in the world for me to do."

"A'ight, but bitch you better handle that shit soon because you know we will if you don't."

Khalil and Jade got out of their ride first. When Dymond and Keeky saw them get out, they got out behind them. Zha stayed in the car.

"Knock, nigga," Keeky told Khalil.

"A'ight," Khalil answered.

Keeky, Dymond, and Jade stood off to the side while Khalil knocked.

"Who dem knock a doors?" a Jamaican voice said from out of the garage. "Naa badda mi."

"It's Khalil, I came to get my shit back, nigga. Open up the motherfuckin' door." Khalil wasn't convincing Keeky with his calm tone of voice.

"You scary bitch," Keeky whispered from the side of the building where she was waiting at. "Nigga, you better ask for that shit like you want it back for real."

The Jamaican swung the door open with a gun pointed at Khalil's head.

"Neegah, dem not yo shit. Dis yah belongs to me."

"No, motherfucka, it belongs to me," Keeky stepped from on the side of the building with an A-K. "Now I suggest you back up inside of this raggedy ass motherfuckin' garage, and give me my shit, or I'm about to get real ugly with your ass."

Dymond stepped up on the side of Keeky, and pointed the Ruger to his head. He dropped his gun. "Don't give us our shit, and you die. Give us our shit, and you still die. Either way, you die tonight motherfucker. Khalil, step your bitch ass in here, too. Nigga, you scary as a motherfucker. You'll be lucky if I don't kill your stupid ass right here with this nigga."

"Wa mek yah dweet fa?" Jade stepped up behind them, and asked the Jamaican.

"Yah set me up, Jade," he said.

"Mi naa waan fi do it. But yah a bad bwoy," Jade explained.

Two other Jamaicans came out of a backroom, and when they noticed Dymond and Keeky had guns pointing at their Jamaican brother, they pulled out straps, and started busting.

Khalil ran, but Jade pulled out a strap and started busting back with Keeky and Dymond. Jade hit one of the Jamaicans with a head shot. He fell, but he squeezed his trigger right before he got hit in the head.

"Ffffuuuuccckkkk," Dymond screamed. The bullet that he let off hit her in the chest.

"Yo, Jade, grab Dymond and slide her to the car. Start that bitch up, I'm gon' be right behind y'all," Keeky was yelling at Jade.

Keeky couldn't find the Jamaican that she originally pulled on. That nigga ran as soon as the other two started busting. She couldn't kill him first because she needed her shit back. The other one was out of sight, too. She didn't have time to search for her shit because she had to get Dymond to the hospital.

Jade was on her way to the car stumbling as she was trying to drag Dymond. She fell backwards, and Dymond's head landed in her lap. She carefully lifted her head, and began to drag her again. It seemed as If Jade was moving in slow motion, but being that she was a nurse she knew that moving her around too fast could cause the bullet to travel in the event that it was still inside of her.

"Yah hang in dere hea?" Jade was trying to talk positively to Dymond. "I got yuh, but yah heavy gal." She chuckled so that she could try and remain on a positive note. Jade fell again, but this time she had to pause to catch her breath. They were almost to the car when Zha noticed them moving in a hurry to get back.

Jade opened the door to put Dymond inside. She looked up, and Zha was staring her dead in the face in shock, "What the fuck happened to cuz, yo?"

"She need a doctah," Jade replied in a hurry.

"Ay-yo, Keeky, let's go. We gotta get Dymond to the hospital," Zha screamed out.

Keeky was almost to the car. When she hopped in, Jade told her that she needed to hurry. Dymond was barely breathing, but she was still alive. The hospital was ten minutes away.

Jade kept the wound covered. She climbed on top of her, and sat with her hands over Dymond's chest in a criss-cross like manner. She pressed down on it firmly. She could feel Dymond taking short breaths.

"Damn, Keeky, we're not there yet? Push this motherfucker." Zha was demanding from the back seat.

"We're about to pull up now."

When they made it, they saw some paramedics standing around outside. Jade ran to get help.

"Please, we need help. My friend has been shot," she was yelling.

One of the paramedics ran inside of the emergency room door, and about two minutes later, he came back with a stretcher, followed by a nurse with some other equipment. The paramedics got Dymond out of the car, put her on the stretcher, and hooked up the other equipment that the nurse brought outside with her. Keeky, Zha, and Jade stood there with their legs shaking, and their minds on overload. Zha was crying uncontrollably, and Keeky was trying to explain to her that everything would be alright. Dymond was a fighter, and they needed to stay positive.

"Open the doors," one of the paramedics yelled. They needed to get Dymond inside.

Bbbbeeeeeepppppp. Dymond flatlined as they took her through the doors.

Chapter 8

"Bliss Heins, Mr. Thompson will see you in his office now," a secretary said.

"Thank you," Bliss responded.

The office building that he went to for his meeting was immaculate. The secretaries had computers surrounding them. The walls were an olive green color, and his furniture was a beautiful beige color. No one could enter this office, or speak to the owner without first going through a secretary. There were security officers surrounding the place in black suits with guns on their waistlines for every eye that entered the building to see. Doing business with Mr. Thompson would definitely be a good look for him and his company.

"Hello, Mr. Thompson, I've been looking forward to meeting you," Bliss said as he walked through Mr. Thompson's office doors. "I've heard great things about your venues, and my company is here to serve you however you may need."

"As you already know, I am in the night club business. I need promoters that can fill my clubs everytime the doors open. I have four of Houston's largest, and most upscale venues. If you believe that you can do that, then I believe that you are the man for me. Your track record speaks for itself, and Bliss Heins, sir, I am very impressed."

"My team and I look forward to doing business with you. I'll have my lawyer draw up a contract, and I'll present it to you in two days."

Bliss' phone vibrated. It was Keeky. "Can you excuse me, sir, while I take this call?" Bliss asked Mr. Thompson.

"Yes, sir, I can. Take all of the time that you need."

"Hey wassup, Keeky?" Bliss asked as he picked up the phone, and walked outside of Mr. Thompson's door.

"Yo, you have to get to the hospital quick, son. Dymond got shot, and she flatlined. I'm goin' fuckin' crazy over here. I don't know what the fuck to do. All I see is blood, yo. The doctors brought her back twice. Now she's going through her second surgery trying to pull through. They can't get the bullet. Son, I'm tellin' you, make way because I'm goin' to tear Houston apart."

"I'm on my way now. I had an important meeting when I left the club. Now was the only time that I could do it. Do you know who is behind this?"

"Some fuckin' Jamaicans, and that bitch ass nigga Khalil."

"Khalil?" Bliss repeated after Keeky in shock. "Yo, see if you can find this niggas whereabouts. I'm on my way."

Bliss hung up the phone and walked back into the office. Mr. Thompson had overheard everything. "You don't have to say a word, Mr. Heins. Go take care of your family. You have my prayers."

"Thank you."

Bliss hurried to the elevator to leave. Mr. Thompson took his cell phone out of his pocket to make a call.

"Hello," said the gentleman on the other end.

"Khalil, I suggest that you get out of town now. A gentleman by the name of Bliss Heins just left my office. Apparently, he's the boyfriend of Dymond. I know this guy's background. My love, it seems that you have pissed off the wrong people."

"I know, Kayne. I'm trying to think of something now," Khalil said. "Damn, I didn't know that Dymond got shot. I took off as soon as the shit started to go sour. I ran down the street to a gas station, and I called a cab to bring me home."

"I'm sorry, but I cannot be the one to help you this time. Right now I need this guy for a very important business deal. All that I can offer you is my prayers. I told you to stay the fuck away from those people after we got rid of Zha." He hung up the phone on Khalil.

***

On the way to the hospital, all Bliss could do was think about these niggas that shot Dymond. If he lost her, he wasn't sure what he would do.

He pulled up to the hospital and burst through the doors. Keeky and Zha was standing around still crying. Jade was off to the side staring in their direction.

"Wassup, is she okay?" Bliss asked nervously.

"She hasn't gotten up yet. The doctors said that she's in a coma. They don't know how long it will last, or even if she will pull through," Zha answered.

Listening to Zha speak made Keeky click out. She punched Jade on the side of the head, then she grabbed her hair and put a knife to her throat. "Bitch, I want answers now, or I will slit your motherfuckin' throat right here." Keeky's eyes were blood shot red, and she was breathing as if she was hyperventilating. "*Speak*," Keeky yelled.

"Yo, we're in the hospital, Keeky. Let her go," Bliss pleaded.

A nurse came walking from the back. "Is everything okay in here?" the nurse asked.

"Yes, ma'am, we're fine," Zha answered. Keeky let go of Jade.

Slap. Jade went across Keeky's face. "Bitch, me no take yuh threats lightly. Ease up uno self. Hit me again, and I'll kill yah dead."

"Bitch, you clapped back, and my sister laying in that motherfuckin' hospital bed fightin' for her life because of you motherfuckas." Keeky lunged at Jade, and they fell. She climbed on top of her, and banged her head on the floor. "In Jamaica you probably was a bad bitch, no doubt, but here, I'm the baddest."

Bliss pulled Keeky off of Jade, and Zha got in between them.

"Bliss, go take care of Dymond, we have some business to handle. Call us in a few with an update," Zha said.

"Fuck all that, I ain't going nowhere until this bitch Jade starts explaining what the fuck is going on," Keeky said, still in a rage. Jade was still trying to get up off of the floor, but she seemed dizzy.

"Yo, let's be out. Keeky, you're tripping. You act like the motherfucking laws ain't in this hospital," Zha snapped back as she helped Jade to gain her composure. She beckoned for them to follow her to the door, and she waved good-bye to Bliss.

He walked towards the receptionist desk to find out which room Dymond was in, and to gain access to her. The receptionist gave him directions to the nurses' station in ICU, and the nurses gave him access to Dymond. His eyes watered up the minute he saw her lying in that bed with tubes coming from everywhere.

He grabbed her hand, "Dymond, baby, it's me. Please pull through. Baby, I love you. You're a fighter. You've always been a fighter. God, if you don't do anything else for me, please bring my baby back. Please God. Dymond, baby, I want you to be my wife after all of this is over with. Nothing else even matters to me. I just need you to pull through for me, baby. If you're going to fight, baby, and if you can hear me, please squeeze my finger." He looked down to see if Dymond would squeeze his finger, but she didn't. He looked back up, and she had blood running out of her mouth.

"Nnnnnuuurrrrssseeeee, she's spittin' up blood." Bliss ran out of her room yelling. He yelled down the hallway so that he could get someone's attention. Two nurses and three doctors came running down the hallway.

The doctors and nurses asked Bliss to step out of the room. He went into the waiting room. While sitting there, all he could do was think about what would make things better for Dymond. He bowed his head, "Dear Lord, there's not much that I've been asking for lately. You've been blessing me beyond what I could ever imagine. God, when you created Dymond, I know that you did so with me in mind. Lord, I'll take her place because I hate to see her in pain. You said in Your word that no weapon formed against us shall prosper. You promised us that by Your stripes we are healed. I know that all things work together for the good of He that lives in me. Lord, wrap your arms around her. For I may as well be dead, if I have to live without the other half of my heart. In Jesus' name I pray, Amen."

Bliss was raised in a home where his father cherished the ground that his mom walked on, and she treated him like a king because of it. Their family was not perfect, but he could barely even remember arguments between his parents. They had busy lives, but his parents always kept God first, and taught him to do so as well. His father was patient with his mom, and he learned to be patient with Dymond. He was always taught that love inspires you to become a patient person.

His phone rang. It was Keeky. "Hello," Bliss answered the phone.

"Waddup, Bliss? Did you hear anything?"

"No, she started spittin' up blood, and they put me out of the room," he said as tears began to fall down his face, and his voice began to tremble. Keeky could hear the hurt in his voice.

"What do you mean she was spittin' up blood? That shit ain't a good sign, yo. I swear on God, bro, if my sister doesn't pull through, I'm causing hell for real. I'm going look for these bitch ass niggas. Hit me up when you hear something."

"That's a bet," responded Bliss, and they hung up the phone.

"What did he say?" Zha asked Keeky.

"She started spittin' up blood, but he'll call if he hears something new."

Zha pulled out her pistol, and put it to Jade's head. "Start talkin'." At this point, Jade was still with them because they needed her to help them find the Jamaicans that jacked them.

"Mi talk fah wat?" Jade asked. "Yuh don't truss mi and mi don't truss yuh. Yah bettah use that pistol if yah pull it out on mi."

Zha cocked the tool, and pushed it deeper into Jade's temple. "Bitch, don't try me. I'm telling you. We just want to know what the fuck is going on."

"When me was in dem streets of Jamaica, as a young guh, me mom got beat and rape by a whole heapa neegahs. Right'n fronta me. Mi dad seen me shakin' and fear fah mi life when him find us. Him was a ganja smuggla so afta we bury mi mom he taught me to slang ganja and how tah protect miself. Mi neva forget what dem dun to mi mudda, so I train miself to shoot dem neegahs and tah kill 'em everytime dey fuck ova one of mi women. Mi fadda brought me yah and mi went tah be a nurse. Him met Khalil and he send mi off wit dat bwoy wen he went tah jail. I recognize Khalil face from sumwea so I went wit him. I come ova yah da day dem planned on killin' yah. I hear him talkin' tah a Kayne and dem was settin' yah up. He was posed tah kill yah dead. Dem lef me tah a hotel in Alabama. I wait fah dem tah leave and I go afta dem dutty neegahs. I radda dem truss mi so i lay low. Undastan? Khalil wutless bwoy and he no shoot ya dead, yah. I called dem ambulance and we save yah life. I asked tah wuk at yah hospital and dem send me tah be yah nurse. When Khalil try tah take mi back to Texas with dem, I say no dem give me a job. Mi stay til yah wake up and then mi left tah come tah Texas. I didn't know dem was yah drugs, but I know dem was supposed tah set up Khalil tah go tah jail wit mi fadda. Dey musta got greedy and dem took yah drugs," Jade explained.

"So you're saying you stayed because you was trying to kill Khalil for me?"

"Mi tellin' yah I stayed because I recognized his face when he meet me fadda. He was in Jamaica when dem bad bwoys kill mi mudda. He nah rememba me, but I rememba him. Mi been stickin' 'round 'til me fadda get outta jail."

"Yo, Keeky, she ain't lying. I remember that nigga used to take trips back and forth to Jamaica to bring back that good. He never slung it though, he was a trafficker."

"This nigga been sheisty all this time?" Keeky said. "This bitch gotta go, and one of y'all need to make that shit happen tonight."

Keeky's phone rang, interrupting their conversation. It was Bliss.

"Dymond just got out of surgery. They found the bullet, but couldn't remove it, and they also stopped the bleeding. She's still in a coma though, so they're monitoring her closely."

"This was her second surgery, right?" Keeky asked.

"Yeah, in the first surgery they couldn't remove the bullet because of the fear that it would cause her to die if they would have moved it around themselves. After x-rays were done, they found that the bullet had dislodged itself, and they may be able to do an emergency surgery to remove it. They need her closest family member's permission to do so because it is a high risk. Call her brother for me, y'all, so that he can come and talk with them and give them permission to remove it."

"Kiss her for me, yo. We'll be back as soon as we get this business handled, but I'm calling Blayden right now so that he can get there ASAP." Keeky hung up with Bliss, and got ready to reach Blayden.

"Zha, call and tell Blayden Dymond is in the hospital. He still doesn't know, but he needs to get there because They need his permission to do suregery to remove the bullet." Zha really didn't want to be the person to have to call and tell Blayden that his sister was in the hospital. She dialed him up anyway.

"Hello," Blayden answered the phone.

"Say cuz, Dymond got shot. She's in the hospital in a coma, but they need you right away for permission to do emergency surgery."

"What the fuck happened to my sister, cuz? Why the fuck am I just now finding out?" Blayden sounded hurt and pissed.

"Khalil got jacked by some Jamaicans. When we went to get the shit back they started busting, and Dymond got hit. We didn't call you right away because the shit went down so fast, and all we wanted to do was get Dymond to the hospital. She flatlined right when we made it there, but they were able to stabilize her. I apologize for not calling sooner, but we have a hell of a lot going on right now," Zha explained.

"I understand that, but that's my sister. I should have been the first nigga that y'all thought about calling. I'm on my way over there right now." Blayden hung up in Zha's face. She knew that Dymond and Blayden had been close all of their lives so it was expected for him to feel some type of way when nobody thought to call him as soon as the shit went down. She knew that he would get over it sooner or later, but they would just have to respect his mind for now.

"Yo, Keeky, Blayden is on his way to the hospital right now, but he sounds hurt and pissed," Zha said.

"This shit is really fucking with me. I can't take seeing my round in that fucking hospital bed. I'm turning this bitch around. We going to that nigga Khalil's spot right now," Keeky said. She whipped the car around and they headed over to Khalil's.

About fifteen minutes later, they arrived in front of Khalil's spot. Keeky started giving out instructions. "I'm gon' hit the front door, Jade you go around the right side, and Zha you hit the left side."

They split up. Everybody did as they were told. Keeky started banging as soon as she hit the front. "Khalil, bitch, open up the door, or we breaking this bitch down."

Khalil wasn't expecting them so soon. He thought that they would still be at the hospital with Dymond. He was inside trying to pack up. He left his belongings, went out of the back door, and closed it lightly. Keeky kicked the door until it burst open, but there was no sign of Khalil.

He crept through the back yard, and Zha stepped in front of him. "Peek-a-boo, motherfucka. I bet you ain't wake up this morning and think that I'd be the one standing over your bitch ass."

Chapter 9

Khalil froze. His eyes were so big that you could see the redveins popping out of them. “Zha’Reign. It can’t be,” he said out loud.

“Yeah, nigga. I’ve been waitin’ to kill your ass for years now. Bitch, you really tried to sleep me.”

“But...” he tried to plead before Zha cut him off.

“Bitch, shut the fuck up, and get on your knees.”

“Yoooo, Zha got this nigga in the back,” Keeky yelled out. Keeky and Jade ran around to where Zha was.

“Jade. Wait a minute. You turned on me for these motherfuckas,” he started yelling. “Bitch, I was good to you. I looked out for you when your daddy went to jail, you sheisty ass gutta rat.”

Jade walked up to him, and squatted down so that they could be face to face. She moved her dreads to the side, and pointed at a scar on her face that she had gotten when she was trying to help her mom.

“Yeyewata. Ya vex’n me. Yah see dis hea. Dem gimme dat when dey kill mi mudda. When yuh helped killed mi mudda in Jamaica. Yah it is me. Dah little guhl yah left fah dead aftah yah rape ha, and yah beat ha. Rhaatid, pussyclot. Me knew yah time soon come when mi link up with yah key hea.” She slid her hand through her hair and pulled out a razor blade. “Chop, chop muddafucka.”

She slit his right eye open. She stood up and stepped back as Khalil grabbed his eye, and screamed in agonizing pain. He was shaking and yelling nonstop while rocking back and forth as if that would ease the pain. He took his hand down, and put it in front of him so that he could see how bad he was bleeding. She went around him, and grabbed his mouth. Keeky and Zha were cocked and ready.

"Wait. Hold up, yo. I have to do something first," Zha demanded.

She was still in her club clothes because they never had a chance to change. She walked up to Khalil's other eye, and she used one hand to expose her tattooed breast. Jade had to hold him up because he was still squirming from the pain of the cut in his eye. She put Khalil's bloody hand on her chest. "You feel the reaper. This is what a cold heart feels like. You made me this way. Because of you, I'll never be able to have a family. Because of you, I'll never trust another nigga again. And because of me, bitch, you die."

Jade let him go, and moved to the side.

"Wait, Zha, baby, I'm..."

He didn't have a chance to finish his statement before the bullets started ringing. Zha and Keeky lit him up.

After their clips emptied, Zha went over, and stuck a knife through his heart. "Sleep tight, ya bitch you. Rest in hell, motherfucka."

"Come on, Zha, let's go," Keeky said.

They ran back to the car before the neighbors could figure out where the shots were coming from. Jade noticed a gas can on the ground outside of Khalil's spot, and she asked Keeky to give her about two minutes. She hurried back over to where they left him, poured the gasoline on him, and set his body on fire.

"Y'all finally got what y'all wanted. We all did," Keeky said out of breath when they made it back to the car. "How you feeling now, Zha?"

Zha sat quietly. She stared out of the window, and then she burst into tears. "I feel like I let that nigga win. He took away my ability to give life. Y'all probably wonder why I don't trip off of being with another nigga. Why should I? I can't give a real nigga shit except a nut. I wasted years with that motherfucker, and then I wasted years letting thoughts of doing that nigga in consume me. I used to ride with that nigga, would have died for that nigga, hustled with that nigga, never cheated on that nigga, and he fucked over me. Why me? What did I do to deserve for the bitch ass nigga to do me like that?"

Keeky and Jade sat quietly because they could see how bad Zha was hurting.

Jade's phone rang. She didn't want to be rude and answer while Zha was having her moment, but she knew that the call was important so she picked up.

"Yah," Jade answered her phone. They were on their way back to the hospital.

"Me tracked down dem bwoy yah say shoot yah fren. Dem address comin' to yah phone. Do ya ting. Reespek."

"Reespek." She hung up the phone. "Keeky, me know wea dem bwoys who got yah drugs."

"Yo, Zha, call Blayden and tell him to meet us at my other spot. He knows where it is," Keeky said. "Bitch, I want his head, and I want my shit back tonight."

"You don't think that Dymond would trip if you bring Blayden around this shit? When she wakes up, we definitely don't need her stressing out? You know she's overprotective of that boy," Zha asked out of concern.

"I don't want him to do anything out of the way. We bring him when we need him to do something extra for us or to be a watch out."

Zha called Blayden, and Jade gave them the address. They met Blayden at the spot about thirty minutes later, packed up the car, and rolled out.

It didn't take them long to make it to the address that Jade gave them. They arrived at what looked to be a Jamaican smoke shop. Keeky made a quick phone call, then told everybody that they needed to wait fifteen minutes before they could go with their move.

"Blayden, you hit the right side. Jade, you go around the back. Zha, you take the left side, and I'm going through the front door of this bitch." Everybody strapped up, and went to their assigned positions.

Bbblllrrrrrrr. Keeky started tearing the front of the shop up with her choppa. She could see the Jamaicans scattering, but they didn't come outside. *Bbbbllllrrrrrrr*. She started blasting again, then she kicked in the front door. Blayden and Zha were right behind her.

"Everybody get down. I came back for my shit, bitch."

"Yah drugs in dha back," the Jamaican who jacked Khalil said.

"Yo, Blayden, go gather up my shit. Zha start offing the rest of these niggas." One by one Zha gave head shots to the other five Jamaicans that were there. "You see, you, I can't kill you," Keeky told the Jamaican she had the gun on. "Ay-yo, Bliss, I got the nigga right here."

Keeky's phone call outside was to Bliss. He told her that he could be there in fifteen minutes, which was why they waited.

Bliss walked through the door with his nine in his hand.

"You're the reason why my baby is laying in that hospital bed, nigga?"

"Mi not shoot ha." The Jamaican stared nervously into Bliss' eyes as he spoke.

"Yeah, but your homie did. I don't allow another nigga to touch what's for me. I ride for mine at all costs. I kill behind that. Sleep, nigga." Bliss shot him straight through the forehead.

"Where's Blayden with my shit so we could go?" Keeky asked. "We gotta find him." She walked in the back of the building, while Bliss and Zha followed. They didn't see Blayden.

"Yo, Bliss burn this bitch down," Keeky said. "We gotta find Blayden." She decided to walk out of the back door, and saw Blayden with a pistol pulled on Jade.

Jade was standing there looking at Blayden with tears rolling down her eyes. Things were happening so fast all of a sudden, but there was something about Jade that seemed to be genuine. Being surrounded by so many snakes though, Blayden was beginning to be confused about who he should trust.

"Blayden, son, what are you doing?" Keeky asked.

"I don't trust this bitch. She's the reason my sister is laying up in that hospital bed," Blayden said as he continued to stare Jade in her eyes.

"Me either, but she did help me to get our shit back," Keeky answered.

"Yo, fuck all this talkin'." *Blowl.* Zha shot Jade through the temple. "The bitch needed to go. We gave her one chance too fucking many."

Chapter 10

"Why did you kill her, Zha?" Keeky asked.

"Because I was sick of y'all talking," Zha answered in a nonchalant manner.

"I know, but damn, you could have at least found out what else she knows."

"Yo, Keeky, bruh, fuck all that. I'm not trying to wait for a bitch to kill me. She had to go."

"Fuck it then, if that's how you feel. Let's roll."

They left and rode back to the hospital in silence. Their motto was to *push it to the limit*. No matter what the situation was, or what it could become. Kill before being killed. Hustle harder than the competition. Never front a nigga what you know they can't afford. In fact, if you have to front the nigga then you know he can't afford it. Never let money consume your thoughts because all sales aren't good sales. Part of this is why Blayden didn't trust her, and why Keeky didn't put up more of a fuss when Zha killed her.

As she pulled into the parking lot of the hospital, Keeky let out a deep sigh. She put the car in park, and sat there in an effort to gather her thoughts. Zha did the same. "Come on, let's go. We have to face this shit someway, somehow." They got out of the car, closed the doors, and walked back to Dymond's room. Blayden was right behind them. Dymond was still lying there full of tubes. He could not keep himself composed. He broke down.

"Dymond, sis, I love you. What the fuck am I gonna do if you don't pull through? You playin', sis. Ain't no way you're not responding to me. I ain't never had to do this shit on my own. We murked the motherfuckers who put you in this position, and you still laying there, baby girl. Come on, sis, wake the fuck up. I'm not trynna hear this Dymond is in a coma shit. Sis, we all we got, bruh. We done been through too much, and now you're trying to step out on me. Wake up, sis, or I'm going to crack the fuck up."

Keeky and Zha broke down. They walked out of the room so that Blayden would not see them cry. While standing in the hallway, Keeky's phone rang. She didn't pay attention to it until it rang a second time.

"Hello," Keeky answered the phone.

"This is a prepaid collect call from... 'Zay' ...an inmate in Houston City Jail. To accept charges, press one," the operator said from the other end.

Keeky immediately pressed one.

"Wassup, baby?" Zay asked Keeky.

"Chillin', worrying 'bout you. Wassup with you?"

"I'm gucci, ma. They got me on some old shit. I should be out as soon as my lawyer clear this shit up."

"How long do you think that shit will take?"

"Not long. Fuck. At least a month. No later than two months."

"You need anything, my nigga?"

"Naaawww, sweetie, but that's wassup. Thanks for asking. I knew you were special."

"Whatever you need, my nigga, just holla."

"I shouldn't need too much, ma. Good to know you don't mind ridin' with a nigga though."

"Awwwready. So, what's goin' on in there with you?"

"Nothing, shit. They put me in the dorm with some Jamaican nigga who's goin' crazy right now. The laws just gave him some bad news. He crackin' up, yo."

"For real? Damn, yo, that's fucked up."

"Whatever the fuck happened, nigga gettin' out in 'bout three months, and it looks like he's going to fuck some shit up."

"Well, that's on that nigga. You straight though, right?"

"Yeah, I'm good, ma. You miss me?"

"You know that, nigga. My pussy still jumpin' from when you left."

"Well, keep that pussy tight, I'll be back soon."

"You have one minute remaining," the operator interrupted.

"Yo, I miss you, girl."

"I miss you, too, Zay."

"I'm gon' holla at you tomorrow."

"Bet that up." The call ended. Keeky hung up with a big smile on her face.

"Was that your lil dip or something? Bitch, you're smiling like you just heard that you hit the lottery or something," Zah joked.

"Yeah, that was him," Keeky said. She was still grinning.

Zha laughed, and they walked back into the room to see Dymond. They pushed open the door, and Blayden stood there looking at them with tears in his eyes. "Y'all can't let my sister leave me."

"We won't," Keeky answered, "let's let her rest up. We all been through a lot today. Let's just come back tomorrow."

"That's a bet. My girl gotta shake back," Zha said. They left. Keeky and Zha went to meet with Bliss. Blayden was really taking this shit with Dymond hard.

"Bliss, we're on our way," Keeky called and said.

"I'm at my office," Bliss answered.

"A'ight, we're on our way." Keeky hung up.

"Yo, you think Dymond gon' be straight?" Zha asked Keeky.

"Man Dymond's been fightin' since we were small. She gon' pull through."

"She better, bruh. I don't know what I'm gon' do if my girl leave, son."

"Don't talk like that. We got business to handle. When she get up out of that coma, she should not have a thing to worry about, for real."

"You right, but what are we going to do about these Jamaicans? Sooner or later it's gonna be beef when they find out what happened to Jade."

"Fuck those Jamaicans, bitch. What they gon' do about us?" They arrived outside of Bliss' office.

"Open the door, we outside." Keeky called to tell Bliss.

"A'ight," he said.

"What's up? What you needed?" they asked him as they walked inside.

"I got a contract for a promoting deal with a rich nigga named Kayne Thompson. Watching y'all in action tonight made me realize that I need y'all on my team. Y'all really are about y'all money, and I need riders like that."

"What did you say that nigga name was again?" Keeky asked Bliss while looking at Zha.

"Kayne Thompson. Why you ask?"

"My nigga, that's the bitch ass motherfucka that sent Zha on the hit for Khalil to try to kill her. This bitch was in love with Khalil."

"That can't be the same nigga." Bliss did not want to believe that they were talking about the same person. He seemed shocked and confused.

"Call him on the phone real quick." Zha wanted to be sure.

"Ai'ght." Bliss dialed Kayne.

"Hello, Mr. Heins. Is your family okay?" Kayne asked from the other end of Bliss' phone.

"Yes, sir. My girl is in a coma, but God will pull her through."

"What is it that you need at this hour?"

"Nothing much. I just wanted to touch basis with you and let you know that everything is still a go. I should still have the contract to you on time."

"Okay. Glad to hear that. Please contact me when you are ready for me to sign. I have an important business matter to handle. I am in the process of finding a friend of mine. I haven't been able to reach him since about the time that you left earlier. Hopefully, he is just ignoring my calls because he is busy."

"Well, okay then. Talk to you soon."

They hung up. Bliss looked at Keeky and Zha.

"That's that motherfucka. Yo, Bliss, he gotta go," Zha said.

"How do you know that it's him?" Bliss asked. "This is the chance of a lifetime for me. I don't wanna fuck it up by going at this nigga, and he's the wrong cat."

"Listen to me, Bliss, I would never forget that voice. That nigga tried to have me killed. He fucked up everything for me. I'm telling you, that's him. The nigga has to go like ASAP."

"I agree," Bliss answered, "but let me do it my way."

"That's a bet, but if I feel like you're taking too long, I'm gon' personally off that nigga on my terms," Zha reassured Bliss.

"I got him," Bliss said. "Hold on, y'all, somebody's calling me."

"Hello," he answered the phone.

"Bliss Heins?" a lady asked from the other end of the phone.

"Yes, ma'am. I am Bliss Heins."

"The police are here, and informed me that I should call you. Please get to the hospital as soon as possible. Someone was here trying to pull the plug on Ms. Dymond."

Bliss hung up the phone.

"We gotta go," he yelled at Keeky and Zha.

"Yo, what's wrong?" Keeky asked.

"Somebody just tried to pull the plug on Dymond." They ran out of the door, and got into their cars.

On the way to the hospital, Keeky called Blayden. "How far are you away from the hospital?"

"About twenty-five minutes, why?"

"Us too. Get back over there. Somebody just tried to pull the plug on your sister."

"I'm on my way."

"Is he coming?" Zha asked.

"Yeah. He's on his way."

Keeky and Zha were trailing Bliss closely. He was going about ninety miles per hour trying to get to the hospital.

When they pulled into the parking lot, Bliss hurried to park, and was the first to jump out and run into the hospital. Keeky, Zha, and Blayden weren't too far behind.

"What the fuck happened? How did y'all even let some shit like this go down?" Bliss was raging.

"Mr. Heins, please calm down. We only let in family members," the nurse explained.

"What do you mean calm down? I almost lost the love of my life because of this fucked up hospital, and you have the nerve to tell me to calm down?"

"Mr. Heins, please keep calm. My name is Officer Byron. We were told that her brother and yourself only wanted family members to visit Ms. Dymond. All that we let in were family members. At least that is what she told us."

"She?" Keeky and Zha said at the same time.

"Yes, ma'am, she," answered the officer.

"Dymond doesn't have any other family members."

"Wait," Keeky said, "somebody better roll back some motherfuckin' cameras or somethin'. I need to know what the fuck is goin' on."

"We did that already, ma'am. We cannot see all of her face due to the roses that she had covering most of it as she walked past the cameras. All that I can remember is that she was very well-dressed, and seemed to be very pretty," the nurse explained.

"Blayden, you spend the rest of the night here, and we're going to go home and get situated for tomorrow. We have to sort some shit out," Keeky said.

"That's a bet," answered Blayden.

"Yo, Zha and Bliss, let's be out. Let me holla at y'all outside real quick."

They left the room and walked outside. Keeky looked around to see if anybody was outside close enough to hear what they were talking about. No one seemed to be out there except for the three of them.

"What you thinkin'?" Zha asked Keeky.

"Son, whoever the fuck was here knows us well. They also know how to get close to us. Fuck lettin' this shit happen again. We'll switch shifts if we have to, but somebody has to be here with Dymond at all times."

"Fasho," Bliss said. "Whatever's going on, I'm all in."

"Bet. We'll holla tomorrow."

They started walking towards their cars. Bliss slowed down to pick up a piece of a paper that he had dropped on the ground.

Booommm.

The car exploded. Keeky and Zha were nowhere to be found. "Oh shit. What the fuck?" Bliss was yelling out as he was running around trying to find Keeky and Zha. Keeky's car was fully engulfed in flames.

The explosion had to send them flying, but Bliss needed to find out where. He looked in the grassy area near the hospital. "Yo, Keeky, you alright, ma?" he said as he was running towards her lying in the grass. The explosion had blown them both away from the car. The hospital staff was now running outside, also.

"I have one of them over here," Bliss was yelling, "please find the other one."

"I see her," a nurse yelled out. Zha was knocked out, but Keeky was starting to come to.

"What... happened... Bliss?" Keeky asked with a shaken up voice.

"Your car exploded, baby girl. Thank God we stopped to talk first, or y'all would have been in there."

"Where's Zha?"

"A nurse just found her on the other side." Bliss helped Keeky up, but she could barely walk. They made their way over to where Zha had been found, with Keeky using Zay to hold her up.

"One... two... three... four... five..." a nurse was doing CPR. "Come on, young lady. Breathe. Breathe. Breathe."

"Come on, Zha. Come on, Zha. Don't you leave me again," Keeky was saying through tears.

"Yo, what the fuck happened?" Blayden was asking as he ran up from behind.

"Somebody put a bomb under Keeky's car. Her shit blew up, and they flew separate ways. Keeky's straight, but they're trying to revive Zha."

"Yo, Zha, you gotta get up, cuz. Get up."

"One... two... three... four... five..."

"Ugh, ugh, ugh," Zha started choking.

"She's back," the nurse said. "Get her inside for observation."

Zha and Keeky were brought inside to get checked out. Both were fine, except for a few scrapes and bruises, and a knot on Zha's head, but they were going to pull through.

"Hello," Blayden walked off to answer his phone.

"Wassup, bae? Where are you? I've been waiting for you to come, and when you never showed up, I got worried," Kenzy, Blayden's girlfriend, said from the other end.

"I had to come back to the hospital with my sister."

"Ok. I was just checking on you."

"A'ight, I'm gon' dip through tomorrow. I gotta stay here tonight."

"Is she doing better? I can't believe that this is happening. I know how close you are to your sister, baby."

"Yeah, she's okay. There's just a lot going on over here at the hospital right now. I'll explain it to you tomorrow when I see you face to face, babe."

"Okay, well call me when you can."

"I will. Love you, baby girl."

"Love you too, boo."

Blayden hung up the phone and looked over towards the others. "One of y'all will have to stay tomorrow for me."

"That's fine," Bliss answered first. "I'll stay."

"Yo, y'all need to tell me what the fuck is going on, though," Blayden said looking at Keeky and Zha confused.

"Nigga, we don't even know ourselves," Keeky answered.

"Whoever the fuck this is must be treading close, yo. Y'all, from this point on, no fuckin' body outside of this circle is to be trusted. I'm telling y'all. We need to keep up with each other at all times if we have to. This shit is real right now. I stay ready for some gangsta shit. But this caught me off guard, yo, I can't lie. I just hope whoever the fuck this is slips up and makes the wrong move because I'm on that ass when they do."

"It's do or fuckin' die right now," Zha added, "I hope that all y'all living like y'all ready to die because these motherfuckers is bringing heat. I'm really 'bout this shit, though. Ain't no nigga or bitch livin' gon' make me hide. I'm not stopping until whoever the fuck this is, is gone. It's either gon' be us, or them.

Everything that looks flakey to me has to die. I'm shooting first and asking questions later. Anybody can get it right now. My mind is all fucked up, and I'm not to be played with."

"I'm feelin' the same way," Keeky said.

"If I find out that this nigga Kayne is behind this shit, I'm rockin' this nigga to sleep on the spot, son," Zha said heated.

"You won't have to because I'll kill the bitch myself," Bliss answered.

Mr. Heins... Mr. Heins... get in here," the nurse called out.

"What's wrong? What is it?" Bliss said as they were all running to Dymond's room.

Dymond was trying to open her eyes.

Chapter 11

"I'm pulling up outside, bae," Blayden told Kenzy when she answered the phone.

"A'ight, I'll be here waiting," Kenzy said.

The night was very humid, and the moon was brightly shining. Everybody needed to wind down, but it seemed as if everything was just happening so fast.

"Man, this shit with my sister has me all fucked up," Blayden said as he walked through the door.

"You want me to make you feel better, daddy?" Kenzy asked. She recognized how tense and flushed her man looked.

"Yeah, do that, ma. I'm so tensed that I don't know what the fuck to do.

"Lay down."

Kenzy had Blayden to lie down across her bed. She unbuckled his pants, and pulled his dick through the hole in them. She grabbed it with her freshly manicured nails, and stroked it up and down. She kissed him softly while she held it, and she whispered in his ears, "I'm gonna relax your mind, bae." Blayden lay still, and didn't move.

"Take off your pants while I take off mine," Kenzy said.

When she returned, she climbed up as far as Blayden's face, and stared at him, while breathing lightly. She started to kiss him, but she went to his chest, and stomach area first. She moved her lips up and down his body slowly. Each kiss and each lick drove Blayden crazy. She used her tongue to make long, sexy strokes from his chest to the the bottom of his stomach. She grabbed his legs, and wrapped her arms around them.

"Don't flinch," she said.

She wrapped both of her lips around his penis, and she went up and down while squeezin' her jaws. Blayden's eyes were rollin' in the back of his head. She lifted his balls with her tongue, and licked the spot that was in between his nut sacks and his bottom. She licked as if she had something to prove. She came back up and let his legs go. She grabbed his dick with her right hand, and stroked it. She used her lips to suck on the head as if it was the only thing that she knew how to suck.

"You like that?" she asked Blayden.

"Fuckin' right," he answered. She took her two forefingers, squeezed his head together just a little, and stuck her tongue in between the hole that he would cum out of. Then she let him go, no hands touching, and went up and down on that dick with her mouth until he couldn't hold back anymore. "Fuuuucccckkkk," Blayden said as he was shakin'. "I'm about to cum." Kenzy kept sucking. She swallowed and sucked as he was coming. Blayden felt as if his soul was leaving his body.

"Damn, ma, that's why I love you."

"I have to make you feel different everytime I touch you, daddy."

Kenzy's phone was going off. "Hold up, bae, I have to answer this."

"Hello," Kenzy said as she walked off.

"Hey, Kenzy, wassup?"

"Hey, dad. I'm a lil busy right now."

"Okay, baby. I was just checking on you."

"I have Blayden over here. Dymond is still in the hospital. Everybody else is okay, too."

"That's okay. We can try something else later."

"Yeah, I waited on them to get to the hospital after I left Dymond's room, but something must have went wrong."

"Okay, baby girl, I love you. Don't fail me now."

"Okay, daddy. I love you, too."

Kayne and Kenzy hung up the phone.

"Who was that, baby?" Blayden asked Kenzy.

"Just my dad. He was checkin' on me."

"Oh okay. When are you going to let me meet your dad?"

"I will when the time is right. How's things with your sister?"

"Fine so far, she's starting to come around. Somebody tried unplugging her at the hospital today."

"Oh no, do they have any idea who it could have been?"

"No, they couldn't see a face on camera."

"Damn, that's fucked up. I'll definitely keep your sis in my prayers."

"Thanks, bae. That's why I love you so much."

"I love you, too. So, did they say when she would be getting out of the hospital?"

"No, they didn't, but Keeky and Zha almost got their asses blown away, too. Some foul shit's going on. I don't know what it is, but something flakey is really going down."

"You damn right. What type of extra shit do they have going on?"

"I'm not sure, but I know them, and they're ready for war. Between this shit and the shit with the Jamaicans, I don't know how the hell they're going to win this one."

"Jamaicans?"

"Yeah, they have beef with some Jamaican niggas who's in jail with Keeky's dude."

"Damn."

"Well, I'm ready to go to bed, baby. I'm tired from all of this extra shit that we have going on."

"Okay, baby. Let me use the restroom real quick." Kenzy went into the bathroom, and texted her dad. *"Get someone to go to the Houston City Jail and find the Jamaican who recently lost his daughter. You all have the same goal in common. Tell him that you know who killed his daughter."* Kenzy powered off her phone, and went to get in bed with Blayden.

Chapter 12

"Yo, Zha, wake up. We have to go to the spot. I have some shit I need to break down, bag, and ship out. Then we have to go see Dymond. I also need to see if they're going to let me see Zay."

"I'm up, fuck," Zha answered. She hated to wake up early because she always had to stay up late for business. Her body was not getting used to the time change. They freshened up and left out the door. Keeky had to ride with Zha today until she could make time to go to a lot to pick out another car.

It was a Saturday morning, and it was not as hot as it had usually been. The wind was blowing, and people were out everywhere. Zha liked to stunt so she put her sound on blast when they passed through the busiest neighborhoods.

"That's my shit," Keeky said. "Yo, louden that shit up." Lil Wayne was pumping through her speakers, *"Please say the motherfuckin'...baby you gotta know that I'm just out here doin' what I gotta do for me and you, and we eatin'. So bitch, why the fuck is you trippin'..."* Keeky was bobbing. She loved to rep her home town's music.

When they arrived to the hospital, Keeky told Zha that they should stop in the gift shop to get some cards, and a balloon for Dymond.

"Wassup, Bliss?" Keeky said as they walked in the room.

"Wassup, y'all?" he answered. "I'm good just was waiting on someone to get here so that I could go home and get me some rest."

"How's she doing?" Zha asked.

"Why don't you ask her yourself?"

"Whhhhaaaatttttt?" Keeky and Zha ran over to the bed.

"Hey, y'all," Dymond said softly.

"Oh my God. Cuz, you shook back. When?"

"Early this morning. I'm in a lot of pain, though. Plus, I feel like I'm exhausted."

"Let me allow y'all to catch up," Bliss said. "Baby, I'll be back later. I love you." He kissed Dymond on the forehead.

"I love you too, daddy." Dymond answered.

"You need anything sis?" Keeky asked Dymond.

"Nawww, I'm good, but check it out, though. Dymond motioned for them to come closer. I kept having these horrible nightmares while I was out. I didn't tell Bliss because I didn't want him to worry."

"What you was dreaming about like that?"

"I dreamt Bliss was praying over me as if I was dying or something. I dreamt that the hospital was going crazy because of a bomb, or something like that. I can't remember the whole thing. I dreamt about a lady, very pretty as a matter of fact. She came into my room, and rubbed my head. She called me beautiful, and then she made a phone call to her dad. She asked him if he was sure he wanted me dead. He must have said yeah because she hung up and said '*may god have mercy on your soul*,' and right before she tried to unplug me, she said something about Blayden not forgiving her if he ever found out. She only got the plug halfway out, and then she heard someone coming, I guess. That shit was crazy. It felt so realistic. It was like I could hear the people, but I couldn't see them."

Keeky looked at Zha in shock. "Yo, Dymond, that shit wasn't a dream. That shit was real."

"What do you mean it was real? You mean somebody came back, and tried to kill me?"

"Yes, and us too."

"Well, y'all, we have to handle that shit quick. I need to get the fuck out of this hospital." She was trying to get up.

"Don't move, yo. Be patient. We have to do some investigating of our own before we make any type of moves," Keeky said.

"Knock, knock," Blayden said as he walked through the door. He was ecstatic when he saw Dymond.

"Yyyooooo, my girl shook back. Just in time too, sis, I have somebody that I want you to meet. It's my girlfriend, Kenzy."

The girls immediately jumped on Blayden. Things were too hectic right now to have anybody that they didn't know getting close to them. No matter who it was. Not a single person was getting near Dymond if they had anything to do with it.

"Yo, Blayden, wassup with that shit? We told you that nobody comes close right now. *Nobody*," Keeky said.

"I know what we discussed, but this is my ol' lady."

"Nigga, I don't give a fuck who she is. I'm sorry, Ms. Kenzy, but right now is not the time. You are going to have to meet Dymond later."

"That's fucked up, Keeky, bruh. A'ight. Come on, bae, let's be out. Sis, I'm gon' holla at you later." Blayden left out of the room, and Keeky apologized to Dymond.

"I'm sorry I had to do that shit, Dymond, but right now we can't trust anybody outside of us, and now is not the time to bring anybody to meet you when you're just getting out of a coma. Shit, we don't know who to trust anyway."

"I understand. Blayden should know better than that shit anyways," Dymond told Keeky.

"Right, and too much shit has been going on, so until we get to the bottom of this shit, I'm not trustin' a fuckin' thing that's walking outside of this circle."

"Real. None of us can."

"Y'all two run it, let me answer my phone," Keeky stepped out of the room. "Hello."

"This is a prepaid collect call from 'Zay,' an inmate in Houston City Jail. To accept charges, press one." Keeky pressed one.

"What's up, baby?" Zay asked Keeky.

"Nothing much, just handling some business as usual."

"That's wassup, ma. You're a true hustler."

"I gotta eat, my nigga."

"Fa-sho. Will you be able to come see me today?"

"Yeah. I'll be over there. I wanted to ask you how am I supposed to come when I never gave you my information to put me on your visitation list."

"Shit is different over here. As long as you come and visit within the first thirty days of me being in this bitch, you're straight. Nobody in here has to make a list until they've been here for thirty days or more."

"Oh okay, that's wassup. Well, I miss you on some shit."

"I miss you, too. Wear something sexy."

"Nigga, everything on my body has to be covered up, but I'll try."

"Yeah, do that for me."

"That's a bet. I'll talk to you when I get there. Sorry I can't stay on the phone with you for the whole fifteen minutes, but my money is calling me."

"A'ight then, Keemari. Don't be late."

"You still calling me Keemari, huh?" She chuckled because she liked that shit. "But okay, I won't be late. I'm coming through on time, my nigga." Keeky went back into the room with Dymond and Zha.

"What y'all two discussing?" she asked, interrupting their conversation.

"Nothing much. Just trying to figure out who this bitch could have been that tried to pull the plug on Dymond," Zha answered.

"Yo, I don't know who the fuck it was, but when I find out, I'm at their top," Keeky quickly answered.

"Right, my girl, but we have to get her better first," Zha said as she stared at Dymond. She hated seeing her cousin this way.

"The doctor said if I'm straight in a week he'll let me up out of this bitch." Dymond decided to answer because she could tell that Keeky and Zha were in their feelings about her still being in the hospital.

"That's good. We're tired of babysitting your ass anyways," Keeky joked.

"I got my nine right here," Dymond laughed. "Bliss gave it to me as soon as I woke up. Daddy always makes sure his Dymond is protected."

"Bitch, please."

They laughed. Keeky hated to interrupt the good time that they were having, but she had to get to the jail on time, or they wouldn't allow her to visit Zay. "Yo, Zha, can you chill with Dymond until I go visit my lil' yea?"

"Yeah, I can chill, bitch. I don't have nothing else to do. Everybody ain't able to go visit their nigga."

"Hahaha, bitch you being funny?" Keeky knew that Zha was being sarcastic. They all played about their relationships that way. "Let me be out. Y'all bitches gon' have me late for my visit."

Keeky smiled and left out of the room. While on her way to the jail, Keeky passed up a Volkswagen car lot and noticed an all-white Audi in the show room. She didn't want to miss her visit with Zay, so she decided that she would make her way back to the lot during the week.

"What am I doing?" she thought to herself. Never in a million years did she think that she would be visiting, and looking out for a nigga in jail. That was going against the grain for her. If he didn't end up in jail behind something concerning her, then he wasn't her concern. She didn't even know this nigga that well, but she felt like it would be worth it in the end. If he fucked up in any way while in jail, at least once, then it was over for them. No way was she going to sit back, and let a nigga play her who wasn't even free.

Keeky arrived at the jail, and the officers searched her. "Got damn, girl, you fine," one of the officers told Keeky.

She had on a black long sleeve fitted shirt, straight legged jeans, and a pair of black Air Max. Her hair was loose and curly. The jeans she wore were fitting her just right, and her ass sat up perfectly in them.

"Sign in right here," the officer told Keeky. "I also need an I.D." Keeky pulled her driver's license out of her back pocket and handed it to the officer. He wrote down her information and told her to have a seat until they finished getting everybody else's information who was there for visitation as well. It was about fifteen minutes before the inmates came walking from the back, and Zay walked up behind the glass. The officers directed all of the visitors towards their seats on the other side of the glass. They picked up the phones.

"Waddup, baby girl?" Zay said with a big smile on his face.

"Nothing much. Wassup witchu?" Keeky answered with a smile on her face as big as Zay's.

"I miss you," he said as he stared into her eyes.

"I miss you, too, dude."

"You look better than you looked the first time I laid eyes on you."

"Well, I try. Have you heard anything about when you're coming home yet?"

"Naawww, not yet. The way my lawyer talkin', it's gon' be soon though."

"That's wassup. The way you had to leave me was fucked up, though. My pussy ain't shake back since," Keeky started laughing, "I need some dick like today."

"You keeping that thing tight for me?"

"Fuckin' right. Why wouldn't I?"

"That's wassup. I thought you would have bounced on me by now."

"For what? I don't have a reason to." Keeky looked around to see if anybody was possibly paying attention to them. Nobody was. "Yo, I need you to do me a favor while you're in this bitch."

"What's that?"

"You remember the Jamaican nigga that you was tellin' me about when were on the phone?"

"Yeah, why?"

"Get real close to that nigga for me. Make him trust you."

"Why?"

"Nigga, I told you that you really ask too many questions. I'm gon' run it to you when you touch down. Just do that for me, please."

"I got you."

"Thanks. I appreciate it, for real."

"Anything for you sweetheart. So, what have you been up to out there?"

"I've just been chilling. My girl Dymond is in the hospital. She got shot in the chest."

"Damn, baby girl, I'm sorry to hear that."

"It's nothing major. Minor setback for a major comeback. Nothing she can't handle."

"Glad to hear that. You been thinking 'bout me and you?"

"Yeah, I have. I just have to see how this jail shit is gonna end up, though. I don't wanna find myself falling for a nigga that can't be out here with me, you feel me? Have you been thinking 'bout us?"

"No doubt about it, sweetie. Honestly, I can't stop thinking about you. I know that it might sound crazy since we haven't been dealing with each other for too long, but I'm telling you, my mind stays occupied with thoughts of you. Shits crazy for real. I guess it might be because I had to leave right after I got that good from you." Zay and Keeky laughed. Their conversation was disrupted by the guard on duty.

"Times up," he yelled.

"I'm gon' call you later," Zay told Keeky.

"Bet that up." They hung up the phone and put their hands on the glass as if they could touch each other. Keeky smiled. She headed out of the jail and back to the car. She had about five missed calls from Zha. *Something must have happened,* she thought to herself. *Let me call back shit. I hope nothing happened to Dymond.*

"Keeky, bruh, get over here. Blayden's pussy whipped ass felt played by what you said earlier, and he's in here going off on Dymond," Zha said as soon as she picked up the phone.

"Okay, I'm on my way. I'll be there in a few. Where is he right now?"

"I don't know. I went to the cafeteria, and when I walked in the room, he was storming out."

"I'm on my way. I'm not too far."

They hung up and Keeky thought to herself, *This bitch must be fuckin' the shit out of this nigga. Dude is really starting to piss me off.*

It was already a hot summer, and Keeky felt as if they didn't need the extra problems. Nothing was more important than Dymond's recovery, and their safety at this moment. What part did Blayden not understand?

When Keeky arrived at the hospital, Blayden had made it back to Dymond's room, and he was going off. Kenzy was standing next to him, quietly.

"Blayden, son, didn't I fuckin' tell you not to do this shit right now. You're really pissing me off, cuz."

"Yo, that shit wasn't right, Keeky. I just wanted my sister to meet my girl."

"Man, fuck that girl."

Blayden slapped Keeky. "Watch that shit, Keeky, bruh. You let your mouth run too loose sometimes."

"Bitch," Keeky yelled. "When the fuck did you get enough heart to play with me like that?" Keeky cocked her gun. "Family or not, if you touch me again I will end you. Nigga, do you fuckin' understand me?" She was furious. "Right now is not the fuckin' time. Son, your sister is laying in a motherfuckin' hospital bed trying to recover from a serious injury, and all the fuck you can think about is having her meet a motherfucker that you're involved with. Honestly, you should have been did this shit, nigga. You're that stuck on pussy that you decide to come at your sister at a time like this. You better get the fuck out of here, I'm telling you. Before you fuck around and piss me off more than you already did."

"Blayden, let's go. It's not that important. Nice to meet you, Dymond. This other bitch is crazy," she said staring towards Keeky.

"Bitch," Keeky looked at her and said, "I got your bitch."

Kenzy grabbed Blayden's hand to leave the room. Blayden turned around, "Yo, Dymond, sis, that's fucked up how you let her do me like that."

"No, Blayden, what's fucked up is how that pussy makin' you forget that it's business over bullshit right now. Nigga, we all we got."

Kenzy pulled Blayden by the arm, and they left.

"I can't believe this shit," Dymond yelled out.

"What?" Keeky said, "Bruh, the nigga shouldn't have hit me."

"Bitch, I'm not worrying about that shit. I knew you wasn't gon' kill him."

"Well, what then?"

"That's the voice that I heard in my dreams."

Chapter 13

"I'm tellin' y'all that's the voice," Dymond said to reassure Keeky and Zha.

"Bitch, you lying. I got this, bitch. I'm goin' catch that hoe outside," Keeky said.

"No," Dymond interrupted Keeky. "I have something special in mind for this bitch."

"Yo, Dymond, I hope that you know what you're doing because it's nothing to pop that bitch real quick, with Blayden or not," Zha added.

"Son, I'm tellin' y'all I got her. Find out who that bitch daddy is first, though. She did call and ask that nigga if he was sure he wanted her to kill me. We kill her now, then we never find out who's behind all of this shit. We have to stay at least ten steps ahead of these motherfuckers."

"You're right. Blayden better get his fuckin' mind right, though. That bitch is flakey. This nigga is sleepin' with the motherfuckin' enemy, and he doesn't even know it."

"Yo, if this bitch kills my brother, I'm gon' sleep her whole fuckin' family. You can bet that shit."

"We can't run this shit to Blayden, though. She got that nigga nose wide the fuck open right now. Brother or not, Dymond, we have to keep this shit right here."

"I agree. I'm not trippin'. I'm just gon' stay on Blayden's ass so that I can keep a close eye on this bitch."

"Yeah do that. The way this bitch is rockin' you never know what type of games she playin'."

Dymond knew that sometimes Blayden could be naïve when it came to women. He was still young, and she always did say that the first female to come along and give him some of the good would have his mind going crazy. Pussy could turn a nigga against his whole family. Sex was a weapon, and she could tell that Kenzy knew that.

"Hold up, y'all. My phone is ringin'," Dymond said.

"Hello. Hey, baby, wassup? Keeky and Zha still there?"

"Yeah, they're here."

"Let me holla at Keeky real quick."

"Yo, Keeky. Bliss wanna holla at you real quick."

"Waddup, nigga?" Keeky asked Bliss.

"Wassup with you? Yo, I have a meeting with that nigga Kayne in a few minutes to sign this contract. Since we've established that the nigga can't be trusted, you and Zha meet me over there, and chill outside until I'm done signing with that bitch. I don't want any flakey shit to go down. If y'all see anything that looks wrong on the outside, come in that bitch spraying."

"We gotchu. We on our way."

They hung up. "Zha, let's dip. Bliss needs us to watch his back while he handles something. You gon' be straight 'til we get back, sis?"

"Yeah, I'm good. I got my nine by my side. She's cocked and ready."

"You don't want to know what Bliss wanted?"

"No, bitch, I trust my nigga. If he called y'all it must be important. My dude is solid, and I know that for sure. Until he shows me otherwise, I don't have a reason not to trust him."

"You sprung ass bitch."

"No, boo. I'm a sprung ass bitch with a good ass nigga that feels the same way about me. You mad, or you jealous?" They laughed.

"Well, we out then." Keeky and Zha left to meet Bliss.

***

"I surely hope that this nigga Bliss hurries up and gets what he has to get out of this nigga because I can't wait to kill that dick in the booty ass bitch," Zha said while they were riding in the car.

"Who you think was pumpin' though, that nigga Khalil or Kayne? That bitch Khalil did look like he could have been the one gettin' jugged, though."

"Bitch, I don't know, shit. I can't believe I let that faggot ass nigga flake me out like that, yo."

"Fuck it. He out of here now." They pulled up about twenty minutes later to meet Bliss.

Bliss signaled them to pull up in the duck off where nobody else could see them. Bliss got out of his car and walked inside to meet Kayne.

When he made it inside, a light pink BMW pulled up and hurriedly came to a stop. The windows were tinted just enough to where you could not see who was inside.

"Whoever that is must be pissed off. You see how fast they pulled up in that bitch?" Zha asked Keeky.

"This nigga Kayne must have fucked over somebody else, too." Keeky and Zha watched as the driver got out of the car.

"Check it out. It's that bitch Kenzy." Keeky couldn't hold her composure. "I got that hoe now. I'm about to make that bitch eat every word she said at that hospital."

Chapter 14

"Hi, baby girl," Kayne said when he called Kenzy. She pulled up, while on the phone with her dad.

"Hey, daddy. Guess what?"

"What?" Kayne wanted to know.

"Dymond is awake, and I went to the hospital with Blayden to see her. They wouldn't let me stay, though. They don't want anybody in the room with her except for a few of them."

"That's fine. We can continue what we started when she gets home. We'll catch them one by one. Are you fuckin' the brother like I told you, too?"

"Yeah. He's really diggin' me, too."

"Good. That's my girl. Now don't you fuck around and fall in love. Love don't love nobody. Don't go puttin' your heart in your mind's position. We have an agenda, and we're sticking to it. Fuck this up, and you answer to me."

"I understand. Business only."

"Well, I found someone that works in the jailhouse to get word to the Jamaican for me."

"That's great. What did he say?"

"Well my connect gave him my number, and he called me. I told him everything. He assured me that he should be getting out in a few days on good behavior."

"Yo, wassup bitch?" Kenzy heard a voice say from behind her. Keeky had taken the opportunity to creep up behind her while she was on the phone with her head down. "That's how it could have happened to your smot mouthed ass. Let me see if you really living like that?" She turned around, and she was standing face to face with Keeky. The phone call with her dad had ended.

"Oh my God, you again?" Kenzy asked in a disgusted manner.

"Yeah, bitch it's me. Let me see if you 'bout that noise you was bringing at the hospital earlier."

Kenzy walked up to Keeky really calm with her purse in her hand, and punched the fuck out of her in her mouth.

"Bitch, you talk too motherfuckin' much. I'm sick of you talkin' stupid to me. You gon' give me my respect, or bitch I will take it." Keeky stumbled. She tried to shake back to swing on Kenzy, but she missed. Kenzy stepped to the side, and hit her in the face. Keeky dropped. "I'm sick of you hoes. I told Blayden not to bring me around you project ass bitches anyways." Zha ran up to hit Kenzy, but she was stopped in her tracks when Kenzy pulled a pink and chrome glock on her. "Bitch, if you swing, I will dead your ass right here."

Zha paused and stared at Kenzy. She was a 5'9" chocolate goddess. Her skin was almost flawless. She reminded you of Naomi Campbell. She had a brain for business with the passion of a porn star. Her mom taught her to act like a lady, and her dad taught her to think like a boss. She was very well established for her age, and had the hustle of a million-dollar nigga. Her dad sent her to the best schools, but also taught her the streets. The bitch was dangerous, book and street smarts. She was part owner of all of her dad's venues, but she also distributed top of the line drugs to wealthy white business owners on the side. She was very well protected because she was the only girl, and the only child. This bitch Kenzy was a fighter, and she was 'bout that pistol play.

"Bitch, don't worry, we'll meet again," Zha said.

"Fuck y'all," Kenzy said back to her. "You bitches ain't as bad as I thought y'all were."

"What's going on?" Bliss asked as he was walked outside.

"These two bitches were just about to leave," Kenzy answered.

"Y'all a'ight? If y'all need to handle business I can wait until y'all handle it. Looks like this is some shit that needs to be addressed right now," Bliss looked at Keeky and asked.

"Yeah we good. Bitch, I got you, remember that," Keeky told Kenzy as she spat blood from her mouth.

"Yeah, I hear you. Do y'all, and I'm gon' do me."

"That's a bet."

"Come on y'all, let's go," Bliss said.

"*Let's go*?" Zha blurted out loudly. "I'm not about to let this bitch pull on me, and I just walk away like that. We'll meet again sure enough, but I want some of this bitch right now."

"I just said that y'all can do y'all if need be. I'm right here. I'm not going anywhere."

"Naaawww, Zha," Keeky said as she put her hand on Zha's shoulder. "Let's be out. We'll meet again, I promise that shit."

They started walking off and Zha asked, "Yo, Bliss, do you know her?"

"Yeah, that's Kayne's daughter, Kenzy."

"Kayne's daughter?" Keeky and Zha said at the same time.

"Yeah, if I would have known y'all knew her, I would have warned y'all about her. That's a bad bitch. He had her trained by the best. How y'all know her anyway?"

"She fucks with Blayden, and Kayne sent her to pull that plug on Dymond."

"He what?" Bliss screamed.

"Yeah, but we got him, though."

"Yeah, me too."

Bliss took off running back towards the building.

Kenzy had already made it inside. She was furious when she walked in. The secretaries and body guards knew not to bother her when she looked as if she was on a rampage. How did she not see this coming? Blayden had already warned her about what types of women his sister, and her people were. Those bitches were the type that just didn't quit once they felt like you'd crossed them wrong.

"Daddy, did you see those bitches you're trying to kill outside?" Kenzy asked Kayne.

"No, what bitches?" he asked.

"Well, Keeky and some other chick. Dymond wasn't with her. She's still in the hospital."

"Keeky doesn't roll with anybody else. What did the other chick look like who was with Keeky?"

"Long hair, nice body..."

"Wait, was she short, and was she dark skinned like you?" Kayne cut her off.

"Yeah, she was. How did you know?"

"Because Keeky only kept two women close to her. It can't be who I think it is, but I can't see Keeky bringing in anybody new. I've been watching their moves for years now. It can't be who I think it is because Khalil was supposed to kill this bitch a long time ago."

"Wait, daddy, what's going on?"

"Baby girl, it's a lot to explain. Tell me what happened outside. Do they have any idea who you are?"

"They only know me as Blayden's girlfriend because they saw me at the hospital, and we passed a few words. Outside just now, that bitch Keeky tried to run up on me, and I hit her ass twice. I pulled out my glock on both of those bitches."

"My God. Let me make a phone call, baby, excuse me."

Chapter 15

"Bliss. Bliss. Bliss. Yo, slow down," Zha was yelling. "You just said yourself that these motherfuckers ain't to be played with. Besides, Dymond said that she wants to be the one to kill Kenzy."

"Well, I'm about to kill her dad," he said still trying to get to Kayne's building. Zha grabbed his arm.

"No. He doesn't know that we're on to him. Don't forget that this motherfucker set me up to have Khalil kill me. We have to tread carefully. That's why Keeky's ass shouldn't have ever went fuckin' with that bitch."

"Man, fuck all that. She got me. It is what it is," Keeky said.

"No, bitch. Dymond asked you to wait, and ol' girl was right. You were talking too much. I don't give a fuck how mad you were, you never let a bitch take you off of your game like that."

"You're right. I can't even be mad and front like you're not."

"Yo, y'all are really not thinking. If y'all keep reacting off of emotions, we'll all end up dead. Keeky, if you were gonna pull a stunt like that, you should have just slept the bitch right there on sight. No talkin'. Now she's going to be watchful of her surroundings."

"You're right. I wasn't thinking. That bitch just does something to me."

"To all of us, but we didn't do our research on the bitch, and she almost did us in."

When Zha started doing hits she quit believing in talking about everything. Her motto was shoot first, and ask questions later.

"Hold up, y'all, this nigga Zay calling."

"Hello."

"You have a prepaid collect call from..." Keeky didn't waste any time, she just pressed one.

"Wassup, ma?"

"Chillin', chillin'. Handling business as usual. What's good, baby?"

"Nothing much. I tried doing what you asked me to do, but that shit wasn't happening. That motherfucker has real life trust issues, and it looks like he shut shit down completely with everybody after his daughter died. I only seen him use the phone about one time since that shit happened."

"Damn. You sure you tried hard enough?"

"Yeah, ma. I put that on God. I tried."

"You can't try one more time for me, please, baby?" Keeky put on her sexy voice.

"No doubt, I would if I could, but it's impossible now."

"Why did you say that?"

"The guard came in and told that nigga that somebody on the outside pulled some strings. They came back here to get the nigga. He's going home."

"Going home? Already?"

"Yup. I don't know who that boy has working on the outside, but he got pull."

"A'ight, that's a bet."

"What's wrong? Sounds like you have beef with the nigga or something."

"Naawww, it ain't like that."

"Well, enough about that nigga then. How you doing, baby?"

"I'm doing fine, so far so good. Everything is tight on my end."

"I can't wait to come home and make love to your sexy ass."

"I can't wait until you come and make love to me, either. You're making my pussy jump just thinking about it."

"That's what I want that pussy to do. Jump when I speak."

"You don't have to worry about that, she's definitely jumping." Keeky spent the next ten minutes running it with Zay. They were loving the vibe that they were getting from each other.

"You have one minute remaining," the operator said, interrupting their conversation.

"Well, hit me up when you can. I say I miss you, girl."

"I say I miss you, boy." That was their new thing that they had started doing before their calls ended. They hung up. Keeky hurried back to Bliss and Zha.

"Yo, Bliss, get to the hospital with Dymond. Holding her nine or not, nobody leaves her. Somebody needs to be there at all times."

"Why? What's wrong?" Bliss asked.

"The fuckin' Jamaican whose daughter that we offed, that nigga checked out of jail a lil while ago."

"Son, are you serious?" Zha asked in shock.

"Yeah, I'm serious, bitch. Trip part is we can't even case the nigga. We don't know what he knows about this girl's murder. A nigga that had boo coo time on his hands to process shit, could be a well-thought out nigga."

"Well, we just have to get on our shit."

"Let's do that shit right now then."

Bliss left to go to the hospital. Keeky and Zha left to go to the spot.

"What type of heat do you think this Jamaican nigga bringin'?" Zha asked Keeky.

"Bitch, I don't know, but I do know that whatever it is, we gotta be ready for it."

"What are you looking at like that?" Zha said as she looked in her rearview because Keeky kept peeking in hers.

"I'm not sure, but I think somebody is following us. I could be tripping though."

Pow... Pow... Pow... Pow...

The person that she was keeping an eye started shootin' at their car.

"Who the fuck is that?" Zha yelled.

"I don't know. Swing this bitch around the corner and pull in the first duck off that you see."

"A'ight," Zha found an alley, she pulled in, and cut her lights off.

"Look, there they go passin' right now."

"You know whose car that is?"

"Fuck no."

"That's a dead end they about to hit so they gotta turn that bitch around, and come back."

The section that they pulled into was dark, and not lit at all. It reeked of alcohol, and wine. The area was quiet except for a few drug addicts walking through an alley on the next street.

"Yo, get out, and we're going to wait for them to get close." As the car approached, they eased up, and made their way directly in front of the car. They lit that bitch up. The car slowed down and came to a stop. Keeky and Zha walked to the window, and a young Jamaican was in the car.

"Who the fuck sent you?" Keeky asked.

"Mi boss," the Jamaican uttered as he was dying.

"What fuckin' boss?"

"Nunya bidness," he answered as blood started to ooze out of the side of his mouth.

"I'm gon' ask you one more time, homeboy. Who the fuck sent you?" Keeky put her gun to his head, and pressed into his temple. It was still hot, and she could see the heat burning the side of his head as he squealed.

"Fuck ya, pussy-clot," the Jamaican said.

"Well," Zha said looking at the Jamaican, "I'm gon' personally let the bitch know that you missed whenever I find out who the fuck he or she is," and his brains splattered all over her top.

Chapter 16

"Dymond Spencer?" a nurse asked. "How are you feeling?"

"I'm okay, still sore," Dymond responded to the nurse.

"Well, the doctor says if your vitals are okay, and your wound looks good, you can go home soon."

"That's wassup. You heard that, huh, daddy? I'm back in affect," Dymond said smiling at Bliss.

"Yeah, I'm happy for you, baby, but you know that I'm going to handle your light weight for you while you're recovering. No worries."

"I know, bae."

The nurse walked out of the room, and Bliss walked over to kiss Dymond. He leaned in slowly, and looked into her eyes.

"Baby, when I heard that you had gotten shot, I immediately thought the worst. Losing you would be one of the hardest things in life for me to ever deal with."

"I know, daddy, I feel the same way about you."

"I cannot wait another moment. When God made you, he specifically took into consideration what I would need and who I would need in my life. He molded you as a perfect fit for me. I cannot live without your touch. My body craves yours. I cherish your thoughts. Everything about you completes me. I cannot see myself callin' another woman my wife. Baby, I never want to lose you, until death do us part. We ride together, we die together. Love is patient, and you've taught me patience. Love is kind, and you've shown me kindness. Love is not selfish, and I have watched you on numerous occasions deny yourself for me."

Dymond was starting to tear up as Bliss continued to speak. "Love is not jealous, and I have watched you become my biggest fan and reject any thoughts on jealousy, or people trying to create a jealous spirit between us. Love is unconditional, and it has no conditions. I've learned that I cannot give you what I don't have. If I never would have had love shown to me, then I would not know how to give you the love that you need. Baby, I am prepared to give you all of the love that God has enabled me to give. All of the hurt, pain, and hard times that you may have endured, baby, I want to be the one to make you forget about all of that. Please allow me to be your forever. Will you do me the honor of becoming Mrs. Bliss Heins?"

Dymond was fully engulfed in tears by the time Bliss had finished. "Daddy, I cannot imagine ever changing my name to anything else. Yes, I will be your wife."

She hugged and kissed him slowly over and over.

"Baby, you might have to chill while we're in this hospital," Bliss told Dymond.

"I'm about to be Mrs. Bliss Heins. Fuck chillin'."

She grabbed Bliss' shirt, and started kissing him again. He ran his hand from her breast to her pussy. He slid two fingers in, and curved them towards her g-spot. "How does that feel?"

"Uuuummmmmm," Dymond moaned.

"You want me to stop? I know that it probably hurts."

"Hell no. Help me up. It's nothing that I can't deal with."

Bliss took out his two fingers, and Dymond sucked her juices clean. That shit was a complete turn on to Bliss. His dick rocked up instantly.

"Come on, daddy, help me up."

"Dymond, you're not supposed to be moving around right now."

"Daddy, help me up. You can just fuck me slowly. The nurse said that the doctor isn't going to release me until I start moving around on my own anyway."

Bliss took her hand to help her up. She leaned over the side of the bed, and lifted up her hospital gown. She needed the side of the bed to help her to stay steady. She moved her ass a little so that his dick could be guided towards her opening.

"Take your time, bae," she told Bliss.

"I will." He slid the head of his penis in, and used it to open her up. He went in and out with the tip of the head until she was ready for the whole thing. He could tell that she was still in lots of pain so he took his time with her as if it was her first time.

"Go ahead, daddy, I'm ready."

"I gotchu, ma." Bliss started to make a circular motion as he grabbed Dymond's ass to pull it more towards him. He reached his hand around the front of her, and massaged her clit. She didn't make too many movements because the pain wouldn't allow her to.

"Hurry up before the nurse comes back," Dymond said.

"I'm about to get it," Bliss said, "but I ain't getting mine without you." He moved in and out slowly, and then he pushed her ass in and back out, in and back out.

Dymond was biting her lips and moaning. "I'm about to come, daddy."

"Get that bitch." He tapped her ass softly. "Get that bitch." He tapped her ass softly. "Get that bitch." He tapped her ass softly.

Dymond started clenching because she was coming, and her pussy was jumping. Bliss came, too, all over her ass. He helped Dymond back into her bed, and went into the restroom to get a soapy towel to clean himself up. Then he cleaned Dymond, as well.

"Your phone is vibrating, bae," Dymond told Bliss.

"I got it," he answered. "Hello."

"Mr. Heins, how are you?"

"I'm doing fine today. I have a client that I would like you to promote for me. His name is Judas. A Jamaican rapper that I just gave a club performance contract, too," Kayne said.

Chapter 17

Kayne was a 35-year-old millionaire. He was dark-skinned, had short nappy hair, and a pearly white smile. He wore only the best suits, and was all about his business. In addition to owning four of the hottest, most talked about venues in Houston, he was also a big time drug distributor. He taught his daughter the game as well, but she was only allowed to distribute certain drugs.

A few years ago, when Keeky came on the scene, she became a threat to him. She came up fast in the game, and he started losing some of his clientele to her. Bringing Dymond and Zha on board made things worse for him. Together, they were a female powerhouse. They were very well organized. His only option was to kill the competition.

He watched their every move, and even sent some customers their way. He learned everything that he needed to know about them, and taught it to his daughter. He taught her their mentality, their hustle, their fight, their drive, everything. He was smart, but he was flakey.

He found out that Khalil had a thing for women and men, so he started a relationship with him, popped him off a couple of bands here and there, and made that nigga turn on his ol' lady.

Most of their inside hustles, he got from Khalil when he pillow-talked. That's how he decided that he needed to split the three of them up by killing Zha. She was the easiest to get to because of the relationship that she he had with Khalil. He was obsessed with getting rid of them by any means. He wanted the streets back, but Keeky and Dymond had already taken them over. The amount of drugs that they were pushing, and the prices that they were dropping them at made it hard for anybody on the streets to compete. Kayne couldn't afford to match or beat their prices at the time so he had to lay back until the time was right to do so. It was hard to get anybody to cross them.

"Him comin' ova yah? " Judas asked Kayne.

"He cannot make it tonight. His ol' lady is still in the hospital. She's one of the bitches you want to kill."

"Jah know I sire dem dead right?"

"Yes, I know that you desire for them to be dead, but you will never catch them one-by-one. Getting Bliss to promote you will definitely get them to the club. I know that it will get Dymond there for sure. We have to split them up. A divided team *can* be conquered. They're always prepared. These bitches are smart."

"Chatty, chatty. Mi have no time tah talk. Dem pussy-clots kill mi daughter. Yah bring me home bwoy and mi cah do dis. Check it deep. One a day mi kill. Coo yah?"

"Yeah one a day is cool. I have two hundred thousand dollars for you once they're all dead."

"Reespek."

Judas seemed to be the edgy type, always ready to move at a quick pace without thinking things through. Taking a chance on this guy could be fatal for Kayne because he had just lost his daughter, and wasn't thinking clearly. He would try to kill based off of his emotions, which could be a bad thing for Kayne in the end.

Judas left, and Kayne called Kenzy.

"Yes, daddy?"

"Hey, baby girl. I need you to talk your little boyfriend into turning against his sister for me. It's time to break up the click."

"No problem, I know just what to do." Kenzy hung up the phone with her dad, and called out for Blayden to come into the room. She knew just what to do, and just what to tell him in order to get him going. He loved her, and she knew just how to use that to her advantage.

"Blayden, can you come here real quick?" Kenzy yelled out.

"Waddup, ma?"

"Nothing much. I just felt like we need to talk."

"About what?"

"The shit that went down with your sister at the hospital."

"Oh, what about it?"

"I don't think that we could be together if your people will keep treating me that way."

"You don't have to worry about that shit. That's only because of what happened with Dymond. My sister ain't normally like that. She cool people. Her, Keeky, and Zha are all cool. They're just dealing with a lot of shit right now."

"Well, I don't like it. I really don't even like you being in their company, anyways. They will get you killed. If you love me like you say you do, you'll put your woman first."

"Yeah, I love you like I say I do, but you're my woman, not my wife, baby girl. My sister, Keeky, and Zha, that's blood. Even though Keeky gets on my motherfuckin' nerves, and she ain't blood by DNA, she's still blood to me. They'll never turn on me no matter what the deal is, so I wouldn't ever turn on them. I could never have them question my loyalty. Family or not, they'll kill me."

"So, you're just going to let me go like that then?"

"Never. I could just fix this shit between y'all."

"I'm tellin' you, they don't like me. I met up with them today at my dad's office, and that bitch Keeky still had it on her mind."

"Yo, you lying. What happened?"

"I hit that bitch with a two-piece, and pulled my strap on their asses."

"I can't believe this shit. They really came at you like that? And you're really still alive. I'm going to have to talk to Dymond because this shit has to stop. I mean, I love you, and they'll have to accept that."

"Well, they threatened me when they left, so I'm sure that they are not trying to hear that shit you talkin'."

"Threatened you?"

"Yeah, but you've made your decision. We're done."

Kenzy got up to walk away with one of Blayden's t-shirts on, and nothing else underneath.

"Wait, babe, come here."

"What?" Kenzy said, pouting in her baby voice.

"I'll talk to my sister tomorrow and try to fix it."

"You will?"

"Yeah, bae, promise. I'm tired though, ma, let's go to bed."

Ding dong. Their doorbell rang.

"Fuck. Who is that?"

"I don't know. I'm sure that it's not for me," Blayden told Kenzy.

"I got it. Let me put some shorts on." She opened the door and there was a package in the front of it. "Must be something from my dad," she said to herself.

"Who was it?" Blayden asked as she walked back into the room.

"Nobody, must be something that my dad sent to me."

"Well, I know that nigga got cake so open it up." She opened it.

"Oooooh shit," they said at the same time.

It was the gun that she had given to the Jamaican to do the hit on Keeky and Zha, with his trigger finger, and a note attached to it that read, "Bitch you missed. We're ready for war."

Chapter 18

Keeky had finally made it over to the car lot. Zha went with her to pick up the Audi that she had seen the day that she was going to visit Zay. She used the money that she had gotten from her insurance claim, plus some money that he had taken from her stash, and paid the Audi out in cash. It was white, with a chrome grill, chrome factory rims, and black lining around her doors, and along the side of the car.

"Dymond would love to stunt in this bitch," she told Zha.

They filled out all of the paperwork, received the keys, and were ready to leave the lot. The day was beautiful, and Keeky knew that it was perfect to get a lot of work done. Switching up her ride was going to be good for business because people could not fuck with a person that they don't know. No one would know that it was her riding in that brand new Audi.

"Wassup y'all?" Keeky asked Dymond and Bliss as she and Zha entered the hospital room.

"Nothing much. We're just chillin'. Waiting on these discharge papers."

"Discharge papers? They're lettin' you out of this bitch?" Keeky asked.

"Yup, and guess what else?"

"What?"

"I'm getting married, y'all."

"Yooooo, congratulations, sis. I'm so fucking happy for you," Keeky said.

"Me, too, cuz. Wish we could have been here for the proposal. Sorry we didn't make it back on yesterday," Zha added in.

"Why didn't y'all come back anyways?"

"We got into some extra shit, but it's handled. That bitch Kenzy is bringing all types of heat our way. We're going to have to lay her down, Dymond, and quick."

"I know. Bliss told me about that lil scuffle y'all got into with the bitch. Keeky, son, you have to learn to calm the fuck down sometimes. You can't win every battle, bruh."

"Right, I told her that if she was going to go at her like that, should have shot that hoe," Zha said.

"Man, look, I know I was wrong. The bitch just pissed me off. That lil baby got hands, though."

Blayden walked in and interrupted their conversation. "Waddup, y'all? Can I holla at y'all real quick?"

"We're listening," Dymond said as everybody mugged him.

"I heard y'all had a lil beef with Kenzy yesterday. I just want to ask y'all to please let that shit die down, for me. Keeky, what happened between you and her at the hospital wasn't all that serious for you to feel like you had to go at her sideways like that. I'm sorry that she pulled a strap on y'all, too. This shit's really stressing me out, yo. And to top it all off, a motherfuckin' package came to the house last night with a gun, a finger, and a war message. I don't know what's going on, but I surely hope that this shit settles down. I would hate to have to choose between y'all, and her."

"Wait, hold up? I know that you didn't just say that you would hate to have to choose," Dymond said. "Well, choose then, motherfucka."

Bliss interrupted, "Hold up, y'all. Don't do, or say some shit that y'all will regret."

"Blayden, my nigga, check it out," Keeky said. "I personally don't give a fuck who you choose because we'll do us regardless. What your green ass need to do is go home, and do a little more research on your bitch. Ask that hoe where the package came from, since it's obvious that you don't know. I'm sure the bitch acted like she don't know either, huh? Ask that bitch to take you to meet the fam. As a matter of fact, how about you drop your nuts on this bitch, and start laying the dick down instead of letting the bitch be the one to fuck you because it's evident who's fucking who. Oh, and nigga, don't make *us* have to choose. Once you fuck over us, our camp ain't gon' stop eating, but you will. Ain't no coming back from that shit."

"Right," Zha said. "I guess your bitch is in her feelings. Let that hoe feel some type of way then, so we can catch the bitch slippin'. I don't feel sorry for the bitch, period."

"You know what, Blayden, when I get out of this bitch in a lil while, bring her to my place," Dymond said. Dymond felt as if she needed Kenzy to be present for all of this.

"You serious, sis?"

"Yeah, I'm serious, but tell that hoe to check her attitude at the door. I'm sore right now, and I don't have the energy to fight, but I will shoot the fuck out of her."

"That's a bet. I'm going to have her together. I'm going call her now. I'll holla at y'all later."

Blayden left.

Keeky couldn't believe what she was hearing.

"Dymond, bitch I know you didn't."

"Yes the fuck I did. I've had a lot of time to think in this bitch. Fuck going at her sideways, I want to study my enemy, which is what you should have done. I'm about to make sure that we do this bitch in, the right way. No sneak shit. Face to face action. Let her get comfortable. She should have killed me the first time."

"Whatever. I hope that you know what you're doing?"

"I got this."

"What about Kayne then? When are we going to do this nigga in?"

"Soon," Bliss answered. "Right after I get the money that I have to get up out of him. As a matter of fact, I have to get going. I'm on my way to meet a new client of his right now. Can y'all chill with Dymond?"

"Yeah, we got her."

"Bliss left and headed over to Kayne's office. An unknown number called Keeky.

"Who this?" She asked as she answered the phone.

"Baby, it's Zay, come pick me up. The judge gave me immediate release when I went to court this morning."

Chapter 19

"It wasn't that long, but I'm glad that I'm finally up out of that bitch," Zay said to himself. He hadn't been to jail in a while, and ending up back in there was not a part of his plans.

He couldn't wait to get next to Keeky. He knew that he had to work on making her softer towards him, but he did understand why her trust was so fucked up in the first place.

"Hello," Zay answered the phone for Keeky.

"Yo, babe. I'm not coming because I'm setting something up right now. It's important. I'm sending my girl Zha to come and pick you up so just be ready. She's on her way as we speak. She should be pulling up in about thirty minutes."

"A'ight, ma. Tell her I'll be waiting. How will she know that it's me?"

"I gave her a description, but if she isn't sure she'll ask every nigga out there, trust me." Keeky laughed because she knew that Zha could be outspoken at times.

"Okay."

"I wonder what the hell she's doing like that to where she couldn't make time to come and get me. I can't believe this shit. This girl acted like she really couldn't wait 'til a nigga touch down, and now she's too busy for me," Zay was saying to himself. He wasn't used to a woman not jumping at his beck and call. He was used to women doing things the way that he liked them to, and when he wanted them to. He waited patiently for the next forty minutes. Zha was a little late, but he didn't want to complain.

"Ay-yo, you Zay?" He was the only person sitting there. She figured that it had to be him, since she was told that he would be waiting on her.

"Yeah, that's me."

"It's me, Zha. Keeky homegirl. You ready?"

"Fuckin' right. I been ready."

Zay got into the car with Zha. They headed out. "So, how long have you and Keeky been cool?" Zay asked Zha.

"All of our lives. She's like a sister to me. One of the realest bitches that I've ever come across."

"No doubt about that. That's the reason why I started fucking with her the long way."

"Fah-sho. She said you was cool people, though. My girl really feelin' you. Don't hurt her nah, or we're going to want your head." They laughed and Zha pulled up in front of The Marriott Suites Houston.

"What are we doing here?" Zay asked.

"This is where Keeky told me to bring you to. She said to go to room 213. Here's the key."

"A'ight. Thanks again, shawty."

Zay got out, and did as he was told. He walked into the hotel, and went to the room. When he slid the key and opened the door, Keeky was standing there with a mask on, red bottom heels, and her body was glistening.

"Welcome to my playroom," she said to Zay. "Please undress, and lie on the bed."

Zay started taking off everything that he had on. He walked over to the bed, and lay down on it. "Turn over," Keeky said.

Zay turned over onto his stomach, and Keeky dripped strawberry massage oil onto his body. She had the kind that heats as you blow on it. She used her hands to spread it around his back, and as she rubbed, she stopped for seconds in between and blew up and down his spine. The oil heated up. Zay had goose bumps all over his body. She used a feather tickler with red feathers and a black end on it to run it from his neck to his ankles.

Zay couldn't take anymore. He tried to turn over, but Keeky pushed him down and pulled out her flogger. She whipped it across his back. “Don’t move,” she whispered in his ear. “This is my time.”

“Now, you can turn over and be still.” Zay turned over and his dick stood straight up.

He had a hook in it that went to the left. His veins were popping out, and it moved back and forth as he breathed harder and harder. Keeky stood up in the bed, walked over to Zay’s face, and turned around to face the back so that he could look up straight at her ass. She stooped down, but didn’t sit in his face. She leaned forward so that her face could be facing his foot area, and her ass was on his chest. She licked the shaft of his penis, and then slowly used her teeth to softly bite on the tip of his head. Her hands were freshly manicured, so they looked pretty rubbing up and down his dick. She let her spit drip from her mouth, and used it to make his penis extra wet. Zay loved the fact that she was aggressive, but gentle. She sucked it sloppily.

Zay smacked her ass, and she moved it off of his chest. She slid onto his dick. She was still facing the end of the bed, so she rode the dick backwards. She used her hands to lean back so that she could see his penis as it went in and out of her. She got on her tippy toes, and bounced until Zay grabbed her down tightly so that he could put all of it in.

“God damn, baby. You miss this dick, huh?”

“I told you that I wasn’t giving this pussy to nobody else.”

“Who pussy this for?”

“Zaaaayyyy,” Keeky moaned, “this pussy is for you. She was getting ready to climax, and so was he. He bit his lip, and she tilted her head back while biting hers.

“Uuuuuhhhhh,” they said at the same time, and it was over. Keeky got up to go to the shower, and Zay was about to follow until Keeky got a call from Dymond.

“Yo, wassup, sis?”

"Keeky, please get over to the hospital. They're about to release me. You and Zha had to go, and Bliss had to leave me to go to that meeting with Kayne."

"Okay, I'm coming. Why do you sound like you're hyperventilating?"

"Because I just received a picture from Bliss' phone. Looks like he never made it by Kayne. He was tied up, and blind-folded with a Jamaican nigga in the background. I know he's Jamaican because I can see the flag in the room. Come on Keeky, bruh, I need to get my baby back."

Keeky hung up with Dymond, and sat on the edge of the tub in the bathroom. She was trying to put a plan together in her head, but she knew that she needed to leave right away in order to go pick up Dymond from the hospital.

"I'm sorry that I have to leave in such a hurry," she looked at Zay and said. "Dymond needs me."

Zay was very understanding about their situation, so he assured her that he was okay with it, and she got ready to leave.

"How the fuck am I going to help my sis?" Keeky said out loud as she was waiting on the elevator. It was a good thing that no one was around to hear her having a conversation with herself. "I guess we'll have to kill anybody involved."

Chapter 20

"Ease up," Judas told Bliss. "Feel no way. Mi no want yah. Mi want yah guhl."

"If you touch my girl, I will kill you."

"Blood clot. Bwoy, mi kill ha dead."

Judas punched Bliss in the face. He was 6'5" and heavy set. His Jamaican accent was very thick and he had dreads that went down just a little past the middle of his back. He was a well-respected Jamaican kingpin. He told Kayne that he would kill each of them one by one. The only way to do it was to separate them. He was supposed to show up at Kayne's office for a meeting with Kayne and Bliss. When he saw Bliss pull up behind Kayne's office building, he pulled a gun on him, and made him get in the car. Bliss was outnumbered, and his strap was in the glove compartment.

"I'm only going to tell you one more time. If you touch my girl, I will kill you."

"Ya see disya? Yah gonna make mi use it and slice ya throat. Mi naa waan fi do it, but mi wud." He hit Bliss again. Kayne was calling his phone.

"Who dem ring?"

"This is Kayne. I've been waiting here at the office for you and Mr. Bliss, but neither one of you has shown up. His phone is going straight to voicemail, and I just signed a contract with this motherfucker."

"Yah hear any ting from his guhl? She no come look fah him?"

"No, she and I have never done any types of business. Why did you ask me that?"

"Wa'ppun mi key? Mi no kya bout dat neegah. Bumboclot. Tahnight one of dem die."

"Well, it better not be Bliss that dies. I need him. This is business." Kayne hung up the phone.

"Long time mi a wait. No more," he said. "Mi do dis tah yah right nah, but mi want yah guhl first."

***

Dymond showed Keeky, Zay, and Zha the picture that she had in her phone. They all analyzed it, but no one could figure out anything.

"Wait, yo. I know this spot," Zay said. "It's on Tallow Point Court."

"How do you know for sure?" Dymond asked.

"When I first started slanging, we used dat spot to trap out of. We used to slang weed, that's why they put the Jamaican flag in there."

"Let's go then. I have to go get my baby back."

"Dymond you have to think. Didn't you tell us to stop thinking off of emotions?" Keeky asked. "Let's just peep shit out, and go with our move when the time is right."

They left the hospital, and everyone hopped in Zha's SUV. Keeky's car was not big enough for them all to ride in. As they headed over there, Dymond was anxious to see if Bliss was really at the spot that Zay said he was in, and to see if he was hurt, or if she could see any signs of immediate danger. They pulled up in front of the spot where Judas was.

"Fuck all that shit you talkin', bitch, I'm going get my nigga," Dymond said.

"Dymond, yo, you spazzing," Keeky said back to her. She left running towards the door with a choppa in her hands.

Keeky took off running behind her. She almost collapsed because she was still fresh out of the hospital. Keeky caught her before she fell. Dymond started crying.

"Keeky, let me go."

"No. I know you're worried, Dymond, but you know that Bliss is a fighter. He's gonna be alright."

"Keeky, let me go."

"Chill, cuz," Zha said. "We got Bliss. You just gotta wait for the right time. This Jamaican nigga ain't playin', baby girl, and neither is Kayne or Kenzy. This shit is real. We can't go to war unprepared." Zha was trying to help Keeky calm Dymond down.

"Y'all right. I just want my baby back. What am I going to do?"

"Start off by getting on your shit for now, man. Don't do anything that's going to make them want to kill Bliss," Keeky said.

They saw a car coming around the corner so they hid on the side of the building. As the car went to park around the back of the building, they crept around.

It was a small red car with tinted windows. The car reminded them of the one that pulled up to kill Ricky on *Boyz in the Hood*. Things were about to either get really messy, or go in their favor. They crossed their fingers. Zha and Keeky walked up to the car, and got the Jamaicans who were in it to try and holla at them. The driver put the window down.

"Yah lost, pretty guhl?"

"Yeah, I think so. My car broke down. We need a ride to the nearest gas station," said Keeky.

"Awwww shit," Zha said, "I dropped everything out of my damn purse."

"We gon' help yah get it."

The three Jamaicans occupying the car got out to help Zha pick up her things. Keeky walked over and said, "Game over, bitch."

She shot each of them execution style in the back of the head. They needed to draw the others out of the building, and they knew that the sounds of a firearm going off would do so. They needed someone from the inside to see the bodies so that they could also put some fear in Judas.

"Yah hear dat?" Judas asked.

"Mi heard it."

"Go see who dem dea." Judas and the others ran to the back door, but all they saw was the car out there.

They walked out a little further, and there they saw the bodies. They were scrambling, and nervous. Dymond, Zay, Keeky, and Zah were peeping from the bushes near the building.

"Yo, that's the nigga Judas that I was locked up with," Zay whispered.

"If this nigga had a meeting with Kayne, then where the fuck is this nigga Kayne at?" Zha asked.

"Dymond, call Blayden and see if he's still coming to your spot? Make sure that nigga brings Kenzy. While she's paying you a visit, Zay you'll go meet with Kayne."

"And what the fuck will I tell him, Keeky? Tell me please."

"Nigga, are you scared?"

"Fuck no, I ain't scared. I just want you to tell me exactly what I'm supposed to say to this nigga."

"Man, y'all be quiet before them niggas see us," Dymond said.

When they were able to leave out of the bushes, Keeky told Zay that she wanted him to go to Kayne's office to act like he was looking for Bliss.

"Tell him that you just got home, and you're looking for him. Be sure that you let the nigga know Bliss' ol' lady told you that he was supposed to be going to his office."

"A'ight," Zay agreed. "This shit better work, Keeky. And tell me exactly why am I going over there if we know where Bliss is?"

"Because I need for this nigga Kayne to be distracted enough not to call Kenzy, and to be nervous enough that when you show up looking for Bliss, he'll call the Jamaican nigga when you leave. He'll be nervous that you showed up there, so he will call, trust me. Judas is the one holding shit together at his camp, once he leaves to go over to Kayne's, we'll go in his shit for Bliss."

"Let me call Blayden to bring Kenzy over," Dymond said.

"Wassup, sis?" Blayden said when he answered the phone.

"Wassup? Y'all still coming fuck with me?"

"Yeah, we'll be there in a few hours."

"A'ight, well hit me up." Blayden hung up the phone.

"He's still coming y'all," she hung up and told the others.

"Well, do your thing."

Dymond was going to prepare for her meeting with Blayden and Kenzy. Kenzy always let her dad know what she was doing, and where she was going. She had to call Kayne to tell him about her meeting at Dymond's place.

"Hey, baby girl," Kayne answered the phone.

"Hey, daddy. I just wanted to let you know that I'll be going over to Dymond's house with Blayden today."

"Okay. Well, you be careful and keep in touch."

"I will."

"I'm working on getting that click of theirs separated right now."

"How?"

"Well, Dymond is distracted with Bliss. I believe Judas has him. I'm still trying to get to the bottom of it, but he was supposed to have Bliss distracted with promotion only so that Dymond could be caught one on one at some point."

"Well, you have to get your Jamaican investment under control. Sounds like he's doing shit his way."

"You're right, but Keeky will be distracted, too. I did a little investigating of my own, and I found out that she had been visiting a guy in a jail. It seems as if she had an intimate relationship with him based on what the officer on my payroll explained to me, so I paid the judge to let her little boyfriend come home. I can't explain all of the steps that I had to take, but I made sure that I could have this bitch distracted for a while. Hopefully, this nigga will take her off of her game."

Chapter 21

Dymond went home and slowly prepared for Blayden and Kenzy. She wasn't fully recovered yet, but she was trying to move around a little in an effort to help her full recovery time. She took a shower, changed the bandages on her wound, and put on some clothes. While changing her bandages, she looked at the hole in her chest and thought about how she almost lost her life. The game changed when she was the one on the other side of the bullet. It felt as if her life was flashing before her eyes.

She sat down on the bed for a second and began to cry.

"Lord, I know that I may not be living exactly as you please, but the one thing that I've done right in my life is choose to marry Bliss. Bliss is the best thing that has ever happened to me, and Lord you know that I will do anything that I have to do in order to get him home to me. Every minute without him feels like I'm dying. I guess what I'm doing, God, is asking you to give me a little help on this one. You know my heart, Lord. Order my steps and guide my feet. Please allow my Bliss to remain safe. Even if it means taking me, Lord, I just want him to be safe. I will fight for, and with him until six people are carrying me, and my casket drops. God, be with us all. In Jesus' name I pray. Amen."

The doorbell rang and Dymond got up to answer it. She wiped her eyes, composed herself, and answered the door.

"Hey, bro," she said as she hugged Blayden.

"Wassup, sis?"

"Hey, Kenzy," Dymond said looking in her eyes.

"Wassup with you?" Kenzy answered.

"Chillin' chillin'. Y'all come in."

"You clutching, huh?" Dymond asked Kenzy.

"Yeah, I have to. When it's beef, it's beef. No matter which way it's coming from."

"That's wassup. I feel you on that. That's why I wanted y'all to come over here."

"Yo, Blayden, let's sit down." They went to the living room, and took a seat. "Kenzy, I know my brother loves you, and I know my brother loves me. I would apologize for Keeky's actions towards you, but I know that it was you who tried to pull the plug on me. Funny thing is, I didn't say anything, and I chose to let you live this lil while because of Blayden. Bitch, I have it on my mind to kill you, especially because of that lil hit you sent on Keeky and Zha, but you're going to help me get Bliss back. You'll walk out of here alive for now, but you better have your mind right."

Keeky and Zha walked up from behind, and put their pistols to her head. "Because, bitch, if you don't, then you die."

Blayden sat there in disbelief.

"Y'all, please don't do this," he pleaded.

Dymond pulled her pistol on Blayden and took Kenzy's pistol off of her side. "Nigga, don't make me choose," she said while staring in her brother's eyes. Blayden could not believe what he was hearing. He was stuck, and lost for words.

"So y'all really want me to turn on my family?" Kenzy asked.

"Bitch, fuck your family. You live by it, you die by it."

"Exactly, so why do you think that I'll choose y'all over my dad? Never."

"We'll see. Bitch, just like you're gonna ride for yours, I'll ride for mine," Dymond explained.

"Kenzy, bruh, chill out," Blayden said. "Dymond you're really going to pull your strap on me? Your brother? Fuck everything that's going on, Dymond, we're blood."

"Nigga, blood only makes us related. Where does your loyalty lie? You're loyal to a bitch who ain't loyal to you. If she was, she wouldn't be hiding so much shit from you. Period. Even snakes can fit into tight circles. Brother or not, nigga, I feel like if you flake me, you'll snake me."

Dymond made Blayden and Kenzy get up. They walked outside to Zha's car with guns still pointing at them.

Dymond and Keeky had their own definitions of what snakes would do to you if you'd let them. After the first time a motherfucker crosses you, you don't give them a second to do it. If you don't make an example out of a snake the first time, you'll be dealing with the same shit out of them forever. Shut it down, and let them know that you're not playing. Once a snake gets comfortable, they'll eventually slip up, but you only allow them to slip up once, no second chances.

They headed over to the building where the Jamaicans were. Dymond made Kenzy call her dad while they were on their way. "Call your motherfuckin' daddy, and if you give the slightest hint that you're with us, Zay goes in and sleeps that nigga on the spot. You 'bout that life, Zay?"

"I gotchu. Whatever y'all need me to do," he answered.

"Hey, daddy," Kenzy said as she made the call. Her skin had formed goosebumps at the thought of betraying her dad. She had never been put in a position like this before. She had hoped that her dad would sense that something was wrong, but she knew that she could not give him any hints about the situation that she was in because she wanted them all to stay safe.

"Hey, baby girl, wassup? How did your visit at Dymond's place go?" Kayne immediately wanted to know.

"It was straight. Are you at the office?"

"Yeah."

"Okay, I may come to visit. I'll talk to you later, I'm with Blayden."

After Kenzy hung up the phone, Keeky called and told Zay to go inside of Kayne's office. He was already outside waiting on her call. He walked up to the secretary and asked for Bliss.

"I'm here for Bliss Heins," Zay told the secretary.

"A Bliss Heins doesn't work in this office, sir."

"I was told by his sister that he would be at this office for a meeting."

"I'll check with Mr. Thompson."

"Okay. Do that, I'll wait."

The secretary walked out and went to Kayne's office.

When she returned she told Zay that Mr. Thompson wanted to see him in his office.

"Hello, Zayvier."

"Wassup, how did you know my name?" Zay asked Kayne.

"I know everything that I need to know about you. I also know that you were trying to get out of jail, and I made that happen for you."

"You made that happen for me?"

"Yes, sir. I have a very large payroll. Your judge is one of the people on it."

"So, you paid the judge for me to come home? Why?"

"Because I need a favor from you. I know that you're a business man, and I know that you're crazy about Ms. Keeky. What would it take for you to deliver her to a partner of mine?"

"It would take nothing. Nigga, I don't rock like that. What the fuck is wrong with you?"

"Well, get the fuck out of my office, and call me when you change your mind. I'm sure a reverse decision by the judge will help you to do so."

"Nigga, whatever," Zay said as he walked towards the door.

"Yeah, whatever. I'll see if you'll be singing the same tune when I'm done with your ass."

"And I'll see if you'll be singing the same tune when I put an end to your ass if you play with my freedom, motherfucker," Zay swung open the door, and he walked out of the office.

Kayne called Judas as soon as he was sure that Zay was gone. “Get to my office now. Do not waste any more of my time. Be here in twenty minutes.” Kayne hung up, and Judas told his crew that he had to leave for an important meeting.

Keeky, Dymond, Blayden, Zha, and Kenzy sat in a parking lot across the street waiting until they saw Judas walk out of the building to leave. When everything was clear, Keeky tied Blayden and Kenzy to the steering wheel. They got out, and eased their way toward the building. Dymond knocked and hid on the side.

“Who dere?” one of the Jamaicans said from the other side of the door.

None of them answered.

“Who dere?” he asked again.

No one answered, so he walked to the door and opened it.

“Who dere?”

Dymond came from the side of the building with a G18. “Bitch, it’s the reaper.” She shot him in the face, and in the neck. He dropped on the spot.

Dymond moved back to the side of the building. The other Jamaicans that were inside started running towards the door after they heard the gunshots. “Keeky, go around the back, and Zha, you come through the front with me.”

There were only four Jamaicans left inside.

“Nigga, drop it,” Dymond said as she walked through the door, and straight into one of them. The one that she was holding her gun on, he seemed more nervous than the others, so she had actually picked the weakest link. He dropped the gun, and didn’t try to shoot her, or move. Bliss was tied up in a corner in the back with his face beat up.

She lifted up the G18 and pointed it at the one in front of her. He tried to run when he saw her attention go on Bliss.

"Bitch, didn't I say don't move." The other two came out from the sides, but Zha was already on them. She hit both of them in the chest. The fourth one had his gun to Bliss' head, and he started yelling at Dymond.

"Yah want him dead?"

"No, no, no. Don't shoot," Dymond said.

Bliss sat there with the gun to his head, and Dymond still had the gun to the other one.

Boom.

The Jamaican holding the gun to Bliss' head was slumped over. Keeky had walked up behind him, and blew his brains all over Bliss.

"It's over for you, nigga," Dymond shot the other one in the face.

"Untie Bliss so we can get out of here," Dymond told Keeky. "We don't know when Judas is coming back."

Keeky untied Bliss, and Dymond ran over to help her. When his hands were loose, he grabbed Dymond. He hugged, and kissed her tightly.

"That's why I love the fuck out of you, girl."

"I love you, too, daddy."

"I love y'all, too, Keeky and Zha."

"We love you, too, nigga, but fuck all this mushy shit, we gotta go."

They ran back to the car. Kenzy and Blayden were gone. Dymond's phone was lighting up. It was a message from Blayden.

"Big sis, you decided to pull a gun on me because you wanted to ride for yours. Forgive me, but I'm riding for mine. Don't forget that I know everything about you. All is fair in love and war."

"Oh my God," Dymond yelled out.

"What's wrong? And where the fuck could these two be?" Keeky asked.

"Bitch, Blayden says he's riding with Kenzy on this one."
"You can't be serious."
"I should have killed that bitch when I had the chance."
"Fuck it, we'll meet again."
"Yeah, like right now. Bitch bring me to Kayne's office building. I'm sick of these motherfuckers."

Chapter 22

"Daddy, where are you?" Kenzy asked Kayne when he answered the phone.

"At the office, baby girl, why do you sound like you're out of breath?"

"Blayden and I are running now. His sister just took us, and went over to where Judas had her ol' man."

"Find safety, and call me when you can to give me an address. I'll be there to get you."

"Okay."

They hung up the phone, and she stopped behind the first building that they could find.

Kayne was nervous for Kenzy because he knew what Dymond, Keeky, and Zha were capable of. Kenzy was taught well, but she had never been put in a position similar to what she was in now. She was thankful at this point for every decision that Blayden had made.

"I can't believe you chose me and not your sister," Kenzy said to Blayden.

"I can't believe it, either. I guess that's love."

"I really didn't think of it that way at first. All I knew is that I was working for, and helping, my daddy. With my dad is where my loyalty was supposed to be. I've never felt like anyone really loved me, and now I see that you do."

"Yes, I really do. I know that you've been taught by your dad not to trust anybody, but let me be the one to show you that I can actually love you."

"We're all that we have right now, babe."

"Well, let's come up with something, and we're just going to leave. No turning back. No talkin' to your dad, my sister, nobody."

"Let's do it."

Blayden and Kenzy called Yellow Cab of Houston Taxi Service, and headed toward the airport.

"My dad is calling."

"Don't answer."

"I won't. I'm pressing ignore. We're going to be alright."

Kenzy was nervous. She never went against her dad for any person, or any circumstance, but if Blayden was willing to stick it out and go against his sister for her, then she may as well try to do the same for him.

"Damn, now my sister's calling. I won't answer."

"Don't, she's probably close around here somewhere." His phone vibrated about a minute after Dymond hung up.

"Oh, wait, she left a voicemail." Blayden pressed one.

"Blayden, you pussy whipped motherfucker. After everything that I told you about this bitch, you still rolled out with the enemy. Nigga, I got you when I catch you. Oh, and tell your fuckin' girlfriend that her dad's a dead man. I'm on my way to his office now. Tell her that I said to choose, it's her, or it's him. She has five minutes." He nervously hung up the phone because he knew that Dymond wasn't playing at all.

***

Kayne was at his office waiting on Judas. He did not like it when he didn't seem to have things under control.

Judas made it to Kayne's office. Kayne was pacing back and forth. He seemed nervous. "Judas, why didn't you show up to the meeting that we were supposed to have with Bliss?"

"Mi had odda bidness tah do," Judas answered sarcastically.

"You're a fucking lie. You took Bliss to get close to Dymond, and I told you that I had a plan already. You did not do what you were supposed to do, and now this bitch has taken my daughter. If I don't get my daughter back in twenty-four hours, and if you don't body bag these bitches, you die."

"Hush yuh mouth. See hea, small up yuhself. Wi hab di ting unda control. Mi lick shot dem all. Booyaka. Booyaka. Dem dead wun by wun. So, hol' yuh cahna or mi kill yah dead, too. U zeemi?"

"Yeah, I hear you, and do not threaten me. Remember, I'm the reason that you're home. I'll never have to touch you myself, but I will make sure that I end you."

Kayne walked over to his door to escort Judas out. Judas looked at his phone while they were walking. He had a picture mail from one of the guys who were killed at his building. The picture was of everyone in the building who was killed, and of the empty chair that Bliss had previously occupied. Dymond was the one who sent it.

It read at the bottom: "Don't you ever touch what's mine. Nigga, it's game time. Bomboclot yah bitch you."

Judas started to panic, so he gave the phone to Kayne. When Kayne saw the picture, he knew that it was about to be a war that wasn't going to end until one, or both sides, ended up dead. Kayne received a text message a little after Judas. It came from Bliss' phone, but it too, was Dymond.

It read: "It's up there. I'm on my way, bitch. I'm tired of playing with you and your motherfucking daughter."

He put the phone down, and began breathing hard. He was having a panic attack. His phone rang again. It was Kenzy.

"Kenzy, baby where are you?"

"Daddy, Blayden and I are on our way."

Kayne and Kenzy hung up the phone. He did not know what to do now that Judas would have to work alone, and Kenzy had not made it back yet.

While Judas was in the lobby of his building flipping out, he slipped out of a back door, and into his 2015 Porsche 911 T. That was the only car that he felt like Dymond would not know. It was yellow, without any tint. If he didn't hurry, he would be seen. His phone was continuously ringing. He finally decided to look at the caller I.D. and it was Kenzy again.

"Kenzy," he said as she answered the phone. "Do not go to my office. Dymond is on her way there, and I've left. Judas is still there, and I do not know if he has realized yet that I am gone. Now is not the time to be a hero. We have to be smart."

"Okay, daddy. Get somewhere safe, and call me when you make it." They hung up.

"Your sister was seriously on her way to my dad's office," Kenzy told Blayden, "but he is gone, and only Judas is there. He told me not to go."

"So my sister is on her way to where Judas is? Is she alone?" Blayden asked.

"I'm not sure. I don't think so. When we left her she was with the others, remember?"

"Maybe we should go check it out."

"Maybe not. Don't you remember that she wants us dead?"

"Yeah, well I guess it is a bad idea. Fuck it. We don't have to go then."

Judas was still at Kayne's office, and had just realized that he was there alone.

"Kaaayynnneee. Mista Kayne," Judas yelled out. He did not get an answer. He searched every office, and Kayne was nowhere to be found. Judas could not believe what was going on. "Wah di rass? Ah suh it set. Me nah sell out, but dat bwoy is. Me needs tah link up or flex." Judas decided that he would flex. He walked out of the back door, and ran to his car. He started up the car to leave, and looked in his rearview.

"Where did you think you were going?" Keeky asked him from the back seat of his car while looking him in his eyes in the rearview. "I finally got you," she said.

Then, Dymond tapped on his window with the pistol, "Get the fuck out."

Chapter 23

Judas opened the door, and got out of the car. Bliss was still inside of Zha's car, too hurt to move. Zha was tending to Bliss. Zay had left the building earlier after his job was done. Dymond was standing outside of the car with her gun pointed at Judas, and Keeky was stepping out of the back of the car that Judas was in.

"Yah want me dead?" Judas asked Dymond.

"No, bitch, I want you," Keeky answered him.

"Naaawwww, chill, Keeky," Dymond said, "I got some shit that I wanna know first." Dymond pointed her pistol to Judas' face. "Where's Kayne?" she asked.

"Mi have no idea. Dat bwoy left wit out me knowin'."

"Where's Kenzy?"

"Mi have no idea. Let me ask yuh sumtin'? Why yah kill mi daughter?"

Dymond lowered her pistol, opened her mouth to answer, and Judas took off. Keeky wasn't listening to all of the small talk, but when she realized that Judas had taken off, she started busting at him while he was running. Judas was dodging bullets, but he was getting tired. He was a little older than the rest of them, so running was not going to work out for him. He was beginning to slow down because he needed to catch his breath. He ran into a field to duck off behind the first set of trees that he could find. He leaned over, and put his hands on his knees as his chest was going in and out at a fast pace because of all the running that he had done. He remembered that he should lift up in an effort to slow down the breaths that he was taking.

"Dead game," Keeky said from behind him. He turned around to look, and she shot him in the face.

"It's over for you boy," said Dymond, and they turned around, and walked away. It didn't take them long to get back to the car because Judas hadn't gotten too far on feet.

"What's good? Y'all rocked that nigga?" Zha asked Keeky and Dymond as they got back in the car.

"Yeah, that shits over with," Keeky answered.

They rode back in silence for a while. Dymond and Bliss held each other in the back seat, and Zha drove while Keeky seemed to be in deep thought, and then it dawned on her.

When they were at the building taking care of the Jamaicans who jacked Khalil and shot Dymond, Zha had killed Jade with no hesitation. Then, when they went to kill Judas, Zha stayed with Bliss, and she usually was one of the first ones to buck when she knew something was about to go down.

"Zha, what really happened to you?" Keeky asked out of the blue.

"What do you mean?" Zha answered. Dymond and Bliss were now sitting up straight staring at the two of them. Keeky pulled her pistol on Zha, and put it to her head.

"Bitch, I fucks with you, but I will fuck clean over you." Keeky was suspicious. Things weren't seeming to add up anymore. "You did more, and you know more than what the fuck you told us. Bitch, talk, or I will blow your whole face out of this car."

"Keeky, so you're really going to pull your strap on me?" Zha asked.

"Motherfuckin' right. Don't make me use this bitch, Zha. I'm tellin' you. I love you, but I'll watch you go. Now talk."

Zha started crying.

"We're waiting," Dymond said.

"Okay, everything about Khalil was true. When I woke up in that hospital with no memory, and Jade told me that I would never be able to have children, she also told me that the baby I was pregnant with died when Khalil shot me in the stomach. Yes, I was pregnant, but not very far. Khalil had found out the same day that he shot me. I did not remember anything about myself, or my life until about two months after I had been in the hospital. When I started to remember everything, I remembered Jade helping me to get to the hospital, but I also remembered her talking on the phone before the ambulance got there."

Zha got really quiet because she didn't know how to explain the rest. She was eventually going to have to tell them anyway, but now was not the time that she had chosen. She needed to make sure that she had all of her evidence straight first before she could just tell them something like this. This was going to have to be a good time since Keeky had a gun held to her head.

She took a deep breath and continued, "It was true that Khalil had helped to rape and kill her mom, but she wasn't just trained to look out for women. Her dad did teach her to hustle ganja, but he was dirty. I remembered her saying to someone that she was helping one of us to the hospital, and that she would get a job at the hospital to watch me closely in case anyone came to visit. They released me, and I really thought that it would be over with her until I ran into her again with y'all. Also, when I recognized Dymond's face, and I killed the chick who sent me to do the hit, I started to kill Dymond, but I wanted to know y'all side. I really thought that y'all never tried to find out what happened to me. I didn't know that y'all were under the impression that I was dead, or had disappeared. I really didn't know where y'all were because y'all had moved to another side of Houston, and I never bothered to look for Khalil because I needed to try and get my money right. I knew that I would run into him again when the opportunity arose. Anyways, not only was the nigga Judas dirty, he was a dirty cop who taught his daughter everything that he knew. The only problem was that she used hers for the better. Jade, was an undercover fed officer. When it dawned on me in the hospital, I never said anything, I just let it blow over because we were separating, I was going my way, and she was going hers. Seeing her in the back of the car when Dymond got shot let me know that after all of these years, she was still watching y'all. That is why her dad sent her to stay with Khalil. So, I killed her as soon as the opportunity presented itself. What better way to do it, than when we killed the other Jamaicans? I decided to end her with her fellow kind. Keeky, my girl, she wasn't working alone. I don't know what you're going to do exactly, but the guy she was running it with on the phone while waiting for the ambulance to arrive for me, was Zay. He found you on purpose. Your man is the feds."

"The feds," Keeky yelled. "Bitch, why did you wait this long to say something? That's fucked up, Zha."

"I was going to tell you when I could kill the bitch like I did Jade, but I hadn't seen him until I picked him up from jail for you. Plus, I didn't know exactly how you felt about the nigga because you never expressed it," Zha answered. "I just wanted to wait until the time was right, and give you the option of letting me know how we should handle the nigga."

Keeky couldn't believe what she was hearing. The first nigga that she decided to trust was the feds. Thinking about all of the shit that he had told her brought tears to her eyes.

"So, this nigga had to go to jail to be next to Judas because all of these motherfuckers are cops. I wonder what the fuck Judas actually went to jail for? That nigga really wanted our heads because he knew his daughter was actually doing her job. I swear on God that as soon as I get everything in perspective, I will murder that snake ass bitch."

"Yo, Keeky, baby, I know you're mad, but listen to me. If he's a fed, that means the feds are watching, and he's not the only one. Jade is dead, and he's the only one that they have close to us right now. Do you know how much time a nigga can get for killing a federal officer? Zha, if you knew that Jade was the feds, you should have considered keeping her alive, baby girl. Killing Zay will only make this shit worse before it gets better. Look, just keep that nigga close for a while, and we'll find out everything that we need to know. We have to play this one smart. Make that nigga fall in love. Keep doing what you're doing. You might not want to do it, but you have to start thinking like a fed, straight up. That's the only way that we can stay one step ahead," Bliss explained.

This time Keeky was going to have to remain level headed. Although, it would be a hard task, she had to remember that putting her freedom in jeopardy for killing a federal officer was one thing, but there was no way that she could do that to everybody else. As of now, they all just needed to focus on staying alive, and staying out of jail.

Chapter 24

Kenzy and Blayden were on their way to California. They didn't have time to pack all of their things, so they left with what they could grab in the little time that they did have. Kenzy had family all over the place, so she made it a priority to get in touch with her first cousins Teena and Teeana. They were twins, and related to her on her mom's side. Kenzy knew of her family on that side, but her dad never let her keep in touch with them. When she was about ten years old, her dad took her away. She still didn't know why, but she'd missed her mom ever since. He cut off all contact, but she was able to find a few cousins via the web about two years ago. She was still very young, and this would be her first time away from her dad.

"Blayden, baby, this is tough," Kenzy said.

"Why? As long as we're together, we should be fine."

"I know, but I miss my daddy already, and I don't like being on the run."

"Well, how do you think I feel about my sister? We are all we've had all of our lives. You think that I like my sister feeling like I betrayed her? I would never betray my sister, but I learned from her to stick by the side of the person that you love. It's kind of fucked up that the person I'm in love with tried to kill my sister, but I do understand that your loyalty was to your blood. I just want you to remember that sometimes your blood doesn't mind seeing you bleed. They would be the ones to do it to you. The streets don't love nobody."

"It took me awhile to realize that, but I'm ready to give us a try now. For real."

She leaned over to kiss Blayden. He gently rubbed the side of her face, and looked into her eyes. "Baby, I love you."

The pilot interrupted over the intercom, "Please buckle up and turn off all electronic devices. Fasten your seatbelts and raise your seats to an upright position. We will be landing shortly."

Kenzy took Blayden's hand, and she began to say a prayer as they prepared to land. The plane hit a few air pockets, and the lights flickered.

"There is a little turbulence ladies and gentlemen," the pilot said. The lights continued to flicker, and the plane ride had begun to be a little rocky. The passengers bobbed back and forth as the turbulence seemed to worsen. The plane began to make a squeaky noise as if something was coming apart, but everything seemed to be under control.

"Ladies and gentlemen, please make sure that you read the emergency instructions in front of you," the pilot seemed to be calm. "Do not panic. *We are going down.*"

Everyone looked to the back of the seat in front of them and prepared for the plane to crash.

"We are close to the airport because he just announced it, so we can't be going down too far from there," Kenzy told Blayden.

"Lord, please be with us," an elderly lady yelled from her seat.

The ride was getting rockier, the lights continued to flicker, the flight attendants prepared to buckle up, and children were crying while the adults were trying to console them. The plane was approaching its designated landing spot. The passengers of the flight were all in tears.

Kenzy looked out of her window, and saw a wing on fire. She started screaming, "Lord, send your angels to keep charge over me. You are greater than anything we are facing. I know that when we pass through the waters, You will be with us, and the river will not overflow us. When we walk through the fire, we will not be burned, nor will the flame touch us. You are our comforter, Lord."

She froze up when the pilot said that everyone should brace themselves. As soon as he was quiet, she began again. "Hear me when I call, God. No matter what happens, lift us above this, and into your presence." All of the other passengers were trying to stay quiet while Kenzy was praying.

"Oh my God, we're about to hit," someone screamed.

The pilot tried his best to keep the plane from crashing onto the runway.

Bbbooooommmm.

The plane went down, cockpit first. All of the airport was watching. Emergency crews took off towards the plane.

Teena and Teeana were being held back as they watched the emergency crews bring body after body from the wreckage.

"We are asking that everyone please back up. There's no possible way that we can detain this situation, if we also have to detain all of you. Please step back as we don't want to have to begin making arrests. As of now, ladies and gentleman, we are assuming that there were no survivors."

***

Dymond, Zha, Keeky, and Bliss had arrived home, and were ready to get comfortable after all of the chaos that they had been through. It was still hot, and it felt as if the heat index would not change no matter what time of day it was. It was hard to get comfortable in that type of weather.

"Let me make y'all something to eat," Bliss said.

"No, baby, you should rest up," said Dymond.

"I got it. I've been sitting still since the day those bitch ass Jamaican niggas took me."

"Okay, well do your thing then, baby."

Keeky, Dymond, and Zha went to sit in the living room. Everybody was quiet. Dymond decided to roll up a blunt.

"What is that? Reggie?" Zha asked Dymond.

"Reggie? If a nigga gives me reggie, I'll shoot that bitch in the head," Dymond said as they laughed. Keeky sat quietly, and in a daze. She was still trying to register the fact that Zay was working with the feds.

"Hold up, y'all, I don't know this number?" Dymond said. "Hello."

"Hello. I am trying to reach a Ms. Dymond Spencer."

"This is she. Who's this?"

"This is the California State Police. We are calling the loved ones of the passengers of Flight 225. We need you to come down to identify a body."

"Identify a body? Ma'am, why would I come to California to identify a body?"

"There's a young man involved who was a passenger on the flight. His identification says Blayden Spencer. His emergency contacts in his cell phone has your name listed first."

"Blayden. Oh my God. I'm on the next flight out."

"Okay, ma'am. Please do not leave the airport once you arrive. Check in with gate number two. That is where you will be able to get all of the information that you will need, and where you will be able to give us all of the information that we need."

"Yes, ma'am. I'm on my way."

"Yo, who was that?" Keeky asked.

"That was the California State Police Department. Blayden was involved in a plane crash," Dymond answered.

"You alright, cuz?" asked Zha. Dymond sat there with tears in her eyes. She didn't answer Zha. All that ran through her head was how shit had taken a turn for the worst all of a sudden.

"Nnnoooooooo, I can't believe this shit," Dymond screamed out. She was shaking uncontrollably. Bliss, Keeky, and Zha were all holding her at the same time.

"Go book us a flight," Bliss whispered to Keeky.

She left out of the room to go book the flight as Bliss stated. Zay was blowing up her phone.

Now was not the time to entertain him, but she decided to stay in town so that she could keep a close eye on him and what he was up to. She found a flight for Dymond and Bliss that would leave in two hours. Zha decided to stay with her.

"I found y'all a flight. It's paid for and everything. It leaves in two hours. Get packed, and we'll drop y'all off," Keeky said.

"Chill, bae. I'll pack everything," Bliss said. "Just try to relax."

Dymond sat down to relax. Her mind was all over the place.

The same officer that called Dymond had to turn around and call Kayne, also.

"Hello," Kayne answered the phone.

"Hello. I am calling from the California State Police Department. Is this the father of Kenzy Thompson?"

"Yes, ma'am, it is. What's going on?"

"There was a crash involving Flight 225. We were able to find a pulse, but your daughter is in critical condition."

Chapter 25

"I wonder why she's not answering the phone," Zay said to himself. He did not expect her to save his life when he met her, and he did not expect the pussy to be that good, either. This shit wasn't supposed to happen.

"Wassup?" Zay asked as he answered the phone.

"Wassup, boo?" Keeky answered.

"I've been trying to reach you for the longest. Where have you been? I've been worried about y'all since I left Kayne's office."

"I've been with Dymond. Her brother just died in a plane crash. Still can't believe this shit. My girl is going through the most."

"Damn, baby girl. I'm sorry to hear that. Do you want to come over? I can make you feel better."

"That's wassup, I'm on my way."

They hung up the phone, and Keeky told Zha that she needed her to stay available in case of an emergency. Zha agreed to stay back because she had a hit to do, also. It was time to get back to business, and to grind as much as they could because money was a major factor right now. It was needed just in case any of them ended up in jail, or in case they needed to get someone touched that they couldn't touch themselves. Why hustle if you can't make enough money to be prepared for the shit that might go down in the future?

It took her about an hour before she pulled up to Zay's place. "Open the door," Keeky told Zay.

"It's open, baby girl. Come in," Zay answered.

Keeky walked up and opened Zay's door. The lights were out, and he had soft music playing.

"Come to the bathroom," Zay yelled out. Keeky walked to the bathroom, and when she opened the door, Zay was sitting in the tub with the water steaming, rose petals all over the floor and in the water, candles surrounding them, and a fruit tray going across the foot of the tub. "Climb in," he said softly to Keeky. His body was glistening with suds and rose petals sticking to him in all of the right places.

"Naaawwww, let me take a seat for a minute. Shit has just been happening so fast. It feels like everything is starting to pop off all at once. I know what it felt like to lose my brother so this shit feels like deja vu. I can definitely feel my girl pain with this one," she said as she held her head down.

"Come on, baby, just climb in. I'll help to ease your mind, even if you only sit here and let me hold you in my arms."

She stood up, and undressed. She climbed in front of Zay, and she still was holding her head down.

"Let me taste that pussy before you sit down." He slid up, and put his head between her legs. He used his forefingers to spread her lips, he licked her clit, and then he put one of her legs up on the side of the tub so that he could suck on it until it swelled. Now, he was grabbing her hands to guide her to sit down in front of him. He took some water in his hands and dripped it down her spine. She grabbed a few grapes to eat, and she leaned back. He kissed her shoulders, and rubbed his hands from her forehead through her hair. He was falling for the poison that could cause him to lose everything. She was supposed to be forbidden. "I think that I'm falling in love with you," Zay told Keeky.

"Really?" Keeky asked.

"Yeah, really."

"I never knew that a fed could fall for the bitch that he's supposed to be watching." She grabbed her nine off of the floor. "Nigga, you really got me fucked up."

"Hold up, baby girl. Put the gun down. Let me explain," Zay said.

"Start talking, bitch," Keeky said with her nine pointed at his face. "I've been keeping it a hundred with you since I met you. I don't do snaky shit, and I told you since day one that my trust is fucked up." Zay started to move so that he could explain. "Move again, motherfucker, and you're done. You started earning my respect, now you've lost it. Your honesty was appreciated, but now I consider you a liar. You started gaining my trust, and now that's gone. I was going to return your loyalty, but now your chances of that are done. Fuck your love, I don't want it," Keeky was yelling, and she was turning fire red.

"Keemari, baby, listen. As bad as you would like to kill me, you can't. Right now you need me. Kill me, and they come looking for you. The day that I came to you, and dude tried to rob me, I didn't expect for you to be everything that I had dreamed of. Don't get me wrong, I am a cop, this is my job, I did lie, and I did not have intentions of being with you, or of falling in love with you. Baby, I apologize for everything. Give me a chance to make it up to you. Allow me to save your life, and everybody who runs with you. Kayne wants to meet up with me, and I'm sure that he'll need me to handle something concerning you. Let me deliver the nigga to you, or I can take the heat off of you, and deliver him to the feds. Either way, you win, and I'm going to try to get them to back off."

Keeky's eyes swelled up with tears, and Zay stood up to grab her. This wasn't supposed to happen. How did she fall in love with the enemy? She had to shake back. Now was the time to get to know her enemy better. Your enemies are defeated when you make them your friends. Zay was begging at this point. Why should she interrupt her enemy when he was making a fatal mistake? From now on, she could let him do all of the talking, and kill two birds with one stone. She wanted Kayne dead just as bad as she wanted Zay dead. She could move in silence. What better way to defeat someone who expects you to go off about how you feel? So many thoughts were running through their heads.

Zay grabbed Keeky's hands, and put the gun down. Once he removed it from her grip, he wiped her eyes, and kissed her lips softly. "Baby, I'm sorry," he whispered. He cut on the shower, and pushed Keeky underneath the water. "Let me make it up to you, baby girl." He lifted her up against the wall of the shower, and eased her down onto his penis.

The water running down the front of Keeky's body made him want her even more. As it splashed on her breasts and down her back, Zay lifted her up and down slowly so that she could feel every inch of every stroke. Because of the water that was running down her face, he could not see her cry. How could a nigga that hurt her so bad, make her feel so good? She guided his hands to the bottom of her ass so that he could grip her more, and she told him not to move. She positioned herself perfectly so that she could ride him at her own pace. He started sucking her titties, and she started riding faster. Up and down with every long stroke, Zay began to shake. He let her breasts go, and she started sucking his lips wildly as she bounced faster. She stopped abruptly, and climbed off. She bent over wit one leg lifted on the side of the tub. She was still positioned where the water could run down her back. Zay put it in, and grabbed her waist line.

Keeky pushed back as he pushed forward. "Fuuuuccckkkk," Zay screamed.

"Don't you come," Keeky said.

"I'm about to," he told her.

"I'm getting me riigghhtt now," Keeky moaned. She pushed back so that it could go in deeper. After she came she looked back at him. "You ready?" she asked.

"Yeah, it's right there, baby."

She hurriedly turned around, got on her knees under the water, wrapped her lips around the head of his dick, and swallowed everything that Zay let out. He got weak as she looked into his eyes as seriously as she could. “I want everything that you promised me, or love will get you killed, and that is what I can promise to you.”

Chapter 26

"Hello," Kayne answered his phone as he was preparing to fly out to see about Kenzy.

"Long time no see," a female voice said from the other end of the phone.

"Who is this?" Kayne asked nervously. He feared the day that he would hear that voice again.

"Nigga, you know my voice. It's Nala."

"Nala?" He tried to act as if he was puzzled. Nala was Kenzy's mom.

"Don't play stupid, bitch. It's me. My nieces called and told me that she was involved in a plane crash. Glad you're coming to Cali. Bitch, if she survives, I'm telling her everything. P.S., I got you when you touch down. For the first time in a long time I'll get to see my baby, and it'll have to be while she's going through a pain such as this. Let me tell you something. I have spent years trying to figure out why you did something like that to me, and now that I have a chance to reunite with my daughter, I will do it at all costs."

Nala hung up in Kayne's face. He knew that it was about to be trouble. Kenzy had not seen her mom in years. Nala was thieteen years old when she found out that she was pregnant with Kenzy. Being that she and Kayne were so young, she could only prepare to give her daughter the little bit that she could. Kayne's family was better off than hers financially. Her family wasn't poor, but a baby simply could not fit into their budget at the time. It was only right that she let her daughter live with her dad so that she could be brought up comfortably.

Nala would go to visit Kenzy daily, and stay over at night as much as she could. As Kenzy grew older, Nala taught her how to be a little lady. She and Kayne had different ideas on how to raise Kenzy. The things that he would teach Kenzy were wrong, and being a teenage father was no excuse for that. Nala's family did not have the same morals when it came to raising kids because of their African decent, and especially because of the mental illness that ran in their family. Although Nala did not grow up in Africa, she was taught the beliefs of her parents. She still considered herself to be African, even if she did not have the accent (but she knew some of the language), or grew up a little more fortunate than other younger members of her family.

When Kenzy was about five years old, Kayne told Nala that his family was going on vacation. He called her over to see them off, and he never returned. He stopped answering phone calls, and lost all contact. The twins held onto his number just in case of an emergency on Kenzy's behalf. They had a closer relationship than other family members knew about. Kenzy trusted them as if they were sisters. The twins held things down for Kenzy on the California end of her hustle.

When Nala received the call from them about Kenzy, she didn't know how to react. For the first time in years, she would see her daughter, and possibly lose her all around the same time. She hated Kayne for taking her child away, but she hated her parents for not helping her to get her child back. For years she treated her parents horribly.

"Hello," Teeana answered her phone.

"Hey, honey. Have you heard anything else about my Kenzy?" Nala asked the twin.

"No, not yet. We can't find out any info until her father arrives."

"Well, let me know as soon as he touches down."

"That's a bet, auntie. I got you."

Nala hung up the phone, went down to her basement, and looked into her mother and father's eyes. "I finally have my daughter back. Now you two can burn in hell." They stared at her, but could not say a word. She was a 5'10" African nightmare. She was beautiful. Her skin was almost a cold black, her hair was in a short natural fro, and her legs were gorgeous. She weighed about one hundred ninety-five pounds, but she was well-toned and in shape. She poured gasoline around them, walked up the stairs, struck a match, and threw it down at her parents.

"God rus jou siel," she said in her African accent, which translates to *God rest your soul* in English.

"Nooooo," her parents yelled. "Nala, pleaaaaaaassseeee," they were screaming. Nala smirked, squinted her eyes, and left out of the basement.

She'd grown heartless since the day that Kayne stopped answering the phone. She was very ill tempered. Her parents tried to help her to understand that allowing Kenzy to leave was the best thing for them all. Nala left the house without putting the fire out on her parents. She walked down the street and watched the house burn from the trail of gasoline that she left behind, until the fire department showed up.

"Yeah, it's done," Nala told the voice on the other end of her phone.

"You sure it's over with? They're gone?" the voice answered back.

"Yes, I'm sure. Meet me over where they have my Kenzy."

"I'm on my way."

Nala hung up the phone and waited for her ride to come by and pick her up. Everything was starting to fall into place. Hopefully, Kenzy would pull through because nothing would go right without her. She hoped that it would not be much longer before she could go forward with her plan. Life as they all knew it was about to turn upside down. Her thoughts were interrupted by a phone call from Teena.

"Hey, auntie, wassup? Where you at?" Teena asked Nala.

"I'm not too far away from y'all, why?" Nala answered.

"Well, check it out. Kayne called and said that he's getting ready to board his flight. He should be here soon. How do you want us to do this?"

"When he arrives, I'm going to need y'all to act distraught. Talk to him until I arrive. Do not allow him to get to Kenzy without me."

"Okay, I'll try. How are we supposed to do that though?"

"I'm not too far away. Think of something."

"I guess so. See you when you get here."

The twins were identical. They were fair skinned, but not too cute. Each of them had an acne issue that it seemed as if they couldn't control. Things were not always on the up and up in their lives because of their run-ins with the law, but overall they were good girls. They did not tell everyone about the relationship that they had with Kenzy because she knew that her dad did not want her mom.

Nala waited for the line to clear and dialed her boss man.

"Are you busy, sir?"

"Yes, I'm with my girl," he hinted over the phone.

"Well, Mr. Zayvier, sir, Kayne is on his way, and I should get to Kenzy in a little while." Zay was Nala's boss.

Chapter 27

It is never easy for anybody to identify the body of a loved one. Although death is a part of life, it's never something that one could get accustomed to. As human beings, we all know that death will come, yet we still find it hard to deal with. Having to identify a close loved one all of a sudden, is detrimental for a lot of people, especially if the death may have occurred suddenly. Dealing with Blayden's death took Dymond by surprise.

"I don't know if I'm equipped to identify my brother. Even though we were not seeing eye to eye, he was still all that I had, baby. We've been all we had for a long time. I can't believe he let a bitch come between us. I never thought that he would fall for such a disloyal motherfucker. I'm hurting so bad right now. My emotions are all over the place. I'm pissed off, I'm scared, I'm losing it, I'm hurt, I'm lost, and I'm feeling like a piece of me is gone," Dymond explained to Bliss on their flight to Cali.

The flight was almost over, and Dymond was getting knots in her stomach. The thought of having to identify her brother was really messing with her.

"Baby, listen. I don't dip into your affairs too often, only if they involve you getting hurt in some way. Since this involves you hurting, let me put something out there for you to think about. The definition of loyalty is the quality of being loyal to someone or something. Your loyalty is to your circle, and Kenzy's loyalty is to hers. You see, baby, you all have to stop making things seem wrong when it doesn't fall in your favor. Kenzy is one of the most loyal people that I can think of. Now, don't get it twisted, I am not taking up for Kenzy. I'm just saying, she's riding with her daddy 51/50 just like you're going to ride with your people 51/50. Her not trusting Blayden enough to be loyal to him simply reminds me of how you and Keeky are. Y'all two most definitely have trust issues. Kenzy was never supposed to be loyal to any of you. Her loyalty is to her father. As far as your brother goes, baby girl, we are promised two things in this life. One is to live, and one is to die. No one is promised tomorrow, so that squabbling you all were doing does not seem to be worth it once a day like today is presented to us," Bliss answered her.

"We have arrived in sunny California. Please exit the plane carefully, and enjoy your trip. Your flight attendants are here to assist you if you need them," the pilot said over the intercom system.

As the passengers started unloading the plane, Dymond began to have a panic attack. She could not breathe, and she was frightened.

"It's almost over, baby. Breathe. It'll be okay. God's will shall be done," Bliss said as he was trying to console Dymond.

They helped her off of the plane. As they entered the terminal, and went toward the proper gate, Bliss pointed to a short Asian guy holding a sign that said "Families of Flight 225."

"Over there, baby. We have to go over to that young man."

"Do you have some form of identification?" the Asian guy asked as they walked up.

"Yes, we do," Dymond and Bliss answered.

They handed him their I.D.'s, and he pointed upwards to the third floor of the airport. That floor had been shut down, and taped off.

"Who are you here for?" asked a female security officer.

"I'm here to identify the body of Blayden Spencer," Dymond answered.

"Right this way, ma'am." Dymond followed the officer. Bodies were laid out as if the third floor was a morgue.

"Is this your loved one, young lady?" the security officer asked as she pointed to the body that was now right in front of them.

Dymond looked and gasped, "No, ma'am, that is not him."

"Not him?" the security officer asked confused. "This has to be a mistake. Follow me."

Dymond and Bliss followed the guard into another section. Dymond broke down crying and screaming when she saw Blayden lying there. He looked so empty and lifeless. He was swollen, and he looked as if he had suffered.

"Jeesssuuuussss," Dymond screamed out. "Jeeesssuuuusssss. Lord, why my brother, Lord? I didn't get a chance to make it right. Blayden, I love you, baby brother. Nooooo, Lord, not my brother, God. That's all I had, Lord."

Bliss had never seen Dymond break down like this. He tried calming her down, but nothing seemed to be working.

"Oh my God, baby, look," Bliss said. He was looking to his right. Dymond was still screaming uncontrollably until Bliss said, "It's Kenzy."

"Kenzie... Kenzy... Kenzy... Fuck Kenzie," she yelled. "This bitch is the reason my brother is gone." Dymond dashed towards the stretcher that was taking Kenzy onto the elevator. It had taken quite some time to get the surviving passengers to a hospital because of the traffic that was in the area due to the plane crash.

As the doors opened for them to push Kenzy in, the paramedic started to scream. She was in shock. The body of an African American male was suffering from gunshot wounds, one to the stomach, and one to the chest.

"Somebody grab another stretcher," the paramedic was yelling.

It was hard to work around the chaos that was already going on. With dead bodies in one section, and severely critical individuals in another, it was hard to find an available stretcher for someone who was found on the elevator when the door opened. The male subject looked to be in his mid-30. When Dymond got close enough to see the individual lying on the floor of the elevator, her mouth gasped open. It was Kayne. She started to back up, and ended up backing into Bliss who was right behind her.

"What is it, baby?" he asked Dymond.

She whispered in his ear, "It's Kayne. Kayne has been shot in the elevator. What the fuck is really going on? I just want to make arrangements to have my brother sent back home. I cannot take any more surprises."

"Kayne? Who the fuck would want to kill Kayne in California?" Bliss asked.

"I'm not sure, but I'm wondering the same thing."

"Miss... Miss... Miss..." the paramedic was beckoning for Dymond to look her way.

"Ma'am, do you know this guy?" the paramedic asked.

"No, I do not," Dymond answered. "I only know the victim that I was brought her to identify, and the young lady that you have on the stretcher right now. She was my brother's girlfriend."

"Okay, well, we are still waiting for her family."

"Coming through, coming through. Excuse us," another paramedic said as they were running to assist the one that was already in the elevator working to stabilize Kayne.

"Back up, baby," Bliss said to Dymond. He pulled Dymond back by her shoulders. She was so distraught that she never realized her phone was blowing up.

"Hello, Zha. Now is not the time, cuz. You wouldn't believe the shit that's going down in Cali right now."

"That's what I'm calling to tell you. I'm getting tired of all the back and forth shit with these motherfuckers. That nigga had Khalil give me one to the chest, and one to the stomach, so I gave that bitch the same fucking thing."

"I'll call you back, Zha. I'm surrounded by police officers on this floor," Dymond hung up. The medical personnel were taking Kenzy and Kayne out of the airport to the ambulance to be transported to the hospital.

***

The twins were still waiting outside.

"Why haven't you called yet? I've been waiting," Nala asked Teeana when she answered the phone.

"We haven't heard from him yet. He was supposed to call us as soon as he got to Kenzy. We've been waiting, too."

"Well, my patience is getting short, and I can't take all of this waiting."

"Hold on real quick, auntie. They're bringing more stretchers out of the building."

Teeana waited and peeped as the paramedics continued to bring more stretchers out of the airport. "Oh my Lord," Teeana said, not realizing that she had the phone to her ear.

"What's happening?" Nala asked.

"Two of the stretchers that just passed in front of me, one had Kenzy on it, and the other had Kayne. Kenzy looked stabilized but out of it. Kayne looked bad. They're running to the ambulance with him."

"I'm on my way. Do you have any idea which hospital they may be taking them too?"

"No, but we're about to follow them."

"Okay. Call me as soon as you figure out exactly where they're taking them."

"Gotcha."

"Okay. Bye."

When Nala hung up the phone, she quickly picked it up again. "Okay. Everything is falling into place, except that now Kayne has been shot."

"Shot? Your daughter's father?" Nala's sister asked in shock.

"Yes. Him. He's been shot."

"Okay. I will schedule a flight as soon as possible. I shall arrive in about two days. I have a few things to take care of here in Africa first. I received the phone call about our parents' death, and about the fire. We should be able to collect our inheritances as soon as everything is finalized. I pray that they suffered much before they passed away. May they rot in hell."

"I'm sure that they suffered just as much as we've had to. I guess we'll see them when we make it to hell. Talk to you later, sis."

"Okay. Hold it together until I get there."

"I will. I'm on my way to the hospital now as we speak. Kayne and Kenzy will both be surprised to see me. The rest will be in shock upon your arrival. Terror doesn't usually come from Africa. Everything that I've discussed with Mr. Zayvier will soon fall into place. We'll start with the one that's trying to take him away from me. She should be an easier target. She can never have my love."

"Okay. Talk to you soon."

Nala was in love with Zayvier. Sad part was, he did not know that her name was even Nala. She was schizophrenic. He knew her as Naomi. There was no one on the other end of her phone call. Nala, herself, was the sister that she was talking to. That was the reason why her parents let Kayne leave with Kenzy. Nala's other personality was from Africa. Her parents could not let her raise a baby that way.

Chapter 28

"I'm about to roll out," Keeky told Zay. "Who was that on the phone?" she asked.

"Nobody special. She works for me. All honesty from now on so here goes. After watching you all for a little while, I started digging for the best way to catch all of you in a position that would allow me to move up in my career. Getting close to you meant that it would be possible to get close to everyone affiliated with you, and that included Kayne and Kenzy as well. The best way to deal with those two was not only through you and your crew, but with the one person that could turn their world upside down, and that is the baby momma from hell. The only problem that I ran into with her was mixing up her name with her sister's name. I didn't even know that she had a sister. Blayden and Kenzy's crash ruined things as far as her coming out here, but plans will resume in California. Only thing is, I'll have her deal with Kayne, and I'll work on protecting you and yours," Zay explained.

"Well, let me break something down to you. Look into my eyes. If I feel like something is wrong from this point forward, then I'm not second guessing it. The same way you were watching me, I'll be watching you. No way in hell will anybody be able save you if you cross me."

"Is that a..." Zay started to say.

"It's a promise," Keeky interrupted.

She continued to get ready to leave. Everything from now on would be do or die for them all. False moves could end it for anybody at this point.

Keeky told Zay that she was leaving to handle some business. She wanted to show her support for Dymond, and start making some surprise arrangements for Blayden's service.

They'd seen some family and friends come and go, but Keeky knew firsthand how it felt to lose a brother. That shit was surreal, especially when a bond was shared. Being taken away by things that went on amongst them was one thing. Going somewhere with plans to kill someone else could always turn out differently than what was expected, but the way Blayden left was not expected at all.

"Before you go, I have something to ask you," Zay said as Keeky was walking towards the door.

"Wassup?" Keeky asked.

"How did you know that I was a fed?"

"Zah recognized you from being affiliated with Jade. When she picked you up for me from the jailhouse, that's when she realized who you were."

"It's funny that you mentioned her name. Don't forget that we've been watching y'all for years. What exactly did she say happened the night that she disappeared?"

"Does it matter what she said?" Keeky asked.

"I guess it doesn't," Zay answered.

"So, are you going to let me know what the deal is, or not?"

Zay had a puzzled look on his face. Things were already crazy, so telling her about Zha couldn't do any more damage than what was already done by them all anyway.

He really loved Keeky, and he needed to gain her trust back, but was snitching on Zha really the way to do it? He had to choose his words, as well as his battles wisely from now on. The games that they all were playing were very dangerous. No one wanted to end up hurt at the end of it, no one wanted to be snaked by the people they were surrounded by every day, and no one wanted to be labeled disloyal, but they all wanted to live the lifestyle.

The lifestyle was surrounded by death, dishonor, and disgrace. Zay's problem was that he started to slip up because he changed the way that he usually moved, and the way that he did his job. He was never supposed to mix business with pleasure. He came from the streets, and that was what made him an almost perfect federal agent. Who better to take a nigga off of the streets than a street nigga? Keeky's problem, as well as the rest of her girls, was that they were heartless, but still tried to have a heart when it came to these niggas.

You cannot let your emotions run your hustle. It's okay to go with your heart sometimes, but you have to take your mind along with you. They were all so busy watching the snakes around them that they never realized snakes attack what they have the time to size up best. They were keeping their enemies outside of their circle, while the people that wanted what they had were keeping their enemies close. Cops couldn't catch what they couldn't see, or touch. A woman was most likely never the intended target of a narcotics team, but when they slipped up, and made emotional moves with their hearts and not their minds, they became an easy target. Easy to turn against each other, easy to make them bicker, easy to set them off, and easy to get to, especially if you could get to their heart. They are loyal creatures, but they fall apart when they are hurt. It would have been better if they thought like men, but presented themselves as ladies, and if they stayed a step ahead of these niggas, and ready to let loose on these bitches.

Keeky stood staring at Zay so he knew that he needed to start talking. "Did she say that Khalil tried to kill her?" Zay asked Keeky.

"Yes, she did," Keeky answered.

"Did she also tell you that she had already met Jade?"

"Yes, she did."

"Well, she was sent to do a hit for Kayne. She took Khalil along with her. They were arguing over something serious about a child, or a baby, but what happened next intrigued me the most.

Khalil pulled out his strap on her, and hit her twice. He popped her with one to the chest, and one to the stomach. Then he took off."

"Yeah, yeah, she told me all of that."

"But did she tell you that Jade ran over to help her, and before she blacked out, Jade tried to get emergency information from her so that she could contact someone. You all were never contacted because she mumbled her biological father's name. Her words were mumbled as follows... *please... get... in touch... with... my... dad...*"

"And why the fuck is that important to me?"

"Because Jade found out that night that she had a sister. Her father was locked up. Zha'Reign is the daughter of Judas."

"Sisters? What the fuck do you mean they're sisters?"

"They are sisters. When Zha came to and Jade realized that she had lost her memory, she never said anything to remind her of what she told her. I'm sure Zha figured it out at some point when she realized that Judas was Jade's father."

Keeky walked away from the door and sat down. She couldn't believe what she was hearing. That's not just something that Zha would forget to tell them. After all of these years, she never said a word about who her real father was.

One can spend years around a person, and still not even know them. This proved it. The same way you could be surrounded by people daily, but still feel like you have no one. It was time to do her research on Zha'Reign once and for all. Friends turn into foes real quick, but what was Zha's motive? Why would she keep secrets? Why would she not speak up about something so valuable and important?

It was getting late and Keeky should have been left Zay's spot. She stood up, and looked out of the window. It was a little darker than usual. The clouds were rolling in front of the moon, and she could hear thunder in the distance. Zay was on the couch laid back snoring, and she couldn't get any rest because her mind was on overload. She knew that she needed to get back to her hustle, but she had too much going on around her right now to know exactly who she should trust. Knowing that Zay was a federal agent also put a damper on things. Making a couple of thousands off of her hustle was not worth spending twenty-five years of her life behind bars. The only way to safely hustle at this point, would be to talk Zay into doing it with her. Now was the perfect time because he was dying to gain her trust back.

Keeky jumped when she saw lightning strike outside of the window. Rain started to pour and the lights began to flicker. Zay turned over and opened his eyes.

"Keeky, baby, you still up? I'm surprised that you didn't leave," he said as he was still trying to wake all the way up.

"Yeah, I'm still working out some shit in my mind before I hit that road."

"Well, you know that you can stay as long as you need to."

"I know."

She continued to stare out of the window. Zay looked down at his cell to check the time. He had a missed text message from an unknown number.

He clicked on it and it read, "Zayvier, time is winding down. We should be just about ready to rap this case up. Report to the office tomorrow at 10:00 am for briefing."

Zay clicked his power button so that his screen could cut off. He had to figure out something quick because they were looking for him to be ready to bust Keeky and the others.

"Looks like you saw a ghost," Keeky told Zay. He didn't notice that she had turned around while he was reading the message.

"Nawww, it ain't that," he answered.

"Well, I've been putting some shit together over here," she said. "If you're working for the feds, why did they show up here to arrest you that day? Exactly why did you go to jail? And if Judas was Jade's dad, that meant you already knew him, very well. You see, I've been trying to register all of this new shit that you just ran down to me, but something still isn't adding up. Why did you tell me about Judas crying over Jade when you were in jail, and most importantly, why did you want him dead? You knew that telling me about him would make me want to kill him before he could kill us. You're a federal agent. You already knew that we killed Jade because you all have been watching us. Who the fuck are you really?" Keeky asked while squinting, and staring Zay directly in his eyes. "You're not just a federal agent, are you?"

"You are right," Zay answered Keeky. "I'm not just a federal agent."

He stood up and started walking over to her. The storm was getting worse. The lights were still flickering off and on from time to time.

Keeky was getting into position to grab her tool. *There's no way I'm going to let this nigga do me in*, she thought to herself.

Zay had no choice except to be straight forward. He told the truth about Zha, he may as well tell it about himself. He was more than sure that Keeky would be understanding. Things really could not possibly get any worse at this point. He never actually expected her to be everything that she had been to him thus far. He actually should have never given anyone else the chance to tell her about him.

When you realize that you are falling in love with someone, the truth should not be one of the things that you hesitate to tell them. After telling them the truth, you give them the option of staying or leaving, but at least you give them that option. Love should never be one sided. You cannot give fifty percent of you, and expect the other person in the relationship to give one hundred percent of them. You cannot have million dollar expectations of them, but settle for minimum wage expectations of yourself. You should set your goals just as high for yourself as you do for your partner. Nothing from nothing leaves nothing. If you cannot add to a person, then you should not be allowed to take away.

At this point Zay was taking away from Keeky. He came along with false intentions, but once he started falling for her, and his intentions changed, his conversations should have changed, also. He should have been capable of at least telling her the truth.

"Well, spill it, nigga. Who the fuck are you?" Keeky asked Zay as he got closer. "If you come any closer, I'll let off on you, nigga," she said as she starting clutching her gun.

"Okay, chill out. I'm about to explain," he said as he paused where he was. "I had been wondering exactly who you were for some time now. Moving the way you all moved, touching the type of work that you touched, knocking out all of your competition, that shit was admirable. Taking on your case just added fuel to the fire for me. Shit, I really thought that you were going to be a nigga when I finally tracked you down. Judas was also a fucked up cop, that's how we actually met. Me landing this job was a way to take all types of other heat off of me. I already had it in for that nigga Judas because he fucked over me at one point when we were on the streets. So, fuck that nigga, yeah I wanted him dead, and it was even sweeter that I ain't have to be the nigga to do it. I couldn't believe that y'all were women pushing the amount of work that y'all were pushing. I'd been watching since before I got your case. You spend big money whenever you re-up, and I had to see exactly who was out here pushing that much work. You came up too fast. That's what drew my attention to you from the start. I never let a nigga see my face before this, which is why you always dealt with my right hand. Baby girl, I'm your plug."

"My plug. Nigga, you've been my plug all of this time. So you knew me before you actually knew me? I was just standing over here trying to figure out how to get you to hustle with me, but all of this time you've been the reason that I've been eating."

"Yeah, my girl. The way you were moving sparked my curiosity. I was arrested because of some past bullshit, and Kayne getting me out only made my people look at him closer. So, it's highly likely that I can get that heat off of y'all, and back onto him. I have a meeting in the morning, I'll figure some shit out to present to them to buy me some more time."

"My plug," Keeky whispered to herself. "Nigga, if you don't get over here and take this pussy. You just made my shit have a heartbeat." Keeky loosened her grip off of her gun.

Zay walked up and picked her up. He carried her to the couch and laid her down. She wrapped her legs around him. He pulled his shirt over his head, and then lifted up hers. She was breathing faster and faster as he sucked her pretty red nipples, and then let them pop out of his mouth. Zay pulled off her pants, and unbuckled his. He let his dick massage her clit as he moved back and forth along her body, kissing every inch of her. "Put it in baby," Keeky moaned.

"If you want this dick, take this dick," he whispered in her ears.

"I gotchu bae," she said.

At this point, Zay had her undivided attention. Keeky stood up, pulled down his pants, and told him to lay down. He laid back, she put his penis in her mouth, but she never stopped looking him in his eyes. She made her tongue fold and roll back and forth from the top of his head to the bottom of his vein on the back side of it. She massaged that vein smoothly with her tongue. Then she squeezed her jaws, and came up off of it. When it popped out of her mouth, she let her saliva drip down the head and then slid it inside of her. She straddled him back and forth, and then turned around. Zay sat up so that Keeky could sit straight up on him as she went up and down. She stroked his sack with her hand as she leaned back on his chest. He nibbled on her ear lobe, "Damn, you riding the fuck out of that dick," he whispered.

"I'm about to turn around... grab that ass," she said back to him.

She spun around with his penis still inside of her, and kissed him slowly. She rode him in circles. He grabbed her ass as he was told, and moved it around in the rhythm that he liked. He pulled her down as he got ready to come.

"Uuuuhhhhhh," Keeky moaned while biting her lip. They came at the same time.

"I can't believe I'm fucking the plug," she smirked.

"Well, believe it, baby girl. Let's get cleaned up. We have business to handle, and moves to make."

"Before we make a move I need you to promise me something."

"What's that?"

"No matter what happens with me, even if you can't get the heat off of my whole crew, promise me that no matter what, Dymond walks free."

Chapter 29

The paramedics finally got Kenzy loaded into the back of the ambulance. Everything about her life was flashing through her head at this moment. Most of the good times that flashed were with Blayden, and most of the messed up shit that she had done in her life involved her daddy. The type of love that you get from family, and the type of love that you get from your partners are not one in the same. Family cannot make you feel the way that a lover does, they cannot give you what a lover can, they cannot fill the void of loneliness that a lover can.

"I think she's going to make it," she could hear a paramedic say.

She was praying, but she could not speak the words. She was going through excruciating pain, but somehow she still felt alright. It's just something about knowing that you know whose you are.

She still could not speak, but Psalm 23 came to mind during her times of trouble as usual: "The Lord is my shepherd. I shall not want. He maketh me to lie down in green pastures. He leadeth me beside the still waters. He restoreth my soul. He leadeth me in the paths of righteousness for His name's sake. Yea, though I walk through the valley of the shadow of death, I will fear no evil. For thou art with me. Thy rod and thy staff, they comfort me. Thou preparest a table for me in the presence of mine enemies. Thou anointed my head with oil, my cup runneth over. Surely goodness and mercy shall follow me all the days of my life. And I will dwell in the house of the Lord forever.

"Cllleeeaaarrrr," the paramedic said as she shocked Kenzy's chest.

"Lo, I am with you always," she heard another voice whisper.

"Cllleeeeaaarrrr. We are losing her," the paramedic said. "Up the voltage."

"Lo, I am with you always," the voice whispered again.

"Clllleeeaaarrrrr. We are losing her. How far away are we?" the paramedic was now yelling.

"Lo, I am with you always," the voice whispered again.

"Clllleeeaaarrrr," the paramedic tried once more. "God must be watching over this one. I have a pulse." The voice of the Holy Spirit reminded Kenzy that she was going to be okay.

They were almost to the hospital when they heard gunshots ring out in front of them. "Oh my God," the driver said.

"What is it?" the others asked. "A car just came from behind us, and shot up the ambulance carrying the guy in front of us."

"Where's the car now?" they asked from the back.

"It sped off. I'm contacting the police now. I didn't get a plate number, though."

They pulled off to the side to check on their co-workers. The right side of the ambulance had numerous bullet holes. They were all standing around on the side of the road in shock.

The driver of the ambulance that had been shot up, opened the doors, and jumped in the back. "Wow. How did this guy not get hit by any of those bullets?"

"He's still alive back there after all of that?" her partner asked.

"Yes, he is. Let's hurry and get him transfered to another ambulance so that we can get him to the hospital right away. I cannot believe that he did not get hit."

They weren't too far from the hospital so it would not take too long for a replacement emergency response vehicle to arrive. "We have to get going with this other one. She's stable for now, but we almost lost her."

"Go ahead. There they are now."

Another ambulance arrived, and they began to unload Kayne. They unhooked everything, and began to roll him out. By this time, Kayne was beginning to look pale, and he had lost a lot of blood. It was a miracle that he was still alive. They opened the doors on the emergency vehicle that had just arrived, and prepared to load Kayne in the back of it.

"Excuse me. Do y'all need any help?" a female voice rang out. They were so busy that they didn't have time to stop and answer her. "Excuse me. Is everything okay? Would you all like some help?" They continued to work because the voice did not sound close enough to even entertain at the moment. It was vital that they moved at a fast but safe pace in order to save Kayne's life. They had already phoned the hospital to have the emergency room doctors to get extra staff, and to prepare for the surviving victims of the plane crash, and for Kayne.

"Please see if he has any identification on him, or a cellular device with information on who he is."

"Excuse me," the voice said as it had gotten closer. "Is there anything that I could do to help? Seems like something is very wrong. Do you all need me for anything?"

Several onlookers were now standing around, and they began to offer a helping hand, also. "Thank you, young lady, and thanks to all of you, but we have the situation under control. What is your name, miss? I would like to address you properly, and to thank you for your concern."

She walked off without giving her name. All she wanted to do was get close enough to see if Kayne was still alive.

"Hello," Dymond answered her phone.

"This nigga just does not want to die. I shot up the whole right side of the back of that motherfucking ambulance, and this bitch is still alive." Zha was furious.

Chapter 30

"This nigga has to go. I'm tired of letting this nigga breathe." Zha's nerves were bad. She never missed. "How the fuck do I keep missing this nigga?"

She hopped back in the car to drive to her hotel. She had already let Dymond know where she would be staying so that she and Bliss could have somewhere to spend the night, and to figure out exactly what they would do about getting Blayden's body back home, and preparing a funeral service for him.

Shooting up that ambulance was kind of sloppy of her because she could have easily been caught down bad if they would have recognized her, or would have gotten her plate number.

Zha really had anger issues because of everything that she had been through. She decided to call an old friend, who was a counselor, for some advice, and to help her to clear her mind. Maybe her stressing could be the reason that her work had gotten sloppy.

"Hello," the counselor said when she answered the phone. "This is Dr. Marshall."

"Hey. This is Zha'Reign. Long time no hear from." Dr. Marshall and Zha had become good friends throughout the years.

"Hi, Zha'Reign. To what do I owe this pleasant surprise?"

"I just needed some words of encouragement, and you came to mind."

"What's the problem?"

"I've just been on an emotional rollercoaster. I also lost someone near and dear to me. My cousin, Blayden, was one of the victims of the Flight 225 crash."

"Oh, ok. I see. I saw something about that accident on the news. Well, my friend, losing a loved one is never easy. You have my condolences. As far as you being on an emotional rollercoaster, we all go through that, especially us women. You see, even when you are going through, you have to make the choice to be happy. Happiness, my friend, is a choice. It all depends on the arrangement of your mind. Your mind itself is a battleground. Happiness is something that you have to choose ahead of time. Put it in your mind early. How you deal with your days are totally up to you. It's not dependent on your circumstances, but on your choices. The difficulties that you face are not there to tear you down. For everything that the Lord allows you to deal with, he has his reasons. Your hard times are there to increase you. You have to know that there is not a circumstance presented to you that can take your peace if you do not allow it to. If you're not receiving what you would like to receive, then, baby girl, you will have to rethink and reevaluate exactly what it is that you are putting out. So smile because you only have better days ahead of you. You just have to choose to have them."

"Thank you so much. I really needed that."

"You are most welcome, but before I let you go, please allow me to say a prayer for you. Father, I want to thank You that we are more than conquerors. That no weapon formed against us shall prosper. Thank You for always causing us to triumph. We want to thank You that we are not only making it through, but that we are making it through better off than before. Lord, we plead Your blood over our minds, our bodies, our spirits, and our souls. We want to thank You that we are free, and have sound minds. In Jesus' name we pray. Amen."

"Thank you so much."

"Talk to you later. Please don't be a stranger."

"Okay, I won't. Thanks again."

Zha felt a sense of relief when she hung up the phone. She cut off her car and opened her door.

"Get the fuck out," two females said. One was in the front of her, and the other one was coming from the side. "Bitch, you could've killed my cousin with that stunt that you pulled on her daddy. Lay down, hoe."

"Bitch, I said get down," Teena yelled. They had followed Zha from the time that she went to see if the paramedics needed any help.

"I'm telling you now, if I get down, you better make sure that I stay down. If I get up, it's over for you," Zha said, mugging them.

The parking lot was empty. It was a perfect scene. Teeana cocked her gun and put it to Zha's head.

All of that praying for what? she thought to herself. She was trying to come up with something quick. She was usually the one on the other side of the gun. Should she beg for her life, and plead her case? But how could she, begging and pleading wasn't in her bloodline. Fuck all the extra shit. She had to think of something, and do it quick.

"This is my last time telling you, homegirl. Either you're going to lay down, or I'm going to lay you down."

"Well, fuck it then, I'm not getting down there, my girl. So, you're just gonna have to lay me down."

"It is what it is then, bitch, your call."

Bow... Bow...

Blood splattered all over Zha's car. The alarm sounded, and Zha stood watching Teena and Teeana as they were lying on the ground.

Bliss and Dymond peeped what was going on as they were going to the hotel to meet Zha. They parked in the front, and creeped around back. They had their .380s cocked and loaded.

"Where the fuck did y'all come from? I thought those bitches was going to kill me?" Zha said still shocked.

"It's a damn good thing that we so happened to be pulling up, and payed attention to what was going on," Bliss answered her.

"You damn right. I owe y'all."

"It's all love, cousin. I wasn't about to lose anybody else," Dymond said.

"Let's move before somebody sees us right here. They'll find these bitches when the other guests come back. Somebody will call the police."

"Let's go to the room then."

They walked to the room, and sat down. Dymond and Bliss took a bed, and Zha took the other. The room wasn't fancy, but it was comfortable. Zha went into the bathroom to take a shower.

"They say I'm a dog, but it takes one to know one, alriiight..." Kevin Gates was playing as Dymond's ringtone.

"Yo, waddup, Keeky?" she asked as she answered the phone.

"Chillin', chillin'. How's things going up there? Is Blayden's body going to be able to be flown back here?"

"Yeah, I'm going to give you the details when we return. We're about to rest up for our flight. It leaves tomorrow. We're at Zha's hotel right now, though."

"Zha? What the fuck is she doing up there?"

"It's a long story. She'll explain it to you when we touch down."

"Yo, Dymond. Don't trust that bitch. I just found out that Judas was her daddy."

"No way. That can't be true. We never met Zha's dad when we were little because her mom said that he had passed away."

"I'm telling you. Jade was her sister."

"Oh shit. Let me hit you back, Keeky. She's getting out of the shower."

Dymond hung up on Keeky. She could hear Zha turn off the shower. She looked at Bliss, and put her finger over her mouth to let him know that he needed to be quiet. Zha opened the bathroom door, and Dymond slid her across the room.

"What the fuck is wrong with you, cuz?" Zha asked grabbing her face.

Dymond hurt herself after she hit Zha so she grabbed her chest in an effort to feel better. "Bitch, why the fuck didn't you tell me that Judas was your daddy?"

"Why the fuck did I have to tell y'all?" Zha answered. She jumped up, and ran towards Dymond. Dymond stepped in the middle of the floor. "Bitch, if you swing on me, I will knock you the fuck out."

Bliss got up and ran in between them before Zha could reach Dymond. "What the fuck is wrong with y'all? Y'all are family."

"Family? Family?" Zha was screaming. "Where the fuck was family when me and my mom were barely making it? Why the fuck didn't family come to look for me when I was missing? Huh?"

"Bitch," Dymond yelled back. "Family formed search parties to look for your ungrateful ass. Family put up towards your reward money when we were looking for you. Together me and Keeky put up over fifty g's apiece, but we didn't have to mention that to you because that was from the heart. Family helped your mom to get into rehab so that she could stop selling you to get her bills paid. Family kept it a thousand with y'all, and all you motherfuckers know how to do is lie."

"Chill," said Bliss. "Stop this shit right now before y'all say some shit that you won't be able to take back." Bliss grabbed Dymond and pulled her to the side. "Baby, you're still recovering so chill out." He went over to Zha. He put his arms around her and gave her a hug. She was crying and packing her things to leave.

"You're not going anywhere, Zha. Fuck all that. We all make mistakes. You just need to figure out how to make this shit right.

Y'all need to talk about this shit like women, and forgive each other. All of y'all have been hurt, but the prisoners in all of this is not the people that hurt y'all, the prisoner is you. When you hold on to hurt, you never let it heal. There's too much ahead of y'all right now to let what somebody did keep y'all from moving forward. Let that shit go, and talk about it."

Dymond went to sit on the bed. She grabbed her bag, and took out her blunt. She was tearing up as Bliss was speaking. "Let's just get some rest, and we'll all talk about this shit together tomorrow when we touch down," she said.

Zha and Bliss agreed. Dymond went to bathe and change her bandages in the restroom. Bliss showered up last. When he walked out of the bathroom, Dymond had finished smoking the last of her blunt, and she and Zha had dozed off.

He heard a knock at the door about ten minutes after they fell asleep, and went to the peephole to see who it was. "Y'all wake up," he went over and whispered. "It's the police."

"The cops?" Zha jumped up. "Why in the hell would the laws be at our door? I didn't see any cameras."

"Just chill. I'm about to see what they want."

Bliss opened the door. Two male officers were standing there in uniform. One officer looked to be in his late 20's. He was an African American officer. He seemed to be uptight. The other cop was Caucasian, and he looked to be in his mid-40. He had a better attitude than the black officer.

"Hello, officers," Bliss said when he answered the door.

"Good evening, sir, we are making rounds to find out if any of the guests here may have seen anything suspicious going on. We found the bodies of two African American females whom were shot to death this evening, but we do not have any leads, or any witnesses. We are asking for everyone's cooperation at this time," the Caucasian officer said.

"No, sir. We did not see anything."

"Okay, well, you all have my condolences. Enjoy the rest of your night."

The police officers walked off and Bliss shut the door. He told Dymond and Zha that they were gone, and that they could finish resting up for their departure on tomorrow. He cut off all of the lights, and got in the bed with Dymond. He pulled the covers back, and grabbed her from behind. She scooted back a little so that Bliss could cuff her closer, and so that she could feel his penis poking her. She loved that feeling. Laying up under her man, and having him hold her closely made her feel safe and secure, like everything would be alright.

Zha turned over, but she couldn't fall asleep right away this time. Her mind was on overload with thoughts of what would happen when they returned home. She hated the fact that she had to explain her relationship with Judas to anybody, but she was also tired of keeping secrets from her circle.

She heard a knock at the door again.

"Who is it?" she said walking up to the door. She didn't have a chance to look out of the peep hole.

"It's the police, ma'am, please open up."

"Okay, I'm coming." She opened the door, and there were six officers standing with guns pointed towards her. "Ma'am, move aside please. We have to search the room."

Zha stepped to the side, and gave the officers room to come in and search the room. They never kept weapons used in a murder with them so they were sure that the officers would not find anything.

"All clear," the African American officer said.

Each cop had searched their bags, and every single inch of their room. As they finished up, they walked out of the room and apologized for disrupting their night.

Dymond and Bliss had awakened, but they never moved because the officers would not allow them to, and Zha never had a chance to wake them as everything happened so fast. Their flights were scheduled to leave early because they needed to get back to get things prepared for Blayden. They picked up their things off of the floor that the police had thrown all over, and then they went back to bed. There was a long day ahead of them. A day full of truth, and pain. This would determine whether their clique would last. Maybe Kayne and Judas had succeeded at separating them after all.

Chapter 31

The ambulance pulled up to Ronald Reagan UCLA Medical Center. The paramedics hurriedly got Kenzy into the hospital.

"Over here. This room right here," the emergency room nurses were yelling. They ran to ER 12.

"What's wrong with this one?" a nurse asked.

"She was involved in the Flight 225 crash. Her vitals are steady, but they were dropping on our way here. She almost crashed. She has been unconscious since the crash happened. We have contacted her father, but he hasn't arrived as of yet."

"Well, I'll tell you one thing. This one is lucky. All of the other passengers that survived had much more serious injuries. Let's get her prepped, and knock this out."

They took Kenzy into the X-ray room, and got started locating the exact areas that she had injuries to. They also needed to make sure that everything was fine with her head.

A few moments later, the other ambulance pulled up with Kayne. They rushed him inside.

"This one is suffering from two gunshot wounds. One to the chest, and another to the stomach. He's losing lots of blood. We have not been able to gather information as of yet on any of his family members."

"Please try to contact someone as soon as possible. We need information on the family."

They rushed Kayne to OR 7. The operating team worked on him for about three hours. They almost lost him twice, but he pulled through. They still hadn't located a family member, but they were still searching his things for some type of identification. Kenzy was down the hall recovering in Room 303.

"How are you today, ma'am? May I help you?" a nurse asked Nala.

"I'm here to see my daughter."

"What is her name?"

"Kenzy Thompson. Here's my identification. My name is Nala Thompson."

"Please give me a moment to find her charts."

"No problem."

The nurse went through all of her charts until she found Kenzy's. It had taken her approximately seven minutes because she had a thick pile to rummage through.

"She's in Room 303. Take a left at the corner."

"Okay. Thank you."

Nala had gotten a fake I.D. made so that she could be able to see Kenzy.

"Ma'am... Ma'am... Ma'am..." the nurse was yelling.

Nala turned around. "Yes, ma'am." she said.

"Ma'am, you cannot go back there right now. I have just been informed that we are waiting for her next of kin to arrive before we can allow any other visitors to go to her room."

"I am her only family. Her father is also here, suffering from a gunshot wound here at this hospital."

***

With a body full of pain, Kenzy was starting to come to. She did not know where she was, and she could not remember all of the details of what had happened to her. She moved her hand around a bit, but it was difficult because of the I.V. that she had inserted into it. She managed to hit the button that buzzed the nurse.

"May I help you?" a nurse said through the speaker.

"Yes, ma'am," Kenzy uttered softly. "Can someone please explain what happened to me. Where am I?"

"We'll be right there." The nurse hung up, grabbed Kenzy's chart, and headed towards her room. She noticed the head nurse walking down the hall with a visitor.

"Excuse me," the nurse yelled out. The head nurse and Nala turned around to see who it was. "Please, can you come along with me to the room of Ms. Kenzy Thompson. It seems that she is awake. She just buzzed for assistance."

"My daughter is awake?" Nala asked excitedly.

"Yes, ma'am, she is. I didn't realize that her mother was here."

"Yes, she is. We were just heading over to her father's room, but we'll come along with you. This is great news."

They headed down the hallway to Kenzy's room. Nala hesitated at first, but she slowly made her way in. The head nurse was speaking.

"Ms. Thompson, you were involved in a plane crash. You sustained a few injuries, but miraculously you are still here. You should pull through just fine in a few days."

"I remember the crash a little. Where's my boyfriend? Which room is he in?"

"If you're referring to the young man that accompanied you on the plane, he succumbed to his injuries, ma'am. He passed away. I'm sorry."

"Passed away? No, that cannot be true. We were going to start over. He wasn't supposed to leave me, not like this." Kenzy was crying uncontrollably.

"Ma'am, we'll leave the room so that you and your mom can talk."

"My what?" Kenzy murmered to herself through the tears. The nurses walked out of the room, and Nala walked over to Kenzy.

"My baby girl," Nala said as her eyes began to water.

"Baby girl? Who are you? My mom doesn't even know me. Don't come any closer." Kenzy was trying to be alert through the pain.

"Kenzy Thompson. I am your mom. I am sorry that I have not been able to be a part of your life, but your father stole off with you, and I've been missing you for years. I had you at a very young age, and my parents allowed him to take you from me, also. There was nothing that I could do. No one would help me to find you."

"Well, how in the fuck did you find me now then?"

"The twins gave me your dad's number, and told me that you had been involved in a crash."

"All of this time you mean to tell me that you couldn't find me? I've been existing for twenty motherfucking years, and you couldn't find me. You did not want to find me, and my sorry ass excuse for a father is the reason for my boyfriend's death. Fuck the both of you. Get the fuck out of my room. You've been dead to me all of this time, you're dead to me now. *Get the fuck out*," Kenzy began to scream at her mom through all of the pain that she was feeling. Nala started to drop tears as she turned to walk out of the room.

"Just in case you would like to know, your dad is also down the hallway, fighting for his life." Nala walked out, and went outside to gather herself.

Down the hallway, Kenzy thought to herself.

The nurse had left crutches near her bed. She called the nurse back into her room for assistance. They came in, and unhooked her I.V.'s so that she could try to go and see about her dad.

They left the room and Kenzy struggled to make her way down the hallway. She opened Kayne's door, and immediately burst into tears. She moved slowly to get to him, but once she made it to him, she straightened up, and was overcome by anger.

"All of my life you've used me. I've done everything that you asked of me to do from the day that I was born. My loyalty was to you, my life was given to you, and all that I've ever gotten from you in return is heartache and pain. The one man that loved me is gone because we had to run from all of you dirty motherfuckers." Her tears were dropping on Kayne. "God rest your soul, daddy," she whispered in his ear, and then she put a pillow over his face. She held it there for about twenty seconds, but she couldn't go through with it. "My God, I do not want to live like this anymore. What do I do? How can I kill my father?"

She could not stomach the fact that killing her father had even come to her mind. She felt weak, and out of options. She thought about Blayden, about the fact that she had just met her mom under circumstances that were beyond her control. She buzzed the nurse because she needed help getting back to her room. Her whole body felt weak all of a sudden. She pressed the button for the nurse to come into Kayne's room.

"May I help you?" asked the nurse over the room speaker.

"Can someone please come and help me back to my room?" Kenzy asked.

"I'm on the way," the nurse said.

Kenzy grabbed the pillow that she had, and put it back under her dad's head. She grabbed her crutches, and waited for the nurse to come in.

"I brought you a wheelchair, Ms. Thompson," the nurse said as she walked into the room. "Ms. Thompson, I have a wheel chair for you." Kenzy did not answer, the nurse looked down, and she had passed out on the floor.

Chapter 32

The alarm on Keeky's phone rang at 8:00am. The storm had cleared up and the sun was trying to peak through the clouds. Keeky had never made it home because she spent most of her night running down their plans with Zay. It was cold inside of Zay's spot so she turned over, pulled up the cover, and laid her head onto his chest.

"Good morning, baby," Zay said when he felt Keeky turn over.

"Good morning to you, too," she answered him.

"It's about that time. Let me get up and get ready for my meeting."

"Yeah, I'll get up, also. I have to make it to the airport on time to pick up Dymond, Bliss, and Zha's lying ass."

"Zha? She went to Cali, too?"

"Yes, she was supposed to be somewhere doing a hit last I checked. I don't know what the bitch is doing in California with Dymond and Bliss. I'll find out later because she has some explaining to do. I promise you that I won't have any remorse for her if I feel like she's still lying."

"Well, just see what she has to say first."

Zay walked into the bathroom to brush his teeth, and prepare for his meeting. Keeky slipped her clothes back on, and waited for him to come out of the bathroom so that she could brush her teeth, and wash her face, also.

He stepped out of the bathroom, and he was looking edible to Keeky. She was seeing him in a different light. He was dressed in a dark gray and black Ermenegildo Zegna suit. He wore a black shirt, and a black tie underneath. He had on black Cole Haan's to accent his suit, also. His badge was in his hand, and he was getting his briefcase in order.

"Got damn you look good," Keeky told Zay.

"Thanks, baby girl. I try. This is just something that I do for the job."

"I hear you. Let me get by you," Keeky said as she walked towards him to go into the bathroom.

She grabbed his dick as she walked by, and Zay smiled. "You want it?" he asked her.

"Nope, I'm good. Besides, we need to leave. You have a meeting to get to, and I have to get to the airport." She went into the bathroom while Zay finished up what he needed to get done for his meeting. "You ready to go," Keeky asked Zay.

"Yeah, I am." They walked to the living room. Zay grabbed Keeky from behind, and kissed her neck. He wrapped his arms around her, "Keeky, baby listen. I wasn't fronting when I told you that I loved you. I'm going to get you out of this. I promise."

"I hope so, Zay, because I love you, too."

He turned her around and kissed her softly. Zay held the door open for Keeky, and locked up once they walked outside. He walked her to her car, and he went to his. Keeky felt better now that she had gotten most of what she needed to tell him off of her chest.

"Damn, if he's the plug, then it won't take much for me to get what I need. We can put Houston, and a couple of other cities, on lock. I can get better prices, so that I can give better prices until I knock my competition off of my level." Keeky was figuring out exactly how she was going to get everything that she needed to get out of Zay's ass.

They had already discussed the possibility of them hustling together. She was going to give him twenty-five thousand dollars to test a new product because if it didn't sell the way that she expected it to, at least she could make her money back off of it, and wouldn't take too much of a loss. Taking losses was a part of the game, so she was ready for that at all times.

She arrived to the airport, and had thirty minutes left until the flight for the others arrived.

She parked in the parking garage, and texted Zay's phone, "Just wanted to say that I love you, and I appreciate what you're doing for me." She smiled, and put her head back.

She knew that it would be a lot that Zay was putting on the line for her by trying to save her, and his job. Her phone vibrated. Zay had hit her back.

His message was short and sweet as usual, "I owe you this. Ready to prove my love."

She wondered if it would even be possible to ever trust, or be in a relationship with a federal officer. She had really fallen in love with Zay, that's why it hurt her so bad to find out that he was a cop. She put her radio on, but not too loud. Whenever she was feeling emotional, she would listen to the same song over and over again. That was how Dymond would know when she was going through something.

"There's a hero, when you look inside your heart. You don't have to be afraid of what you are. There's an answer, if you reach into your soul. And the sorrow that you know will melt away," Mariah Carey played softly as she lay back.

She looked at her phone, and a message had just come through from Dymond. "We just got here."

"Pulling up now, leaving the parking garage," she sent a message back. She sat up, put her car in reverse, and pulled out. She saw Dymond walking towards the exit door, so she parked as close as she could get. Bliss and Zha weren't too far behind.

"Yo, Dymond," she yelled.

Dymond looked over and made her way to Keeky. Keeky had already popped her trunk. Dymond could hear Mariah playing through the trunk speakers, "Bitch, are you depressed?" Dymond asked Keeky.

"Don't start, Dymond. I'm telling you." Keeky rolled her eyes.

"Well, fuck you, too," Dymond said back to her. Bliss loaded their things, and they hopped into the car with Keeky to leave.

"What's up with Blayden?" Keeky asked in an effort to break the silence.

"His body should be here on tomorrow," Dymond answered. "This shit will be hard. I'll start contacting the rest of the family that we do have, and I'll try to get in touch with my dad. I'll have his funeral on Saturday. This will be the hardest thing that I have ever had to do." Her eyes were beginning to swell with tears.

"Sis, don't worry. We're here every step of the way. Anything that you may need, we got you. My homegirl is in a choir down at Mount Calvary Baptist Church. I have already talked to her pastor about you having the funeral there, and I've already ordered all of the flower arrangements that you need from five different florists. I just need to call them all back with dates."

"Thank you so much. I know that my family members will want to bring food. I just need to go to the funeral home to pick out a casket, and do whatever other last minute things that may need to be done." Dymond had her phone on silence. She never noticed that she had a missed call from a California phone number. Before she could listen to the voicemail, the number was calling back. "Hello," Dymond said as she answered the phone.

"Hi, Dymond. It's me, Kenzy."

"What the fuck do you want? My brother is dead, isn't that what the fuck you wanted?"

"No, I didn't. That wasn't necessary. Besides, the last time that I checked, we were running because of you and my father. So, you were the one that wanted him dead, not me."

"Bitch, fuck you," Dymond said in a nonchalant manner, and she simply ended the phone call.

Chapter 33

"Good morning, Zayvier," a bald-headed, stocky guy told Zay.

"Good morning, sir," he answered.

"Are you ready for briefing?"

"Yes, I am." Zay sat down with some of his colleagues. He took pictures out of his briefcase of Keeky, Dymond, Bliss, Zha, Kayne, and Kenzy. He passed the copies around, and then he tacked them to the wall.

"Good morning everyone," he said as he began his briefing. "The photos that you are looking at are of the current group of people that we have been investigating, and trying to get solid evidence on for an arrest for years now. This first group, their names are Keemari, also known Keeky on the streets, Dymond, Zha, also known as Reign or Zha'Reign, and Bliss. The second two people that you see are Kayne and Kenzy Thompson, the father/daughter duo. Originally, we believed that Dymond and Keeky were the suppliers, but through our on-going investigation, it has been discovered that Kayne and Kenzy are the two that supply the Houston area. They will be hard to put our hands on because Kayne is a multi-millionaire with a large payroll. His daughter is just as slick. I believe that we may be able to catch her in a vulnerable state right now, though. She just lost her boyfriend in a plane crash that they were both involved in. She will be emotional, and she will make mistakes. This first group of people, however, we will need to get closer to them in order to find a conviction, but as of now I do not see them as a threat. Bliss is a business owner, and the girls have been laying back. Our focus should be on the big dog. We remove him off of the streets, we remove a lot of the drugs, and stop most of the murders."

"Well done, Zayvier," his supervisor said. "We will investigate a little further, and then we make a solid arrest. Also, we need to find out exactly who is responsible for the murder of Jade. Someone has to go down for it. Jade was a good officer, one of the ones that actually had morals and did things right."

They concluded the meeting and everyone packed up their briefcases with their notes to leave the briefing room. Zay asked his supervisor to wait a second so that they could talk. Zay gave him a piece of paper attached to an important document, and he told him to read it thoroughly word for word. His supervisor agreed, and they went their separate ways.

Zay walked outside of the building to call Keeky and let her know the news. She would be able to start trusting him again once she realized that he had taken the heat off of her.

The day was pretty, but it looked as if it would storm again because of the wind blowing and the clouds that were starting to form outside.

"Wassup, baby?" Keeky asked Zay as she answered the phone.

"Nothing much. I just got out of the briefing with my colleagues."

"How did it go?"

"Everything went fine. Their attention should be geared more towards Kayne and Kenzy as of now. You all just need to stay clear of the radar."

"That's wassup. That's what the fuck I'm talking about. Well, are you ready to get this money now?"

"You know that, sweetie. When can we meet?"

"In a few hours. I'm pulling up into Dymond's driveway right now. We have some shit to handle, and then I'll be out and about. I'll call you when I can make a move."

"That's a bet, babygirl. Talk to you later."

They hung up the phone and Zay hit up his right hand. He needed him to pick up the twenty-five thousand dollars that he had gotten from Keeky so that he could break down what she needed, and he could have it for their meeting.

"Hello," he said when he answered his phone.

"Mr. Zayvier, hello, how are you?" Nala said through her tears.

"I am fine. What's wrong with you. It sounds as if you are crying, Naomi."

"I'll be okay. I'm just having problems with my family. My daughter is upset with me for some reason, and her dad is in critical condition. Those are minor problems. Nothing for you to be concerned with, sir. I just called to let you know that I will be coming to Houston in a few days. I have business there to take care of. I am coming to see the love of my life."

"Okay. Well, feel free to stop by."

"I will. Thanks for the invite."

"You're welcome. See you soon."

Nala hung up with Zay. He wondered who could be the love of her life miles away in Houston. Maybe it would turn out to be a good thing that she is visiting because now he could introduce her and Keeky. If he was going to gain Keeky's trust back, he may as well keep everything out in the open with her from now on. The only problem that he would have with the two of them meeting is that Keeky wants Kayne and Kenzy dead, and Nala's love for Kenzy will not let that happen.

Chapter 34

"Bliss, baby, can you take our bags out of the car?" Dymond asked as they pulled into the driveway. The sky was getting darker, and the sun was hiding behind the clouds. No way was any of them leaving Dymond's spot any time soon. The weather was about to get bad, they had a funeral to finish planning, and answers to get from Zha. The three of them walked inside while Bliss unloaded the car. Dymond poured them all a glass of water, and sat it on the table.

"Come on, y'all," she said. "We may as well get this shit over with."

"So, what's the deal, Zha? You've been keeping a lot of secrets. Spill that shit, but make sure that you tell everything this time because I don't think that I'm willing to tolerate anymore lies." Keeky was ready to put everything on the table.

Zha took a deep breath. She decided that she may as well be honest because she was tired of all of the lying her damn self.

"First things first," Zha began to say. "I'm asking y'all ahead of time not to judge me, and to know that I am the same Zha'Reign through and through. I'll speak my mind, but please listen, and allow me to finish because this is hard."

"You got that," Dymond said.

"I'm all ears," Keeky answered.

Bliss was walking through the door, and he happened to hear the end of what Zha was saying. He sat down the last of their bags, and walked over to the table.

"Mind if I join y'all?" he asked.

Keeky and Dymond looked at Zha. "No, I don't mind. Have a seat," she said.

"Okay. Here goes nothing. My mom has been a drug addict ever since I can remember. As we all know, Judas was a dirty cop, and also a hustler. My mom slept with him when she went on a trip to Jamaica with a guy who was using her to traffick drugs for him. Judas was married, and he was being with my mom on the side. I never understood when I was younger, why my mom would tell me that I couldn't tell anyone abut my daddy. If I mentioned him at home, she would hit me so hard that I wouldn't want to speak of him again. I did not know that Jade was my sister until the day that we went to see what was up with Bliss, and Zay called Judas' name. I knew that we had beef with a Jamaican nigga because I killed his daughter, but I never thought in a million years that the nigga would be my daddy. I had never met Jade in my life until I saw her at that hospital, and I never knew that we had the same father. I was a bastard child, I guess," Zha started to tear up, but she wiped her eyes, and continued.

"When I realized that he was the nigga that we were beefing with, I didn't say anything, and I didn't try to stop y'all from killing him because all of my life he's been hiding me. He was making enough money to take me out of that situation with my mom, but instead he let me continue to go through what I was going through. I have so much anger built up inside of me because I feel lost, confused, and hurt. Not only did he allow me to stay in a situation where my mom was selling me, he would have me, also, when he came to visit. I was a young girl, and I didn't just love my father, I was in love with my father. He was my first. When I got old enough to realize what was going on, I hated my mom, but I was still in love with my dad. He stopped answering my phone calls, stopped coming around, and basically stopped loving me. I met Khalil and tried to get over it, but we still would have problems every now and again because I could not love him like I knew I was supposed to. I actually feel a little bit of peace now that my dad is gone. I also never told y'all because I didn't want y'all to look at me as if I'm not even supposed to be here today because I was my mom and dad's mistake. Besides, I felt like y'all would have never told me something like that about yourselves, so I decided to keep it to myself. Keeky, I also noticed that you're still talking to Zay. Using him for information or not, you made me wonder how is it that you are so ready to take me out, and not so easy to forgive me, but yet you forgave Zay so quickly. Not that I am upset with you, but it made me realize that as women, we can forgive a man over and over who has hurt us, but we cut the people in our lives short whom we've known forever because of one mistake. Anyways, I really hope that you all can forgive me because I was not open from the beginning, but I am truly sorry."

When Zha stopped talking, Keeky and Dymond were both in tears. They could not believe that they had known her all of these years, and yet they still did not know what she was dealing with.

Bliss looked on in amazement. Zha looked at them crying, and she finally let her tears fall. They got up, and went over to hug her. Bliss loved the bond that they all had, and he knew that things between them would be better from this day forward.

"Ready to start planning this funeral? We have to send my lil cuz out the right way," Zha said trying to stop the tears, and change the subject.

"Yeah, let's do that," Dymond said. "I have to order him an Armani suit because he always did say that if something ever happened to him, he wanted to be buried in the best so that every nigga at the funeral could be jealous." She was laughing at the thought.

She made all phone calls that needed to be made pertaining to the funeral, and now they just needed to prepare themselves for that day. Dymond just wanted to get it all over with.

Chapter 35

Kenzy sat up in her bed to analyze everything that had gone on. Until today, she thought that she had it all together. Of course she had days in her life when she would want to ask the twins to help her to meet her mom, but she would always change her mind because she felt as if it was not even worth the pain that would come along with it. Having her mom come into her life now, at this time, didn't feel fair to her. She lost her boyfriend, she did not want anything to do with her dad, and now she had to go through the pain of meeting a woman who had waited years to even try and contact her. This wasn't fair at all. She did not choose this life, but she couldn't help but question why it was chosen for her.

Knock. Knock. Knock. Someone was at Kenzy's door.

"Come in," she said.

She turned around to see who it was, and it was Nala.

"What do you want?" Kenzy asked in a disgusted manner.

"Can I please talk to you?" Nala asked.

"You know what, go ahead. I'll listen. It's not like either one of my parents can fuck me up anymore than you've already done."

"Well, first off, let me apologize to you for showing up in your life the way that I did today."

Nala dried her eyes as tears began to fall, and she began talking again. "Kenzy, I've loved you from the moment that I laid eyes on you. Although I was young, it seemed like I was supposed to have you, at that moment, and that time. Becoming a teenage parent was never a part of my plans, but I know that it all had to be a part of God's perfect plan. My parents could not stomach that their baby girl ended up pregnant so young because of the way that their lives were in Africa. I've been trying to get you back for years, but no one would help me. I was too young to do it on my own when you left me, and I guess that I was too late when you had gotten older. If you would let me, Kenzy, I want to be a part of your life now, baby. I know that I cannot make up for all of the time that I've lost, but I can promise that I won't lose anymore time from this day forward."

Kenzy leaned up. She was crying nonstop, and so was Nala. She plucked off the television, and she asked Nala to have a seat on the bed. At first she grabbed her hand, but then she pulled her, and hugged her.

"Mom, I cannot say that it will be easy to do, but I can say that I am willing to try. You could not help a situation that you could no longer control. You may not have been here all of this time, but you are here now, and that's what matters the most to me," Kenzy was sobbing and trying to get out her words at the same time.

They sat on the bed holding each other until a nurse walked in. The nurse could tell that they needed to have their moment. She did not want to be the reason that their time with each other came to an end, so she dropped off the tray of food that she had brought for Kenzy, and gave her a message.

"Ms. Thompson," the nurse said. "I am sorry for any interruptions that I may be causing. I just wanted to let you know that your dad is awake."

Chapter 36

The week had passed, and it was the day of Blayden's funeral. Dymond woke up extra early so that she could make sure that everything was going to be on time. She didn't want anything to go wrong. It was a beautifully sunny day, and the birds were chirping happily outside. Bliss was fixing breakfast for the two of them because he wanted Dymond to eat before they left. Her wound had healed really well, except for the nasty scar that it left on her chest.

"You ready to eat, baby?" Bliss asked Dymond.

"We still have a little while left before it's time to leave, right?" Dymond wanted to know.

"Yeah, we do. About an hour and a half."

"Well, come give me some of that dick so that I could calm down."

"Really, Dymond? Right now?"

"Yes. Right now, daddy."

Dymond motioned her forefinger for Bliss to come to her bedroom. He walked in, and began to undress. Dymond was already naked with a bonnet covering her hair. He laid her down on the bed, kissed her, and began playing with her clitoris. He went down, and began to kiss her clit the same way that he was kissing her lips. He took his tongue and stroked it up and down her clit, then sucked it and slurped it.

"That's the shit I like," Dymond moaned.

Bliss picked up his head, and slid in his dick. He took his time because Dymond didn't like it rough. She hated the pain of when his penis first entered, but he loved the way that she squealed, and ran from the dick because that pussy was extra tight. Once Bliss finally got it all the way in, he slow stroked Dymond until she was dripping wet and he could feel her juices trickling. He turned over, and told her to lay flat on her stomach. She did as she was told while he stroked her from the behind.

"Ouch, Bliss, that hurts," she squealed in the softest voice that she could conjure up. Bliss told her to turn her head to the side, and he went closer to whisper in her ear. She didn't let him talk to her right away because she was still complaining about the pain. "Bliss, daddy, that hurts," she repeated herself.

"Take that dick," he said as he stroked her. "Take that dick," he said again.

He was riding her ass faster and faster. He sat up on his knees, and put his hands on Dymond's ass. "Take that dick, bae," he said again.

"I'm taking it, daddy. Fuck meeeee," she was saying. She was biting her lips, and her head was buried in the pillow. He slowed down as they got ready to come, "Oooowwwwwoooooo, there it goes, baby," Dymond said.

"I'm about to come, too, keep that ass right there."

Bliss pumped about four times, and he fell backwards. They hurried to get up and shower so that they could be ready when the limo arrived to take them to the funeral. Dymond's dad, her two aunts, and her uncle would be at her dad's house waiting on them to pick them up, also.

They finished everything in the nick of time because the limo had arrived on time. It was 10:15am, and the funeral service was scheduled to begin at 11.

She had rented a crème colored stretch Cadillac Escalade, and she had champagne stocked in the bar. They hopped in and made their way over to her dad's house. Everyone was ready on time, and they reminisced on the ride to the church about their childhood. Their family hadn't been together in a while, and it was sad that it took the death of a loved one to bring them together.

Dymond noticed the hurse in the front of the church, and she instantly felt weak. Her stomach was balling in knots. It was time for the family to walk inside. Keeky, Zha, and Zay met them at the church. They were waiting outside for Dymond, and the rest of the family to arrive. The pianist played a soft hymn for the family to march in off of. They made it to their seats, and the mistress of service welcomed everyone, and read the program.

Blayden lay there, in front of the church, with a red and black Armani suit. His hair was neatly pushed back, and spread onto his pillow a little. His makeup was done perfectly because it was not too much for him. His undershirt was red, and his necktie was black. His coffin was a golden color, and his flower arrangements represented the things that he liked.

The church had gotten quiet as the choir stood up to sing, "Will your heart and soul say yes? Will your spirit still say yes? There is more that I require of thee. Will your heart and soul say yes?"

The whole church quietly listened to the words. The liturgical dance team stood up as the intro of the song was flowing into the next part. A young lady lifted her hands for them to begin, and the dance attire began to flow beautifully, they looked like angels.

The words were beautiful, "Yeeesss, open up your heart, and tell the Lord yes. I'll obey Jesus, I won't stray Jesus, but this time I've made up in my mind, I'll say yes..."

Dymond started to scream. The choir kept going. Her dad broke down right after she did. Keeky and Zha stood up to console her. Bliss was fanning her, and her aunts consoled her father. The music broke down as the choir sang, "My soul says yes, he's saying there is more that I require of thee. He's calling you higher..." Dymond started to jump up and down. She fainted.

Bliss carried her to the back of the church, and away from the service. Keeky and Zha broke down. Zay comforted them. Their family was taking his death harder than expected.

"Hallelujjjaaaaahhhh," one of Dymond's aunts started screaming. "Your will, Lord. Your will, Lord. Not our will, Lord, but your will be done," she was shouting and crying.

The lead singer was now saying the words, "I'll do what you want me to, Jesus. I might have to give some relationships, but my soul says yes. I might have to give up some things that I hold dear to me, but my soul says yes…" The song was coming to an end, the pastor got up to speak, and to calm down the church.

Bliss had gotten Dymond to come to. She walked from the back, and reentered the church. As she walked in, she looked towards the entrance of the church, and Kenzy was walking in with Nala. She did not want to cause a scene in the church. Kenzy was still on crutches, and Nala was helping her to find a seat.

"Good afternoon, everyone," the pastor began to say. Dymond was making her way back to her seat, and the church had finally calmed down. "The title of my sermon is, Let It Go." He looked out into the crowd to make sure that he had everyone's attention. "Again, the title of my sermon is, Let It Go. Before I begin, I would like to say that I chose this title because the brother here, who is the deceased, died before he and his sister here could make it right. I just want to say to you all here today, let it go.

"Turn your bibles to 2 Corinthians, Chapter 2 verse 10. It reads, *what I have forgiven, if I have forgiven anything, I did it for your sakes in the presence of Christ*. When you think of unforgiveness, think of yourself in a prison-like setting. There are cells surrounding you with everyone, and everything that has ever hurt you. The prison you see is a room in your heart. Jesus is standing by handing you a key that could release every inmate.

"He's telling you that if you take the key, you're forgiving them all. You choose not to take the key and set them free because they've hurt you too bad. You try to run, but you realize that you can't go anywhere because all of the unforgiveness, anger, and bitterness that you have inside has caused you to become a prisoner, as well. This story was told to me by another pastor. You see, forgiving those people is not for them, it's really to set you free. You cannot go on in life, or move forward, if you are holding onto everything that everybody else has done to you.

"How can you ever move forward if you have that much weight holding you back? How can you ever truly be happy if everytime you see the person that hurt you, you get upset? When you forgive others, you take away their power to hurt you. What others have done to you should not be enough to keep you away from your destiny? If you forgive, let God handle the battle for you. He'll take what was meant to harm you, and use it for your advantage.

"When you don't forgive, it's easy to become what you hate. Joel Osteen once said, 'Many airlines now charge you for baggage. It's the same in life. You can carry around baggage, but it will cost you. You can carry unforgiveness, but it will cost you day-to-day happiness and joy you desire. You can carry bitterness, but it will cost you peace. You can haul that bag of *They Owe Me Something* around with you, but it's not free.' If you do it long enough, there will be a very heavy price. It will keep you from your destiny.

"Also, you have to learn to speak life. If you simply change your words, you can also change your life. Remember, that God has ways of turning everything around. The same God that he was back then, he is still Him right now. Learn to let it go because tomorrow is not promised. Once a person is gone, they're gone. They cannot hear or respond to your sorries, and I love you's. You cannot ask God to forgive you once you are gone, and you cannot expect to enter into the gates of heaven if you cannot forgive your brothers and sisters here on Earth. Forgive and you shall be forgiven. My people, you have to learn to let it go. Thank you."

The pastor went to take his seat, and the church gave him a standing ovation.

Nala and Kenzy slipped out of the back door while the rest of the church took their final viewings.

Chapter 37

"Did you read the documents that I gave to you, sir?" Zay called to ask his supervisor as he was on his way to his private office.

"Yes, Zayvier, I did. Is there anything special that you would like for me to do with these?" his supervisor answered.

"Yes, hold onto them for me. You will know when the time is right to present them."

"Okay, well, I'll speak with you later."

"Okay. Talk to you soon."

Zay hung up with his supervisor, and continued to head over to his office. He decided that he would keep the twenty-five thousand dollars for now, until he could get the order that he needed his right hand to pick up for Keeky. He felt his phone vibrate.

"Hi, Naomi," he said when he answered.

"Hello, Mr. Zayvier. I was calling to find out if we can meet somewhere. I am in town."

"Yes, we can. If you are not busy, you can meet me at my office. How is your daughter, and her father?"

"That is fine. I can meet you. Please text me the address. My daughter is fine. As a matter of fact, she was released from the hospital, and she flew here with me. Her dad is still in California recovering. He doesn't know that we've left. He never even had a chance to talk to, or see us. We left before he could find out which room that she was in. He doesn't know that we are together at this time."

"Okay. That is fine. Meet me at my office in twenty minutes."

"Yes, sir."

Zay hung up the phone and sent a text to Nala with his office address. This would be their third meeting. The first two times they met in California, and Zay stayed at Nala's place. She was courteous enough to save him money on hotel fees, although money wasn't a problem for him.

He pulled up to his office, and Nala was already there waiting outside in her car. She was alone. Zay got out of his car, and motioned for her to come inside with him.

"Nice to see you again, Naomi," Zayvier said.

"Same here," she answered.

They walked inside of the building, and Nala took a seat. Zay sat behind his desk. Nala opened her legs a little, and Zay peeked. "You like what you see?" she asked Zay.

"I can't lie, I do, but I can't mix business with pleasure."

"Well, let's not talk business, and focus on pleasure."

Nala stood up, and walked over to Zay's desk. "I've been trying to fuck you since the day that I met you." Nala didn't hold back because in her mind she had pictured this happening over and over.

"I have a special lady in my life already. I'm sorry, I can't. I won't say that I haven't thought about it, but I can't."

Nala wouldn't take no for an answer, and she was not about to let Zay slip away his time. She leaned in to kiss him, but Zay shoved her back a little. She grabbed his belt, and started to unbuckle it. She pushed him back in his chair, and unzipped his pants. Zay loved her fight, so he chose not to fight it anymore. He laid back in his chair, and let her take control. She pulled off his shirt, and started to lick and kiss on his chest. She used her fingers to rub up his sides softly, and that ran chills through his body. She whispered in his ears in her African language, "Liefde maak my."

"What does that mean?" Zay asked.

"In my native language, it means make love to me."

He was turned on by the African language that she spoke. He thought about fighting her off, but he also figured that it could be a one time thing. Why fight off such a sexy lady? He picked her up, and sat her on top of his desk. He put his penis inside of her, and began to fuck her at a quick pace.

"Oooooohhhhh, Zayvier," she moaned. "I've been waiting for this."

"Do you like the way that it feels?" he asked her.

"Yes, sir, I do."

She scooted forward a little more, and kissed his neck. He was able to push deeper inside of her. Her wetness was all over his desk, and running down the insides of her legs. His dick popped out, but he let Nala grab it, and put it back in. She rode it back and forth until she got that feeling that a woman's clitoris gets when she's about to come. Her pussy was jumping. Zay put her breasts in his mouth, and she locked her arms around his neck.

"Right there," she was yelling.

"I'm right there. I'm right there," he said back. She came and then Zay pulled out, and skeeted on her thighs. She looked at him with sweet eyes as she hopped up to go to the restroom, and clean herself. Zay followed her, and cleaned himself as well.

"We'll discuss business on tomorrow," he said. "I was supposed to meet my girl about an hour ago."

He locked up his office, and they left. He went to his car, and grabbed his cell phone out of his back pocket so that he could call and tell Keeky that he was on his way. He pressed the power button so that he could make the phone call, but he didn't dial her because he had pocket dialed her since the moment that Nala had pushed him backwards in the chair. Keeky had heard everything. He searched his car for the money that he had gotten from her for the product that she wanted, so that he could at least show up with something that could keep her calm. His briefcase was on the back seat of his car, but the money was gone.

Chapter 38

She was pacing back and forth in his apartment. He had given her the key while they were at the funeral so that they could meet up when it was time. Her fists were balled so tight her nails dug into her palms, but her anger blocked out the pain.

How in the fuck could this bitch ass nigga try to play me like this? What type of flunky ass bitch does he take me for? He better have my money so that I can get the fuck on. He has me all the way fucked up.

Her eyes watered as she thought about what he had just done. She started to tremble at the thought of him touching another woman after he told her that he would never hurt her again.

Lying, no good bastard.

Taking a deep breath then exhaling slowly, she tried to calm herself as she made her way over to his living room window, parted the blinds, and looked out just in time to see him pull up.

Hurry up, motherfucker.

Breathing out of her nose, she briskly walked back across the room and snatched her bag off of the couch. Inside of it, she found exactly what she was searching for. Yesterday, her home-girl, who was a pharmacist, had provided her with the needle that was now in her hand. It was filled with something that would neutralize the size and strength advantage he had over her when she struck.

Today, his ass would pay for every single dishonest act he had made against her.

When she heard him put his key in the door, she slid the needle into her pocket, and stood ready to pop off on him. She couldn't believe that she had to hear her nigga fucking another bitch. After all of the chances that she gave this motherfucker, he still tried to play her to the left.

He walked in the door as if he didn't know that she had already heard everything. But when he looked up at her, her expression confirmed what he already suspected. He was busted.

She was extremely red in the face, and breathing frantically.

"Nigga, you got me fucked up," she yelled as he closed and locked the door behind him and turned to face her again.

In three strides she was up in his chest, swinging a hand at him violently.

He tried to move but reacted too slow. The phone in her left hand caught him upside the head, opening a small gash over his brow. "Ah," he winced.

"You bitch ass motherfucker." Her arms flailed widely as she pummeled him with punch after vicious punch.

He threw his arms up to cover his face. "Baby, chill the fuck out."

"No, nigga, you should have chilled. Bitch, where the fuck is my money?" she spat.

"Let me explain."

"Explain? Explain? Nigga, either you better have my drugs or my motherfuckin' money. If you don't, I don't want to hear shit else that you have to say. Tell it to the bitch I heard you fucking on the phone."

"What the fuck are you talking about?" he dummied up.

"I'ma show you what the fuck I'm talking about." She backed up a few steps and pulled a gun from her waist. With a scowl on her face, she cocked the *glizzy* and pointed it at him. She was looking him dead in his eyes, no blinking, with a clip full of bullets. "First, you break my heart, and then you play with my money?" she asked gripping her lips with her front teeth.

"Baby, listen to me," he pleaded softly while deciding to admit to what she'd obviously heard. "I didn't mean for it to go there. It—it—it just happened. That bitch meant nothing to me. I love *you*."

His claim sounded sincere, maybe because she desperately wanted to believe him. Her heart shattered all over again and tears poured down her face.

Sensing her weakness, he cautiously stepped toward her, and then leaned in to hug her. “Baby, we can get through this. Let me make it up to you.” He pressed his lips against her cheek and kissed away a few tears.

“I don’t know if I can trust you.” She sniffled back fresh tears that threatened to escape from her watery eyes.

“You can trust me, baby. I promise you. Please put down that gun before something bad happens.”

She hesitated a moment then let the gun slip from her hand and fall to the floor. His body relaxed against hers and he placed a trail of kisses down her face.

Usually his lips set her body on fire, but she had just heard another bitch moaning from his touch. Add to that, all the other shit she had forgiven him for.

She felt him hardening against her, and that shit pissed her off. The motherfucka had just taken his dick out of another bitch, now he had the nerve to get rocked up for her!

That sealed his fucking fate.

She eased her hand in her pocket and retrieved the syringe. “You wanna try again?” she asked in a forgiving tone. “You promise?” Her arms went around his neck.

“Yeah, baby. And this time I won’t let you down.”

“Ha. Nigga, do I look like a fool?”

Her sudden change of tone confused him. “Say what?” he asked.

“Bruh, you got the wrong bitch.” With her thumb she flicked the cap off of the needle head.

In one swift motion she jabbed the needle into his neck and released the fluid. He let out a pained cry and pushed her away.

"Bitch, what the fuck did you do?" His hand shot up to his neck, where the needle was still lodged. A second later, his body hit the floor and he began to lose feeling in his limbs. She had injected him with an instant paralysis drug.

She looked down at him unmercifully. "Nigga, I told you not to play with my money, but you thought a bitch was playing with you. Bruh, I do this, and I'm tired of telling you niggas not to play with me."

Spittle ran from the corners of his mouth. He tried to say something but his jaws locked up. She shook her head at him in pity, but only because he had tried her one too many times.

Moving with purpose, she began to ransack the house. She went from his living room to the attic, destroying everything. Finally, she stepped onto a loose piece of wood on his bedroom floor. She stopped, lifted it up, and found stacks of money.

Flipping through the bands of cash, she saw that it was mostly large bills. With a trained eye, she estimated it to be at least fifty thousand dollars, which was double what he owed her. In addition to the money, she found a whole brick of cocaine.

A smile crept on her face as she stuffed everything into a pillowcase and exited the room. She stormed into the living room and gathered up her bag and the gun she had dropped on the floor. It was only a few feet away from where that nigga lay, so she couldn't help but look down at him again.

A pang of regret shot from her head to her heart, and a tear stung her eye. *Why did it have to come to this?* she couldn't help but wonder.

She had to force her legs to move or she might've stood there for hours pondering the answer to that question.

Finally, she headed to the door, leaving him motionless on the carpet. He was temporarily paralyzed but not dead. In an hour, or so, he would slowly began to regain use of his limbs. Maybe now he would realize how bad he had fucked up.

As she opened the door, she thought about how letting this nigga slide would have other niggas thinking that they could test her. *You can't have that. These streets ain't no joke. You gotta make niggas respect the way you operate, and nothing earns their respect faster than cold-blooded murder.*

She shut the door, took a silencer out of her bag, and screwed it onto the glizzy. *Fuck it. I'ma do his ass,* she decided as she retraced her steps.

His eyes widened when he saw her return with the nine in her grip and a murderous look on her face.

"Why did you have to do me like that?" she asked. "I forgave you for everything. I never planned to hurt you. You've been lying to me since the day that I met your fake ass. I really fell for you."

Saliva was pouring from his mouth onto the floor. He never answered her because he could not form the words.

She cocked her tool and aimed it at his head. "You're a real bitch ass nigga. When you reach the other side, say hello to the other niggas I sent there."

She squeezed the trigger, letting off one shot. Pieces of skull and brain splattered onto the floor and blood splashed up on her face and her clothing. A pool of blood began to drain from his head, and she breathed out a deep sigh.

"Fuck it, the nigga had to go," she said as she turned and headed for the door.

She had never loved a man as much as she loved him, but his deceit had turned her heart cold against him. She looked over her shoulder and caught one final glance at his dead body.

"All grimy motherfuckers get dealt with, eventually," she uttered to herself as she slipped out of the door.

***

"Waddup, sis?" Dymond asked as she answered the phone for Keeky.

"I'm fifteen minutes away from the spot. Meet me there, it's important," Keeky said.

Keeky just hung up the phone without saying another word. As she rode to their trap spot in silence, Keeky thought about her life with Zay and all the shit that led up to tonight. "I can't believe I rocked that nigga to sleep," she thought to herself as she began to cry. For a minute, she just wanted it all to be over, but she was in way too deep now and there was no coming back.

Keeky saw flashing lights. When she looked in her rearview, cop cars were coming from everywhere. She pulled over, and they surrounded her.

"Keemari Brown, please step out of the vehicle with your hands up," an officer yelled over the loud speaker.

"Ain't this a bitch. This motherfucker was still setting me up after all of this time, and I'm pregnant with that bitch ass nigga's baby," she said. She looked down at the nine on her seat, and put her hand on it.

It's either do or die because jail isn't an option right now.

She looked in her rearview one last time, clutched her gun, and made a decision similar to the one that Cleo made when she was surrounded on *Set It Off*.

"Fuck it. I might as well war it out with these motherfuckas. Push it to the limit. Ain't no coming back from this," she said as she clutched the gun tightly, and grabbed her door handle.

To Be Continued…
Push It To The Limit 2
Coming Soon

Coming Soon From Lock Down Publications

RESTRAINING ORDER **II**

By **CA$H & Coffee**

NO LOYALTY NO LOVE

By **CA$H & Reds Johnson**

GANGSTA SHYT **III**

By **CATO**

PUSH IT TO THE LIMIT **II**

By **Bre' Hayes**

BLOOD OF A BOSS **IV**

By **Askari**

SHE DON'T DESERVE THE DICK

SILVER PLATTER HOE **III**

By **Reds Johnson**

BROOKLYN ON LOCK **III**

By **Sonovia Alexander**

CONFESSIONS OF A DOPEMAN'S DAUGHTER **III**

By **Rasstrina**

NEVER LOVE AGAIN **II**

WHAT ABOUT US **III**

By **Kim Kaye**

A GANGSTER'S REVENGE **IV**

By **Aryanna**

LAY IT DOWN **III**

By **Jamaica**

Available Now

RESTRAING ORDER

By **CA$H & Coffee**

LOVE KNOWS NO BOUNDARIES **I II & III**

By **Coffee**

SILVER PLATTER HOE **I & II**

HONEY DIPP **I & II**

CLOSED LEGS DON'T GET FED **I & II**

A BITCH NAMED KOCAINE

NEVER TRUST A RATCHET BITCH **I & II**

By **Reds Johnson**

CUM FOR ME

An **LDP Erotica Collaboration**

A GANGSTER'S REVENGE **I II & III**

By **Aryanna**

WHAT ABOUT US **I & II**

NEVER LOVE AGAIN

THUG ADDICTION

By **Kim Kaye**

THE KING CARTEL **I, II & III**

By **Frank Gresham**

BLOOD OF A BOSS **I II & III**

By **Askari**

THESE NIGGAS AIN'T LOYAL **I, II & III**

By **Nikki Tee**

THE STREETS BLEED MURDER **I, II & III**

By **Jerry Jackson**

GANGSTA SHYT

By **CATO**

THE ULTIMATE BETRAYAL

By **Phoenix**

BROOKLYN ON LOCK **I & II**

By **Sonovia Alexander**

DON'T FU#K WITH MY HEART **I & II**

By **Linnea**

BOSS'N UP **I & II**

By **Royal Nicole**

I LOVE YOU TO DEATH

By Destiny J

BOOKS BY LDP'S CEO, CA$H

TRUST NO MAN

TRUST NO MAN 2

TRUST NO MAN 3

BONDED BY BLOOD

SHORTY GOT A THUG

A DIRTY SOUTH LOVE

THUGS CRY

THUGS CRY 2

TRUST NO BITCH

TRUST NO BITCH 2

TRUST NO BITCH 3

TIL MY CASKET DROPS

RESTRAINING ORDER

IN LOVE WITH HIS GANGSTA

Coming Soon

TRUST NO BITCH (KIAM EYEZ' STORY)

THUGS CRY 3

BONDED BY BLOOD 2

RESTRANING ORDER 2

NO LOYALTY NO LOVE

CPSIA information can be obtained at www.ICGtesting.com
Printed in the USA
LVOW10s1532280416

485769LV00018B/645/P